The Flower of Scotland

Martin Westhead

http://theflowerofscotland.com

For Ashley, Faelan, Taye and Una

Connor gasped for breath as he struggled up the steep slope. Behind him the fading sun had turned a blood red as it set slowly against a crimson sky. It bathed the rolling hills and glens behind him in an eerie, alien light, beautiful and terrifying.

The sharp gorse scratched at his threadbare wax jacket and he leant heavily on his willow staff as he forced himself upwards. This path was all but forgotten, and he had trodden it only once, many years before. He had been much younger then and had less tar in his lungs.

"What the hell could they want?" he muttered angrily to himself. He had seen the sign; there could be no doubt about that, but after all this time...

The climb was both steep and dangerous. His worn boots had slipped more than once on patches of loose shale sending tiny rocks skittering dramatically down the scree.

He glanced apprehensively at the setting sun. It would be getting cold soon. It would be embarrassing to die up here of exposure like some clueless English tourist.

Finally he forced his way through a narrow crack between two rocks and into a flat, roughly circular area of ground. It was about the size of a tennis court and surrounded on all sides by steep rock walls. On the north side lay a large flat rock that had fallen to form a crude table.

Connor leant against the entrance for nearly a minute trying to catch his breath.

"Alright." He walked forward. "I'm here. You can come out."

He waited; only the sound of his wheezing broke the silence.

"Oh, for god's sake!" He yelled finally.

Walking up to the table he raised his staff above his head. Then in a loud clear voice he cried out:

"O Talisker, mo Thighearn, earbam riut:
  O thusa dhia ud m'ionracais,
  èisd rium tràth èigheam riut;
  'S tu dh'fhuasgail orm 's mi ann an teinn;
  fòir orm, is èisd mo scread."

As he finished he lowered the staff, sinking to one knee and bowing his head... again, silence.

Then he heard the clap, clap, clap of a solitary round of applause. "Oh very good, really, very, very good," called a voice with more than a tinge of superiority. "I do think it's important to keep the old traditions alive. Don't you?"

The speaker was leaning nonchalantly against the rock wall on the far side of the circle. He was dressed in an immaculate buttercup yellow three-piece suit, with Italian patent leather shoes and spats. The incongruity of the outfit was not lost on Connor, but he was trying to ignore it.

"Well? What's up O *great* Talisker?" he said standing up. "I was supposed to be at a gig twenty minutes ago."

"You know that is really at the heart of the troubles in today's world. No one has any time for the important things in life. Once, a man's relationship with his god was sacred. Gods were given the sort of respect they deserve."

Connor said nothing; he was not in the mood for this.

"Do you like my outfit?" asked Talisker, turning theatrically on the spot. "It's inspired by the very latest continental fashions."

"It looks very..." Connor began. He would have liked to tell his god exactly what he thought of the outfit, but he also wanted this conversation to get to the point.

"Um...chic," he finished eventually.

Talisker smiled quietly as if he had won a small victory. Then he moved closer to Connor and his tone changed abruptly.

"I bring grave tidings," he said quietly. "It has started. They will have the Stone tomorrow. Then the Leviathan will be called."

"How long do we have?" Connor's voice had lost all trace of impatience. If his face were visible in the dimming light, an observer might have noticed it had turned a shade or two whiter.

"Three nights, at most."

"The girl?"

"She is our only hope now. You *must* keep her safe."

✻✻✻✻✻

Mari McLeod hated washing up. The never-ending succession of caked egg yolk, ketchup stains and cold food scraps in lukewarm water reminded her too much of the rest of her life – mundane drudgery.

As she worked at scraping the encrusted cereal from the side of another bowl, her father sat, or rather sprawled, in a threadbare armchair in the front room of the small cottage. Even asleep he did not relax his grip on the glass in his hand. The cheap bottle of whisky by his feet was almost empty.

In his lap lay a small black cat. Across the room, the TV news talked to itself.

"...third day of rioting, the violence has now moved to the capital. Edinburgh was the scene of violent clashes between police and demonstrators. The Scottish Separatist Army website is claiming responsibility for instigating the riots.

"There is speculation that at least two of the recent deaths were caused by police firearms. Earlier in the day we spoke with Assistant Chief Constable Mark Struthers of Lothian and Borders police about their new policy on the police use of firearms in these difficult times..."

Mari switched off the TV. The news troubled her these days. She felt as if she should care more, but everyone felt it, everyone hated the English. As a girl she remembered there used to be a lot of English visitors to the island. There had always been jokes about the English, of course. Folks *talked* about how they hated them and there had been some animosity, under the surface, but never outright violence. The English didn't come here now, not since the bombings started.

"It's their own fault," she told the cat, who was the only one listening. Rob Roy scowled at her, jumped lightly to the floor and slunk out of the room.

Mari shrugged to herself as she climbed the narrow stairs to check on her cousin. Katie was already asleep in the bed, tired from the day's exertions. The child's soft breathing made the blankets rise and fall gently.

Mari loved her cousin's visits. When she was happy, Katie glowed with a joy to her that was beautiful and infectious. This afternoon they had taken a walk on the beach together. Katie had collected shells and chased seagulls. When she was with Katie, Mari felt that little girl inside her come to life again. Katie was still so young. Mari wanted to protect her, to keep her from the bitter pain of the real world.

A few years ago, Mari had been chasing gulls on the same beach, but that seemed a lifetime ago – before their "loss," as her father put it.

They found the body on a beach a few miles farther up the coast. They hadn't let her see it. The newspapers said that it had been bloated with water and battered against the rocks.

That was a long time ago now and she had accepted that her mother was dead. She had accepted the "what" but she continued to be mercilessly drawn back to the loose tooth of "why." Even though it hurt so much she just couldn't stop wiggling at it. No one could give her a "why."

The official story was that her mother had been walking along the cliff top and lost her footing. Some rumours had hinted of suicide, others of an affair. One thing was for sure, her father wasn't telling her everything he knew, and that had been the cause of a bitter dispute between them. If only she knew, even if it were something dreadful, just knowing *why* would let her close the book.

Tomorrow she and Katie had planned their usual trip to Dunvegan Castle; it was a sort of tradition. They would wander round the museum, see the Faerie Flag and Rory Mor's horn, take a boat trip out to see the seals, then up to Portree for a pub meal. Katie would be leaving the following day to return to Glasgow.

Katie stirred in her sleep. Without thinking, Mari started softly crooning a snippet of a song that her mother had always sung to her to put her to sleep:

Hush now, hear the silence.
Let it wash your fears aside.
Hush now, feel the stillness,
The gentle strength inside.

Keep the darkness from the threshold,
Fill your heart with light.
Love will triumph over darkness,
Softness over might.

The little girl turned over and settled back to sleep. Mari took one last look and then headed back downstairs. She was going to be late.

She grabbed her leather jacket and lifted her keys from the mantle where they sat next to the cheap porcelain vase that had been her mother's favourite. It had a dark green thistle painted on it, badly. She'd never understood why her mother liked it.

She opened the front door quietly, to avoid the usual evening row with her father. As she pulled the door shut behind her, the catch caught with a sharp *click*.

"Don't you be back late," bellowed her father from his chair. "You and me need to talk. You have to find yourself a better..."

His words were drowned out by the roar of the engine as Mari kicked the Yamaha 250 to life. She slipped the clutch and took off a little faster than she expected down the rough track to the road.

The Bonnie Prince Charlie was a soulless establishment. Its previous owner had neglected it for years and when he retired, he sold it to one of the big breweries. They had refurbished it with the sort of "quality" wood fittings and curios that made it look indistinguishable from any of their other 200 or so pubs. The locals grumbled but kept coming. The area afforded few alternatives.

Mari brought the bike to a jarring halt at the back of the *Bonnie Prince*, spraying pebbles all over the frosted glass door.

The old off-road Yamaha was rusty, scratched and dented but, rather like her mother's vase, it was special to her. Not only had she earned every penny that paid for it but, she had had to fight for it, enduring three days of ranting from her father and then three weeks of bitter silence, but she had prevailed. It had been her first major victory over her father. Since then, the beaten-up old Yamaha had become her personal icon of freedom.

"You're late again," yelled Barry, glaring at her as she walked in. Barry was the bar manager – young, keen and officious. "You know the deal, three strikes." He held up three fingers to emphasise the point.

"Sorry," she said as humbly as she could. "Arsehole!" she added under her breath resisting the temptation to hold up a single middle finger in response. She needed the money.

Avoiding his gaze she moved out into the room and started collecting empty glasses for the washer.

*****

"Never underestimate the dangers associated with the practice of magick. Few novices appreciate that the invocation of magickal forces, in even the most minor of rituals, involves the summoning and subjugation of a sprite, daemon or other ethereal being. It is rarely the desire of the daemon to be summoned and never to be bent to the summoner's will. This is why there are such dire warnings against the dangers of "dabbling." Meticulous adherence to both intention and practice is essential, as is an absolute focus and concentration if the novice mage is to survive their early training. It takes courage, fortitude and talent for a new student of the art to overcome the challenges and progress to a point where they can begin to work alone."

— *The Practice and Art of Ritual Magick*
James Hatherway

*****

The wind whistled eerily around the dark clearing, as if it knew what was about to transpire. It stirred the branches of the old pines, which swayed wildly, casting menacing silhouettes against the starlit sky.

This was an ancient place – one of many stone circles that had been built by the Druids in times lost. Most were unremarkable – their power had long since dissipated. Not so this circle.

It had retained a great deal of its power over the centuries. It was also remarkable for unlike all but a very few such circles it was a focus for dark chaotic power and tonight the air practically hummed with that force.

A woman clothed in a hooded black robe stood in the centre of the circle. She held in her hand a thick jet-black rod about eighteen inches long. It was ornately carved and bore, at its top, a slender, almost, feline dog's head. The bottom of the rod tapered to a sharp point.

The woman took the sharp point of the rod and dug it deep into her palm until blood flowed from the cut. She smeared the sticky red liquid over the smooth black stone of the rod. Then holding it above her head she made several passes with it, carving signs and symbols into the air, and began growling a strange dirge, the guttural sounds of some long forgotten language. Her antics became wilder and more manic until she stopped still, rigid with power. In this position, she opened her throat and screamed a wild, animal sound that echoed around the clearing. It was a scream of ecstasy, of pain, and of terror.

The scream went on for uncountable seconds, echoing over the surrounding hills, until finally it ended with her gasping for breath. Then she fell to the ground and began to buck and twist, writhing in the grass, though whether in agony or ecstasy it was impossible to say. She spread her legs wide and from beneath the folds of her robes dark vapours began to appear. They curled out from under the heavy cloth. The wind blew hard now, snatching at her clothing and hair but the curling wisps of smoke were unaffected.

Gradually the vapour became thicker, more substantial and started to take shape. Three clouds began to form, amorphous at first but almost imperceptibly they started to condense in front of the woman, taking the shape of strange cruel beasts. Their heads were dog-like, savage and brutal with ugly sharp teeth. Their bodies were large almost like bears, but instead of paws, at the end of each limb, they had human hands.

As they took shape they found voices – snarls, growls, barks and howls, terrible unearthly sounds that had not been heard by human ears for centuries.

The creatures stared fiercely at the woman as if they were ready to tear her to shreds. Something was stopping them but that just fuelled their anger and frustration.

As the last of the vapours dispersed, she stopped writhing and climbed weakly to her feet.

"Silence," she said at last, her voice hoarse but commanding. They obeyed.

"Now, my daughters," she gasped. "You know what to do. Go!"

She pointed sharply into the trees and the beasts took off at a run.

*****

The dark-clothed figure slipped over the high brick wall, dropped silently to the ground just out of sight of the security camera and with practised grace melted into the shadows. It was followed by a second, a little less silent, a little less confident and considerably less graceful.

It was raining lightly, a soft patter of droplets that fell gently across the dockyard, spattering on the corrugated iron roofs and splashing into small greasy puddles in the concrete alleys.

The security office was just next to the gate. It was a small port-a-cabin, a bit like a large shoebox. It had one wide window that looked in their direction. The inside was lit with the bright ugly glow of neon strip-lights. From where they stood they could just see the single guard sitting at his desk. He was smiling at something. Occasionally he would glance vaguely across in the direction of the CCTV monitors on the wall.

The guard chuckled. It was an easy job. Nothing ever happened here. He'd heard from the dayshift that some kids had broken onto the site earlier that day and smashed a few windows and a couple of floodlights with stones. That was about as exciting as it got.

He chuckled again. He was watching a documentary on a small portable TV on his desk. It was about the rising anti-English sentiment in Scotland. They were showing a slogan painted on the side of Waverly Bridge, that read: *"Go home ya English bastards"*. He glanced at the clock. He was overdue for a patrol round the docks, but it was a quiet night. He might as well wait until the program finished.

Outside, the two figures began moving stealthily between the warehouses. They stayed in the deep shadows, as they covered the rain-spattered dockyard.

The Pride of the Firth was an old, but powerful, tug that had been used to tow the large tankers past the sandbanks, up the river to the Grangemouth refinery.

She was moored at her usual birth on Prince Albert dock on a small service pier away from the cargo vessels. Usually the pier was well lit but the vandalism earlier in that day left it in gloom.

The two figures reached the pier and went straight over to a pile of crates covered with a worn tarpaulin. One of them pulled the heavy cover aside.

"Thank god for that. Stuffs still 'ere Dougie!" said one in a forced whisper.

"Shut up ya arse 'ol'!" replied the other urgently, glaring at his companion through the eye-holes of his balaclava helmet, "An' fa god sake diney use my name."

Dougie was a plumber by trade. His passion for the cause and his quick wits had allowed him to rise rapidly through the ranks of the Scottish Separatist Army. This was his first mission as corporal in charge of a Fireteam. If all went well he was set to lead two more in as many nights. He was small but athletic with a sort of intent, wired energy. The black balaclava framed his penetrating blue-gray eyes and aside from a few strands his short light-brown hair was hidden.

"Oh, right – aye, sorry, sorry!" said Alex hastily.

Alex had only been recruited to the group in the last month. He had worked for nearly a year at the helm of one of the *Pride*'s sister boats and that gave him unique qualifications for this particular project. Alex carried considerably more extra weight than Dougie. He was not exactly fat but definitely well rounded. He had an untidy mop of red hair that was escaping the sides of his balaclava and slightly vacant blue eyes.

Together they began to lift the crates and equipment onto the tug. The missing lights helped to cover their activities but they moved urgently nonetheless.

*****

Mari loaded the last dirty glass into the washer and set it going again. The evening had picked up a little and the pub was now thick with the din of conversation. It was amazing how loud the sound of people talking could be. Nevertheless there was something convivial about the place, despite what the brewery had done to it. The pubs were the social centres on the island, and there were definitely some worse than this.

Overall she didn't mind the job that much and she needed the money. Her father was on her back about applying to University, but she had missed the deadline this year – on purpose. She had had enough of school, at least for now. She had three Highers and she could use them later — if she wanted to.

Most of her friends had left for the new term already and somehow the place was starting to feel a bit empty without them. She had been thinking about travelling, if she could save some cash. After that, who knows, maybe she would go back to school. One of her friends was doing a course in photography. That didn't sound too bad. One thing was for sure though, despite her father's fears, there was no way she was going to be stuck in jobs like this for the rest of her life. She was better than that and she knew it.

"Hey Mari, do a' pay ya ta day dream?" asked Barry emerging from the cellar. She didn't even look at him but crossed to the bar, where there were several people waiting to be served.

She recognised the one at the front, Connor McColl a local folksinger, eccentric and general philanderer. He lived on a boat and sailed around the Highlands and Islands, doing odd jobs for people to make some sort of a living. He was middle-aged but not unattractive and there were more than a few rumours about his carryings on with the local female population.

"What'll it be, Connor?" she asked, with disinterest.

"Actually, I'm not here for a drink, Mari. I need to talk to you."

"To me? Are you joking?"

Something about Connor's manner made it clear that he was not.

"What is it?" she asked, uncertain.

"Not here. Take your break..."

"Two pints o' heavy and a packet a crisps hen," interrupted a short man with thick black-rimmed glasses and a deep monotone voice.

As she pulled the foaming beers, Mari glanced across at Connor. He was looking intently across the bar at the far door. He looked sober although perhaps a little more ragged than usual. She had no idea what he could possibly want to talk to her about – god forbid it was any kind of romantic proposal.

She gave the man with the glasses his change and returned her attention to Connor.

"Alright," she said, "but this had better be good."

She told one of the other bar staff she was taking her break and then slipped out before Barry noticed.

Outside the pub the gravel and concrete area around the building was brightly lit for about 20 feet and then it disappeared into the darkness of the night. The only other light came from the stars and the headlights of the occasional passing car.

It was freezing. She hadn't brought her jacket out – this had better not take long.

Connor stood for a moment in silence as if trying to decide what to say.

"Well?" asked Mari, impatiently.

"Well..." Connor paused again "Mari, there's a lot I have to tell you but we don't have time now..."

He paused again.

Mari was starting to feel increasingly uncomfortable, not to mention cold.

"Here," Connor went on. "I have something for you."

After fumbling in his pockets for a moment, he drew out something wrapped in dark purple velvet. He handed it to Mari. It was large and heavy. She began to unwrap it.

"It's from your mother," he explained. "She wanted you to have it... when you were ready."

She pulled back the cloth to reveal a brooch with an ornate Celtic cross fashioned from interwoven strands of silver. At its centre was a very large, pure white pearl.

"It's beautiful," said Mari, unable to take her eyes off the brooch. Then her brain caught up with her. "What do you mean it's from my mother? How did you know my mother?"

The mention of her mother was painful, and it angered her to think of what sort of relationship her mother might have with Connor. What was this all about and what was he after?

"There's no time, Mari. You are in danger. There are people after you."

"What do you mean?"

"Come with me now, to my boat. We need to get off this island as soon as possible."

The image this statement conjured was enough to snap Mari back to a reality that she felt she understood.

"You can take your fancy gifts and your offer of a midnight cruise, Connor McColl, and you can shove them right where the sun don't shine. I'm not goin' on no boat with you." Mari thrust the brooch back at him.

"The brooch is yours, Mari, and I'm trying to look after you," replied Connor with a disturbingly earnest look.

"I can look after myself," said Mari with fire in her eyes. She spun around and stormed back into the pub, the brooch still clutched in her hand.

Connor stood there for a moment and sighed. It had been a long night and this was not how it was supposed to be going.

Inside the pub, Mari looked at the brooch one more time and slipped it into her pocket. Maybe it was her mother's, who knows? Something inside her told her she had been a little harsh with Connor but she pushed those feelings quickly aside.   He was a rogue and that's all there was to it.

*****

"What news, Talisker?" the voice was gruff, but not unkind. The speaker had white hair and a neatly trimmed beard. He wore a black jacket and bow-tie and a kilt of rich purple and green with a snow-white fur-covered sporran that matched his beard and hair. He sat in a moss-green wing-backed leather chair in the traditional off-lobby bar of the Balmoral Hotel on Prince's Street, in Edinburgh city centre. There were several other people in the bar similarly attired in traditional Scottish evening-wear.

His left hand toyed with a very pale wooden walking stick shod in silver and in his right hand he held a heavy crystal cut glass containing a generous measure of a fabulously expensive single malt whisky. At his feet, on either side of the chair lay two enormous dogs, gracious and noble beasts, grey with white markings. Anyone looking closely enough would have probably noticed that they were extremely wolf-like in their appearance, though strangely, in the crowded bar, no one seemed to have noticed them at all – not even the bar staff.

Talisker sat to one side of the old man at the near-end of a chesterfield couch made from the same green leather. He also wore a kilt and black tie, though the tartan was a different, more flamboyant design in white, green and blue. Before him on the rosewood table was a pale yellow Martini in a cocktail glass.

"He speaks with the girl, presently," replied Talisker, absently stirring his Martini with an olive on a little wooden stick.

"She doesn't know yet?" asked the first.

"We thought it best that way."

The older man sat back in his chair and thought for a moment, his eyes staring intently into the glass.

"We need to call a council," he announced finally.

"But father," exclaimed Talisker, "we have not called a council in centuries. The situation is under control."

"Talisker, we do not need to have this discussion again. My decision has been taken."

"I fear, father, that involving the others will just complicate things. You know how they bicker. It would be faster and simpler if we just manage this ourselves."

"Talisker, you know, as I do, what is at stake here. Not just all this," he gestured vaguely out of the window at the rain-washed Edinburgh street outside, "but, us. Our very existence could be threatened. Events are moving rapidly now. The others must have their say, and will have their parts to play."

"Few will heed the call. Many of them have passed on and will not wake again."

"All things pass, my son, even gods. Let those who can, join us. We need not worry about the others."

"I still think father..."

The old man set aside his stick and gently held up his hand for silence. He leant forward and looked Talisker directly in the eye.

"Enough. It is time you and your brother found peace. This is more important than your squabbles. Now, rouse the others, or as many as will come."

"Yes, my liege," replied Talisker with resignation. He stood up, plucked the olive from the end of its stick with his teeth and threw back the drink. Without another word, he left the bar and disappeared into the night.

Oban returned to his whisky and reached down to scratch one of the wolves behind the ear with his free hand.

"Will there be anything else, sir, or should I get you the bill?" asked a waiter.

"That's everything, thank you," replied Oban. "Just put it on my tab, would you, and buy yourself one while you're at it."

"Thank you, sir. Very kind of you," said the waiter, clearly pleased with such a generous tip. Although as he walked away he was suddenly aware that he did not know exactly to which tab the considerable bill should be applied and, unfortunately, when he turned back around, the old man seemed to have disappeared.

*****

The Bonnie Prince Charlie was not huge. It had two bars, the main bar at the front and a smaller 'lounge' bar in the back. It had once been furnished with red carpet and velvet upholstered seats and the walls had been filled with framed pictures of local people and local events.

All that had gone. The floor was now 'rustic flagstones', the seats of hard wood, and the walls decorated with a random selection of brass horse tack and old fishing nets. It was pattern number 17 in the brewery selection. Coastal Cottage it was called, supposedly "hard wearing, easy to clean, yet rich with old world charm." In the words of one of the regulars visiting the pub for the first time after its refurbishment, "The seats are so hard that your bum goes numb within a few minutes, but at least they dinae smell of stale beer and puke like they used to."

In the corner of the smoky wood-panelled front bar, a small group of musicians, Connor amongst them, staked out a table and began to play some simple folk tunes. There was often music in the Bonnie Prince Charlie, local amateurs mostly who liked to play and liked to have an audience.

Barry didn't like it much. When he first took over, he used to mutter a lot about liability and insurance and kept trying to turn up the jukebox but his patrons made it very clear that it was something they expected. He was enough of a business man to see that this might be one of those special situations where brewery rules could, according to the manual, be applied 'selectively at the manager's discretion in order to meet local needs and expectations.'

Connor kept throwing glances over at Mari.

The tune they were playing came to an end as Mari was passing the table, picking up glasses and ignoring Connor.

"Sing us a song, Mari?"

It was Connor, but the request was echoed by a couple of others.

"Yeah, Mari, sing us a song."

Mari loved to sing. When she was younger, she had dreamed of running away to be a pop star. She had a good voice, and she knew it, but she also knew that such dreams were for little kids. Every now and again she would sing in the pub or at a Ceilidh or even a wedding – only for friends, though.

"She's getting paid to collect dirty glasses, not sing songs." snarled Barry, from across the room. "Isn't that right, Mari?"

Mari said nothing but pushed her search for soiled glassware deeper into the clutter of tables.

Suddenly there was a loud crash. All eyes turned towards the noise. Someone had fallen to the ground, knocking over a table as he went. Above the prone figure towered the form of Iain MacDonald, a burly local farmer. He looked down at the fallen man with hate in his eyes.

The man on the ground was young with curly blond hair. His hand covered his nose and blood ran through his fingers.

"C'mon then, ya English bastard!" roared the farmer. He grabbed a beer bottle by its neck and smashed it against the solid wooden counter-top of the bar sending beer and shards of glass flying in all directions. Brandishing the broken bottleneck, he started to advance on the young man on the floor.

There were a few grins on the faces watching, but all the same, everyone who could, was giving them as much room as possible.

Mari set down the glasses she was carrying and strode calmly but determinedly between the two men.

"Iain MacDonald you stop that right now," she said, looking up at the big, red haired Scot. But the farmer's blood was up. "You get out of ma way right now, Mari, or I swear I'll cut you, too."

He feigned a lunge with the bottle at her that stopped inches from her chest.

Mari reached out for the huge hand that was holding the neck of the broken bottle. Her slender white fingers gripped the huge hairy fist and she lifted the bottle so that the jagged edge was just in front of her face. She looked him straight in the eye.

"Do you want to cut me, Iain? Is that what you want?"

Her voice was quiet, but her words carried across the still, heavy silence in the room as everyone held their breath. The glass shards in front of Mari's pale skin wavered.

"Take a look at yerself, Iain. Take a good look."

The farmer's gaze dropped. His fingers slipped from the remains of the bottle and it fell to the floor.

"He's not worth it," he mumbled, making for the exit.

"You," she said, pointing to the young man on the floor. "You get out, too. There'll be no fighting in this pub."

The young man rose to his feet unsteadily and started to shuffle out.

"English bastard!" Someone called out from the back of the room as he crossed toward the door.

Gradually, conversation resumed, but there was an ugly feeling in the air. Mari got a lot of looks, some in admiration; some in disappointment; some in disgust.

"Sing us a song, girl?"

It was Connor again. Was he mad? She wanted to crawl into a hole somewhere and cry. The last thing she wanted was to draw everyone's attention again.

She looked around in exasperation. All eyes were still on her, expectantly. Then something deep inside her found a voice. Almost without her volition, her mouth opened and she found herself singing.

It was an old Gaelic ballad, a haunting melody that told the story of two lovers from rival clans who ran away together. Connor found the key and picked out a gentle accompaniment on his guitar.

Everyone in the pub was silent as Mari's voice lifted them and carried them away.

As the final notes of her song subsided, the whole room burst into a round of applause that went on and on.

Mari smiled for a moment and wiped a tear from each cheek before bending to retrieve the dirty glasses she had put down and continue her round of the pub.

*****

"Get the boat ready. I'll be back in a minute," Dougie whispered, "There's somethin' I need to do."

"Right y'are," replied Alex, carrying aboard the last box.

Dougie slipped quietly off the boat and crossed the open. In the shadows of the corner of a warehouse, he took out a wad of cloth, and carefully soaked it in chloroform. Then, pressing his back against the wall, he waited. It did not take long.

A few moments later the guard came around the corner. This was the last round of his shift and he was keen to get out of the drizzle and back to his warm dry hut. He smiled gently to himself as he thought back to the scenes in the documentary. He knew that it was kind of wrong, but he had to admit he loved what the SSA do – someone had to make a stand, after all.

A movement on one of the boats shook him from his revere. There was someone out there. He swore silently to himself – so much for a quiet night. Reaching for his torch he was just about the yell, when Dougie's hand reached out from the darkness of the shadows and covered his nose and mouth with the cloth. The move was quick but the guard fought back, frantically tearing at the hand holding the cloth in place. It was all Dougie could do to hold on. Then the heavy man threw his whole weight against Dougie, driving him hard into the rough concrete wall, crushing his elbow and sending a searing pain up his arm. Eventually, the big man's struggles weakened and he went limp.

Dougie pulled an old hip flask from his pocket. It was filled with cheap whisky – the cheapest he could find. He opened it and poured some of its contents down the big man's front, then opened his mouth and tipped some in. He wiped the flask clean of fingerprints and then placed it carefully in the unconscious guard's hand. If he was found it might buy them a few extra minutes.

As he turned, he heard the engines of the *Pride* fire up. He lifted the heavy bowline off its worn steel mooring and as the tug started gently forward, he stepped gracefully on board. Glancing back, he satisfied himself that there were no signs of alarm. By the time anyone realised the boat had gone, it would be too late.

The boat chugged gently though the dark water making its way out of the dock and then upstream against the slow-moving current. He could still feel his heart beating fast with fear and excitement. This was it, the real deal; desperate freedom fighters striking a blow against the oppressive establishment. What he had done was *illegal* but it was nothing compared to what they were about to do.

"How did you know?" asked Alex suddenly, glancing at Dougie. "Aboot the guard, like. How did you know he'd be coming around that corner just then?"

"Och, after a while ya develop a sort of instinct for these things," Dougie lied.

"Oh a' see," said Alex, who clearly didn't at all.

Dougie had to admit he was actually a little spooked by the experience himself. His instructions had been *very* specific. She always gave very specific instructions. After they had loaded the crates, she had said, the guard would walk round the corner of the warehouse. He was to lay him out with the chloroform and make it look as if he had been drinking.

But how had she known? How could she possibly have known that the guard would come around the corner just then? It was weird. He pushed the thoughts aside – they had a job to do.

After only fifteen minutes, Alex pulled up at the rear of a much larger vessel that was moored all alone against the side of the estuary. Dougie put his fingers to his lips and let out a long low whistle. After a moment, from the dark deck above them came a rope with a large iron hook on the end and next to this a Jacob's ladder unrolled, its steel rungs clanging sharply against the metal hull as it fell. Dougie attached one of the large crates to the hook and gave a sharp tug. Then he started scaling the ladder. After a few feet, he paused.

"Be ready for the tow line," he said to Alex in a low voice. The crate rose up majestically next to him, swaying slightly. From the darkness far above came the gentle squeak of a pulley wheel.

By the time he reached the gunwale, he was out of breath, his arms and legs burning. He threw his leg up over the side and a pair of hands reached out and helped haul him on board. He sat for a moment catching his breath and feeling the blood return to his limbs.

Just above his head, mounted on a bulkhead was a large brass ships bell, carefully polished so that even in the low light it gleamed. The bell bore a beautifully engraved inscription, which read: "E II R, H.M. Yacht, Britannia."

*****

"Britannia was the 83rd Royal Yacht in a long line that dates back to 1660 in the reign of Charles II. She was over 400 feet long, weighed nearly 6000 tons and had a permanent staff of around 240 naval officers and crew, whose duties ranged from polishing silverware to checking the underside of the hull for explosives.

She was decommissioned on December 11th 1997. Now, permanently moored at Leith, in Edinburgh, the Britannia, a majestic monument of British history, is open to the public. It is maintained to its original standard and visitors can tour the decks from the laundry to the royal apartments and discover what life was like on board..."

— *Tourists guide to historic Scotland*

*****

The royal party arrived hurriedly at the gangplank. Their dash through the dark streets lit by the two flickering torches held by servants. Without waiting on ceremony, Neferubity rushed aboard.

The *Promise of Fortune* was a small merchant ship. It had been deliberately moored in this quiet pier away from busier parts of the city docks. With luck, they may have arrived unseen.

Her eyes looked east. It was still dark in the sky but on the horizon the silhouette of the distant desert hills could be made out against the pre-dawn light. It would be dawn soon and the river would be full of fishermen and people starting their day as the city of Memphis woke up. They did not have much time.

A door opened onto the deck and a man stepped out.

"Aristos, my love," cried Neferubity, running to his waiting arms.

The newly-weds embraced warmly. Their secret marriage had happened a few hours earlier, administered by a priest from the Temple of Ra, where Neferubity herself was a high priestess.

The ceremony was held in a small chamber deep in the temple, a far cry from the splendid three-week public celebration that the marriage of a Pharaoh's daughter would normally demand, but Neferubity didn't care. It was a great favour the priest had done her, since he may well lose his life for it.

She looked into the deep brown eyes of Aristos. This was what she wanted, and if her father was too much of a fool to see how special this man was, then she would just have to take matters into her own hands.

Aristos was a merchant and he had no royal blood, but he was honest, upstanding, successful and brave. Few men, it must be said, had the courage to stand up to Thutmose II. Who, after all, would defy a god incarnate?

"Your belongings are loaded my dear," said Aristos, clearly eager to be underway. "Bring your people aboard and let us flee this place."

"I bring but one last thing. Here, it comes aboard now."

Four burly sailors were struggling to lift a large object up the gangplank. It was clearly very heavy and wrapped loosely in a cloth tie.

"What is it, my dear?" asked the merchant cautiously.

"Husband, it is a stone block."

"A stone?" said Aristos, more sceptically than he had intended.

"Not just any stone. I had a dream two nights hence. I heard a voice from this stone. It told me that I would take it with me to a far land, and that while it was in our care we would be safe from my father."

"It is magic?" he asked, his brow furrowing. He was a practical man and she knew that he was not very trusting or knowledgeable about the ways of the Egyptian priests.

"It is powerful, but few know of it. It is the magic of the slaves. It is said to have shown one of their prophets the path to heaven when he slept one night with his head upon it. It has spoken to me."

Aristos looked dubiously at the heavy load being set down on his deck. He lifted the corner of the cloth wrapping it.

"But my dear it has no markings. How do you know it from any other stone?"

Neferubity's eyes flashed dangerously for a moment.

"Husband, trust me. This stone has a long history. It was gifted to me by a very special man. As a baby, my mother found him by the river and saved his life when all others born that year were put to death by my father.

"He came to us three years ago and begged us to help him hide a chest, a holy item of great power. For these years that chest rested upon this stone in a secret room deep in the temple. When he took the chest he told me to keep the stone. He said that it has great power and, husband, I have felt it."

For a moment Aristos looked unconvinced, but then his priorities asserted themselves.

"My dear, for you, I would carry an entire pyramid to the ends of the earth.

"Strap it down, quickly." he instructed one of the sailors. "All hands make sail."

They were far from the city by the time the sun started climbing up into the sky, baking the land with its fierce heat. Before them lay a long and perilous journey. They had only a short lead and they knew that the Pharaoh would stop at nothing to catch them. The fact that Neferubity was his daughter was unlikely to stay his hand if he did. Their marriage had been expressly forbidden and there was only one punishment for disobeying the Pharaoh – death.

*****

The Bonnie Prince Charlie had closed. Barry had turned the lights up full to dispel the "genuine friendly atmosphere," as it said in the manual, and let the patrons know that the party was over and it was time for them to sod-off home. The last few stragglers were finishing up their drinks; most had already left into the cold dark night.

Mari swept up the broken glass on the floor, stacking stools up on tables as she went.

Connor was the last one there. He watched her from the bar.

"I was serious, you know," he said quietly. "You really are in danger and you need my help."

She looked at him for a moment. He seemed sincere. Even more surprisingly he seemed sober. Come to think of it, she had not seen him drinking anything all night.

"Look, Connor," she said firmly. "I'm a big girl. *Okay*. I can take care of myself."

To illustrate her point she lifted the broken bottle out of the dustpan and waggled it at him.

"Mari, you don't understand," he said but she had already turned her back and was moving away.

She dropped the contents of the dustpan into one of the large bins.

"I'm all done here, Barry." She yelled in the general direction of the office. Then without even a glance in Connor's direction she picked up her helmet and strode out of the back door pulling on her heavy leather jacket as she went.

She straddled the motorbike and strapped on her helmet.

"Mari, can I at least see you home?" It was Connor again. He had followed her out of the pub. He put his hand on her arm. Infuriated by the touch, she ripped it away.

"You just don't give up do ya? Just give me a break, *okay*?" She kicked the engine to life and sped away, throwing out a small spray of gravel in her wake.

Conner watched her go helplessly. With a deep sigh he picked up his staff and started to trudge along the road after the bike.

The ride home was cold. She felt her fingers numbing in the chill wind. But she didn't really care. It had been a strange evening; she was exhausted and wanted to be home and in bed. She was troubled by what Connor had said. If he had been try- ing out a chat-up line on her, it had to be the weirdest one she had ever encountered. Perhaps he was on drugs? Or just mad? The trouble was he had seemed more sober and lucid than she had ever seen him. What kind of trouble did he think she might be in? There wasn't really much that happened on a little island like Skye.

After a few miles she turned onto a single-track road that headed west across the island. The engine growled as she leant the bike through the twists and turns. Eventually she came to the broken gate that marked the boundary of the croft. The heavy wooden gate had once kept sheep from straying across the road, but for as long as she could remember it had lain at a crazy angle, sticking out into the track. From the gate it was a short ride up the dirt track that led to the little cottage that was home.

As she came over the rise and approached the building, she saw that there were lights on. Her father would often leave a light on in the front for her, but *all* the lights were on – odd.

She stopped the bike in front of the house and pulled her helmet off.

The front door was ajar.

She felt a mounting dread within her as she approached, sud- denly wishing she had let Connor see her home after all. She pushed open the door. The house was quiet.

"Hello?" she called.

Silence.

She crossed the hall and opened the door to the front room. The place was in chaos. The TV was on its side. Her mother's favourite vase lay smashed on the floor.

"Dad!" she called out. She thought she heard a noise. There, in the corner, behind his armchair lay her father. She gasped in horror at the sight. He lay in a pool of sticky red-black blood that had come from an ugly head wound.

She rushed over to him. It seemed he had stopped bleeding but it was clear that the old man had lost a lot of blood.

"Dad. Da. Can you hear me?" she touched his cheek.

His eyelids fluttered but failed to open.

"Mari, is that you?... Katie, they took Katie ... all these years, Tara. I didn't ... you were right."

The sound of her mother's name sent a physical jolt through Mari. She had hardly ever heard her father use it since her death.

"Da, it's me, Mari."

"Mari, you must...," he gasped, his voice once again filled with urgency, "...Farrow, Cynthia Farrow..."

The rest of his words were lost as he slipped from consciousness.

"Da!" she cried out. He did not respond, but she could just make out a fitful rise and fall of his chest. He was, at least, still breathing. She moved to lift him, and then thought better of it. He needed medical help.

She tried to force herself to be calm. She needed to think. Who could have done this? And why? They had nothing worth stealing. Who the hell was Cynthia Farrow? The name sounded familiar but she couldn't place it... *Katie!* She dashed upstairs and burst in through the door of the spare room. It was empty – Katie was gone. There were signs of a struggle — the bedclothes and pillows had fallen to the floor. The bed had been pulled away from the wall.

Mari's mind reeled. She stumbled back down the stairs to the living room and grabbed the phone. She needed to get her father to a hospital fast. The nearest hospital was in Portree, over half an hour away. It would take at least that long for an ambulance just to get here. Instead Mari dialled the number for her neighbours, the Thornley's, who owned a farm just over the hill, half a mile away. They had a car.

"Hello Mrs Thornley? This is Mari McLeod here. Sorry to

call you so late but this is an emergency. Someone has broken into our house. My father is seriously injured. Do you think Jim could drive him up to Portree? ... yes... yes he is...

"Thank you, I'll see you in a few minutes."

She started to dial for the police when suddenly she heard a noise outside. It sounded like a dog and seemed to come from the field behind the house. A chill descended down Mari's spine as she peered out of the window into the black night.

*****

"Gods, or god-forms can be thought of as collective personifications of cultural archetypes. They are created not, as some observers suggest, purely from the belief of their worshippers, although this may be a factor, but arise primarily from the collective unconscious of a self-identified social group.

Many of the ancient gods, such as those of Egypt, Rome, Greece, and Scandinavia were deeply empowered by the energy their followers invested in them through rites and rituals. The stories and myths of these gods are so strong that they are still conscious today. Much less is known of the lesser gods, but their mark is found in the every day world, if we know where to look. Many of our modern day icons, brand names and trademarks are, in fact emerging god-forms. Some even have a conscious existence and followers..."

— *Wherefore Gods and Daemons, L. G. Theapolus*

*****

The boardroom was sumptuous. Three of the walls were panelled with rich dark wood, ornately inlaid with silver Celtic knots; the fourth wall was a window, glass from floor to ceiling with a view that looked out from an impossible height through clouds and over mountain tops to the rich luminous tapestry of yellow winking lights marking a distant cityscape. In the centre of the room was a large oval table beautifully surfaced in walnut.

Around the table sat the council of Uisge Beatha, the council of the gods, seated in soft brown leather executive chairs. They were all dressed in modern formal business attire and were rubbing their eyes or looking around as if they had just woken up. At the head of the table sat Oban. The chair next him lay empty.

Talisker stood by the window in a purple silk suit, with a shirt and tie that toned exquisitely, if he were any judge. His back was turned to the others as he deliberately admired the view. His blue eyes glinted gently in the starlight as his family and extended family began to awake, yawn, stretch, scratch and then, inevitably, complain.

"Wha' is this place?" demanded a gruff, angry Scottish voice from behind him. "An' what on earth is this ponsey, stupid outfit you've put me in Talisker?"

Talisker turned towards the speaker, his brother, Laphroaig. The broad hairy war-god was dressed in a black, double-breasted business suit and white shirt with gold cuff links and red silk tie.

"I look ridiculous," complained Laphroaig, "I mean how am I going to swing an axe with these shoulder pads... and, by the way, where is my axe. I always have an axe!"

"I left it behind. I didn't want you to scratch the table," replied Talisker provocatively.

Laphroaig glared at him, "I'm no stayin' like this," he announced loudly, spitting dramatically onto the thick wool carpet. The brown phlegm sat there rebelliously on the lush cream-coloured pile. He folded his huge arms. The other gods shifted uncomfortably.

Oban turned around with a pained expression. "Talisker," he said, "I think our usual meeting arrangements would be more suitable for the present."

"I was just trying to bring us up-to-date, " pouted Talisker. "We have been meeting in that draughty old shack for centuries. Don't you think it's time for a change?"

"I don't like change," exclaimed Ardbeg, flatly. She was a stern looking goddess, sitting next to Laphroaig, patron of the highlands and mountains. Her face was worn and craggy as a mountainside with a long and sharply pointed nose, and yet she had a mysterious elegance about her.

"Talisker, dear, *please...*" implored Jura, a confident woman with straight light brown hair and hazel eyes sitting to Oban's left. It was phrased as a question but it carried the hard steel of a maternal directive.

"Very well, mother," sighed Talisker, with resignation, and he snapped his fingers and, immediately, the scene shifted.

The wood panels were replaced by stone walls. The walnut tabletop was became a six-inch-thick slab of unfinished oak and the leather chairs turned into rough wooden stools. Unglazed apertures in the stonewalls looked out on one side over a dark loch.

Laphroaig stood up, admiring his kilt, coarse cotton shirt and leather jerkin. His hands found the leather-bound handle of the heavy two-headed black battle-axe by his side.

"Arrrrgggh!," he roared, heaving it over his head in a mighty arc and burying the sharp, curved blade deep into the oak table. The heavy wood let out a deep crack like a roll of thunder and split along its length. The two separated pieces flew apart and fell to the floor, narrowly missing several of the assembly.

"Now, that's more like it," he said, with a big grin.

"When you children have quite finished, I've better things to do than watch you two fighting" declared MacAllan, Lord of the Oceans, in exasperation. He had a grave, clean shaven face with serious blue eyes and grey flecked hair. He was broad, almost as broad as Laphroaig but handsome like Talisker.

"Sorry, uncle," said Talisker with deep irony in his tone.

"I always find a little testosterone helps me start the day," inserted Dalwhinnie, with an impish smile on her glossed red lips. The Goddess of Love was clothed in a long, revealing powder blue dress that she filled splendidly. Her raven black hair was tied up exposing her delicate white neck and shoulders.

"And you would know," said Ardbeg, sourly.

"Talisker, dear, would you fix the table?" asked Lagavulin. She sat at the far end of the table. She was one of the oldest there; older even than Ardbeg, although her smooth skin and sparkling eyes give the impression that she was the younger of the two. She wore a long wool dress and a white blouse with a lace front. Her long, grey hair was tied in a neat bun.

Opposite her sat Dufftown, the Keeper of Time, the oldest and wisest of them all, he was dressed in a long brown hooded robe. His head was bald save for a few curly white wisps around his ears, but he had a long, white beard that extended well past his waist. His chin rested gently on his chest, his eyes closed as if he were still fast asleep.

Indifferently, Talisker waved his hand and the table returned to its former state without even a scratch to show where the axe had fallen.

Jura turned to the head of the table. "Oban, my dear, much as I love these little family gatherings, perhaps you should start by telling us why you called the council?"

There was a murmur of agreement from the assembled gods.

*****

The Royal Yacht Britannia was as much a symbol of the British monarchy as any true Scot could ever wish to vandalise. It had always struck Dougie as ironic that this icon of the English Royal Family had found its last resting place in a city where there was such unanimous disrespect for that institution.

"C'mon hurry it up. I'm freezin' ma nuts off here," said a voice ahead of him. It was Brian; he was tall, lanky and balding with very short brown hair. By day he worked in a call centre. He wanted to be a professional footballer but wasn't really good enough. His work with the SSA gave him a new sense of purpose.

Beside him, the third operative, Gail, opened the crate. She was small and slim with a bleach-blond bob. Dougie didn't like Gail much, she was not clever enough to be interesting and not pretty enough to be attractive. She was their explosives expert, but he didn't rate her as much of an expert in anything. In his opinion, it was not a job for a girl.

Dougie joined them quickly and rapidly started passing out the contents of the crate. He gave one pack to Gail, and passed another to Brian.

"Check 'em," he said.

Brian began rummaging frantically through his pack. "Aw man, where's the saw?" he cried. "We can ne go anywhere withou' the saw."

"It's in there, alright. Check again," Dougie told him.

"It is no. Look fer yerself."

"It's here, in the crate," said Gail flatly, passing the power tool to Brian.

"Alright," said Dougie, "You know the plan, back on the tug in fourteen minutes. Go!"

The three of them split up. Brian was to head to the bow, Dougie to the royal apartments in the stern and Gail to the engine room.

The operation had been meticulously planned. All three had rehearsed this part until they could have done it in their sleep. And they had taken the tour of the yacht so many times in the last month that they could almost recite the audio commentary for each room by heart.

Brian tossed one end of the towline over the side to Alex who was waiting on the tug below. As he made for the bow, he paid out the remaining line. He secured the other end to a bollard at the bow and then started work on releasing the vessel from its moorings. He had to move fast; the boat had five gangplanks and six dock-lines.

The power saw cut smoothly through the steel-reinforced ropes holding the boat to the wharf. The severed fibres frayed and sprang apart as he sliced and in under three minutes the first three cables fell away into the firth.

Dougie moved quickly around the rooms of the royal apartments, his bag filled with home-made firebombs, each with a radio-controlled detonator.

He moved between the spacious rooms and suites, smashing glass viewing panels with a small hammer and tossing in his incendiary devices as he went. He revelled in the wanton destruction he was wreaking. This place was the absolute epitome of what he hated most about Britain and the English. It was a floating microcosm of the British class system. Two hundred hand-picked staff endured long uncomfortable days in cramped quarters doing demeaning duties just to provide this fantasy experience of perfection to a handful of toffee-nosed, jobless layabouts who lounged around in these grand, expansive suites. It made his blood boil.

"And this is the only double bed on the yacht, which was used by Prince Charles and Lady Diana on their honeymoon," he muttered to himself, imitating the dry tone of the audio tour. "As if anyone deserved a two week holiday on their own personal cruise ship with hundreds of servants waitin' on em. Well, take tha' Chuck ol' boy," he said as threw in one of the canisters onto the blankets.

His time was nearly up, but he was about done. It was a big boat and there was no way they could rig the whole thing, so the plan was to set the fire bombs in the fancy bedrooms, the huge state dining room and parlour, the bits that were most symbolic and of course had the most expensive stuff in them.

Brian watched the seconds tick past as his saw bit into the last of the dock-lines. At fourteen minutes exactly, he cut the cable, and watched it slide over the side. He jammed the saw back in his pack and legged it back to the ladder. Dougie and Gail were already waiting for him in the tug.

With the team back on board, Alex edged the tug slowly away from the Britannia, taking up the slack in the towline that connected them. The Pride of the Firth slowed to almost a stand still as the line went taught and, with a noticeable lurch, started to take the strain of the yacht. Alex revved up the engine and started applying the full power of the little boat. The engine roared and for a long time it seemed as if nothing were happening. Then, agonisingly slowly the two vessels began to move together away from the dock. The gangplanks fell away as they started to pick up speed towards the open estuary.

"Aw, this is gonna be so bloody beautiful," said Brian, his voice tripping with excitement.

As the tug chugged slowly out into the middle of the wide waterway, Dougie's team busied themselves with the remaining equipment.

Timing at this point was critical. They knew that by now

someone would have spotted the theft. You can't go far with a four-hundred foot yacht without someone missing it. It would not be long before they were challenged. Their destination was a sandbank out in the Firth where the grounded yacht would be visible from the centre of Edinburgh.

They were within a minute or so of their destination when the challenge came. From the West they heard the distant, but rapidly approaching, rhythmic throb of helicopter rotors.

"Here they come," said Dougie. "Stay down, we just need to finish the job and we'll be away."

The two police helicopters swooped out of the sky. Their powerful searchlights played over the length of the Britannia and picked out the tug.

"Armed police," announced the tinny voice from the loud-speaker. "Stop the boat. Turn around, and raise your hands in the air. "

The tug kept going.

"Almost there," yelled Alex over the sound of the rotors.

"I repeat: This is the police. We have weapons trained on you. Stop the vessel and raise your hands in the air or we are authorised to open fire."

"Keep going, they're bluffing," called Dougie. He had two radio detonators set out on the seat in front of him. He stared defiantly into the blinding white of the searchlight and pushed the red button. The explosion was deafening. Glass shattered as all of the windows on the top two decks at the rear of the yacht were blown out and flames began to consume the fine interior décor. The dark swirling waters around the boat became liquid fire as they reflected the bright orange blaze above.

All four conspirators stared in awe at the spectacular orgy of destruction they had perpetrated.

As if in response, a pair of gunshots rang out from the he-licopter. One of the windows on the tug smashed as a bullet screamed passed Alex.

"They're shootin' at us!" screamed Brian. "They're bloody shootin'. You English Bastards!"

"Now!" cried Alex.

Dougie's hand slapped down on the second detonator button. At first, it seemed as if nothing had happened and then they heard or felt a barely perceptible rumble, and the water around the sides of the Britannia became clouded with tiny air bubbles. Slowly at first, and then more rapidly, the stern of the massive yacht started to sink majestically into the cold waters of the Firth.

*****

"And so," concluded Talisker, "the signs are clear, events are already progressing rapidly."

Silence fell across the council as the assembled gods considered his words. The only sound was the gentle gurgle of the brook outside the torch-lit council chamber.

Jura broke the silence "How long do we have?" she asked, seriously.

"The Leviathan will be called three nights, hence. That is the point of confluence. We have until then to either redirect events onto a path that can avoid it or to find a way to pass through without any discontinuities."

"Too late to avoid it now, young Talisker," said Dufftown, slowly from the far end of the table. He held a wizened finger aloft. "The confluence has already begun. Every path will be drawn in. Even those that appear to diverge from it now will be very easy to redirect into its heart by whoever is behind all this."

"Which brings us to a very interesting question," interposed MacAllan's rich voice. "Who is behind all this?"

Oban sighed. "I can only conclude that it is Anput once again. I fear she considers herself to have unfinished business in our realm."

"Well, I say we go and punch that ol' dog faced bitch in the nose," exclaimed Laphroaig, aggressively raising a fist the size of a melon. "We saw her off once and we can do it again."

"I'd like to see ya try, young-un," sneered Ardbeg. "She is an old god with deep power. She'd leave you with more than a bloody nose."

There were murmurs of approval from around the table. They all remembered the last time they had crossed paths with Anput. It had been hundreds of years ago but they had faced near annihilation. It would be centuries more before the memory started to fade.

"Bring it on!" Exclaimed Laphroaig. "I could use a straight fight instead of all the usual skulking around."

"Laphroaig, Ardbeg is right," declared Oban quietly. "Anput is a dangerous adversary. Besides, you know the rules, no direct confrontations. If we break them, she can too and I fear she is still too powerful for us to take on."

"Oh for the love of peat! Are we just going to sit around here then?" cried the war-god in frustration.

"No, my friend, we will fight but we must work together. We are fewer than we were and it will take your brawn with Jura's wisdom, Ardbeg's cunning and the strength and skills of all rest of all of us together, if we are to win."

Laphroaig folded his arms in a half-sulk and said nothing.

"Jura, could you let us have the benefit of your glass?" asked Oban.

"Of course, my dear," replied Jura drawing forth a leather pouch from inside her shawl. She opened it and drew out a small silver mirror, oval in shape and about the size of her palm. She set it down on the table, muttered a few words and passed her hand over it, as she did so it grew to fill the oak surface.

The gods peered curiously down as their reflections slowly misted up and then the mirror cleared to show a young woman. She was slight with a pale face and dark hair. Her brow was furrowed with concern. She stood in the room of a small cottage. It was a scene of destruction. A man lay on the floor bleeding from a serious head wound.

It looked as if a sound outside the window had just startled her.

*****

Mari hesitated. Had she really heard something? The sight of her poor beaten father at her feet reminded her that she could be in real danger here. Why had she not had the sense to listen to Connor? What could he possibly know about this?

The darkness through the window was impenetrable. All she could see what her own reflection in the glass. All she could hear was the sound of her own breathing. But she knew she had heard something and on some deeper level she could feel it. There was something out there, something angry, hateful.

She had to get out, get away. She started for the front door, crossing the room in a few strides. As she reached for the door the back window burst inwards, showering the room behind her with shards of broken glass. A dark form sailed through the jagged opening and landed in front of the hearth.

The creature before her was like nothing Mari had ever seen. Somewhere between a dog and a bear, it was as black as the night with a long canine face and massive muscular body and torso. Instead of paws, on the end of each leg it had human-like hands. It shook the glass fragments from its coarse coat and then turned on Mari with a snarl that bared dozens of pointed white teeth.

Mari ran. She burst out of the front door, making for her bike. She could hear the creature follow her, its deep savage growl sounded almost on top of her. She turned to look back and tripped, stubbing her toe on a loose flagstone and sprawled roughly on the hard-packed dirt. Something sharp in her jeans pocket dug into her leg. Without thinking she reached down and pulled it out. It was the brooch that Connor had given her.

The creature behind her was almost on her but it suddenly reeled back at the sight of the brooch.

The large silver talisman felt heavy in her hand. In the soft light the massive milky-white pearl at its centre seemed to almost glow with a feint luminescence of its own. Monsters? Magic talismans? This was all just too weird. She had to get out of here.

Warding the creature off with the brooch, Mari picked herself up and started backing towards her bike. It watched her with pure hatred in its eyes, but made no move. Something was wrong. Again, that feeling, she could sense something. There was another of these creatures behind her, in the shadows outside the light from the house.

She could feel her attackers were waiting to pounce, but she needed both hands to get the bike started. With a deep breath she jammed the brooch back into her jeans pulled the bike off its stand and kicked the engine to life.

Both of the creatures leapt at the motorcycle as Mari slipped the clutch. The first was too slow and fell to one side. The second was better positioned and managed to get one arm over the saddle behind Mari, and grab her leg with its hand. The bike wobbled wildly with the change of weight but Mari kept control, dragging the beast along with her.

The bony fingers dug into her leg as it tried to pull itself up. The creature howled as it was dragged bodily over the stony track but it did not let go. She had to get rid of the thing or it was going to pull her off.

She was almost to the road. Just ahead, illuminated in the dancing headlight, she caught sight of the broken gate lying in the grass at its drunken angle. She leant the bike over and swung it around in an arc that took it within inches of the rotting wooden structure. There was a splintering thud and then a blood-curdling howl as the trailing body of the creature struck the edge of the gate. With a wrench, the fingers gripping her leg fell away.

Mari turned the bike unsteadily onto tarmac and sped away without looking back. Behind her, the broken gate that had for so long marked the track to her home finally fell from it rusted hinges and collapsed into the long grass.

*****

Grash-Tharl (c. Shadow Beast, Hell Hound) The Shadow Beast is a daemon from the time of the great pyramids. It is said that powerful Egyptian Magi would summon them for royal hunting trips as a display of power. They are part dog or jackal, part human or ape, the result was something rather like a canine baboon. They are creatures of the abyss that need neither sleep nor sustenance. They cannot be killed, although their corporeal form can be destroyed and like many such daemons they can only remain in the material world for a few hours — possibly days, depending on the strength of the binding spell. Once bound, these beasts are fiercely loyal.

— Gimwald's Cyclopedic
Daemons and Demi-gods
of the Ancients.

*****

In the pale light of her headlamp, the narrow road flowed like a grey-black river under her front tire.

Mari was starting to feel tired and cold. The adrenalin was wearing off. Her blouse, damp with sweat, clung to her back underneath the heavy leather jacket. She wanted to put a few more miles between her and those dreadful creatures before she would let herself feel safe. She was still a couple of miles from the main road and the twist and turns on this little stretch meant she couldn't get much above thirty miles an hour.

She crested a blind rise, and there, standing in the middle of the road, waiting, was another one of these dog-beasts. Instinctively, she hit the brakes and the motorbike started to skid. The beast crouched down ready to pounce.

To one side of the road, just before where the animal hunkered down, a rough farm track led off across the open countryside. Mari leant the bike over hard and let go of the front brake. She had just enough control left to slide the bike round and take off down the bumpy uneven surface. The beast instantly leapt after her.

The bike bounced wildly down the deeply rutted track like a marble down a drainpipe, skittering crazily from side to side. It was all Mari could do to keep it in roughly the right direction. If she hit a rock or a deep pothole now, she'd be toast. The beast was right behind her and it was gaining. Even over the sound of the engine she could hear the angry snarls getting louder.

Then, from the crest of a hill in front of her came a long pale beam of light, as if someone had just released a single ray of sunlight into the dark night. It shone first on her and she felt warmth and joy at its touch. Then it fell on the beast and

Mari heard a strangled howl as the creature fell to the ground; doubled up in pain.

She did not look back but focussed all her attention on navigating the rough path. She desperately needed to get off this old farm track and back onto a proper road; with tarmac under her tires again she could easily outdistance these monsters. The track she was on would meet the main Portree road in another mile or so of potholes and bumps. On the other hand, the road itself was not far away now. Down to her left, across the field, she could catch glimpses of it when the land dipped down. It could not be more than a few hundred yards away. The rough grass was fairly firm — maybe she should cut across? If she took it steadily, watching out for foxholes and gorse bushes, she could get to the road much faster.

She made the decision and turned the bike off the track to cut across the open country. The bike rose to the challenge. If anything, it was easier going than it had been on the track, the surface was softer but far more even and predictable. The engine roared as she ate up the distance.

She was almost to safety when disaster struck. There was a drainage ditch running alongside the road. It was well hidden, choked with weeds and long grass. By the time she saw it, she was almost on top of it and had no time to react. Her front wheel dropped instantly into the ditch and hit the far side hard, bringing the bike to a jarring halt.

Mari was thrown over the handlebars, and landed roughly on the soft peaty turf of the roadside.

*****

"Aristos, I can take little more of this," exclaimed Neferubity, with uncharacteristic frustration. "We have been at sea for months. I would rather face my father than remain incarcerated on this floating gaol any longer." It was getting late in the evening. The days were longer here and the sunsets slower. The first stars were starting to appear in the sky as the light of Ra's great eye dimmed beyond the horizon.

Their voyage had been long and perilous. They stopped only when they had to, to take on water and provisions and Neferubity had to remain inside the stuffy confines of the Captain's cabin. As they sailed, the blazing sun grew weaker and yellower in the sky. The weather grew colder and the seas grew rougher.

Aristos took her hand. "Patience, my dear. It will not be long now. We should arrive at our new home soon – tomorrow, if the gods bless us with a good wind." He had known where he was heading but he was careful not to go straight there. He travelled widely, leaving false trails behind him as he went, for he knew they would be followed.

"I know that it will please you," he went on. "It is a beautiful land and far, far from your father. He will not find us there — he will never find us."

They embraced, finding safety and comfort in the closeness of each other.

Aristos wondered, not for the first time, at the turn his life had taken. He loved Neferubity more than he could say, more than he could understand, but he was afraid. Things would be different here. He had had to leave so much behind. It would be worth it he told himself as he felt the warmth of Neferubity's soft body against his.

Neferubity said nothing, but hugged Aristos a little tighter. She would not go so far as to say that she had *the sight*, but she knew things — about the world and about the future. One thing she knew for certain was that one-day her father would find them.

"It is not for us," she whispered, softly. "It is for our children. We must find a safe place for them."

*****

"Stupid, bloody-minded headstrong girl," muttered Connor to himself as he staggered after the rapidly retreating motorbike.

This is really not how it is supposed to go, he kept telling himself. He had seriously considered forcibly abducting Mari in the pub, but fundamental to the problem here was the absence of trust and unfortunately kidnapping her was not going to help with that. Instead, he had started out on foot to cross the fields to Mari's cottage, hoping that he could get there in time to help when the danger eventually presented itself. The trouble is that you can't help someone until they know they need help. Tragically, by the time that pig-headed girl understood that she had a problem; there was a very real chance that it would be too late.

He heard Mari's motorcycle before he saw it and rushed to the top of the nearest rise. In the far distance, he could make out the bouncing headlight and the dark shape of the Shadow creature in pursuit.

He had to admit, it had been pretty effin' cool to see the white Light of Làthair pour from his staff and weaken the beast. There's not many as could do tha', he thought to himself with a small grin.

And yet despite his help, Mari had utterly failed to take the only sensible course of action and ride *toward* him. Instead, she had headed off in completely the other direction, at *high speed.*

"Mari! Mari!" he yelled in frustration, but there was no way she could hear him at that distance, with the noise of that confounded smelly machine ringing in her ears. "Mari, ya daft bitch come here!"

Connor was not given much to exercise and following the speeding bike seemed fairly futile. It felt like he had been plodding around the island all night. His feet ached and his trousers were wet and he really needed a smoke. However, there wasn't much else he could do and so he started off in the direction of the whining engine as rapidly as his tired legs would allow. The sound gradually became more distant and then suddenly, ominously, it went quiet. He tried, ineffectively, to pick up his pace.

*****

"Hey Tal, looks like yer man could use a work-out" said Laphroaig, laughing coarsely at the image in the glass of the hyperventilating folk singer, half running, half staggering across the field.

"Is he really the best you have, Talisker?" asked Ardbeg, regarding Talisker sharply. "If our fate hangs in his hands, we are truly in trouble."

"C'mon, you guy's. He's not that bad," piped Dalwhinnie, touching Talisker's arm in a conciliatory fashion. "I think he's cute; in an earnest, troubled sort of a way."

"He wielded the Light of Làthair, did he not?" said Talisker, defensively, not sure that Dalwhinnie's comments were helping. "There's been few who could have done that for centuries."

"Aye, but it'll take more than that to get us through this," replied Laphroaig, dismissively. He was enjoying needling his brother. "Face it Tal, he's just not hero material."

"Heroes can sprout from even the most unlikely of seeds, Laphroaig," put in Lagavulin. "Do you eemember William Wallace when he was young? He seemed hopeless."

"Dishey, though!" exclaimed Dalwhinnie, with a grin.

"He did give her the brooch," went on Talisker, containing his frustration.

"But he didn't teach her how to use it," countered MacAllan. "He'd have been better keeping it. It can't help her yet and she might loose it and then where would we be?"

"He has a strong heart," insisted Talisker.

"Maybe," replied Laphroaig, watching the middle-aged man in the oversized looking-glass staggering across the fields, "but he has weak lungs."

*****

Dougie coughed involuntarily as the smoke from the inferno before him drifted over the tug. The flames from the sinking Royal Yacht lit up the dark waters of the Firth with an orange blaze. This will be the perfect symbol of the separatist struggle: the burnt out husk of the English monarchy scuttled in the Firth for all to see. The charred remains would be visible from the High Street in the centre of Edinburgh, like a dark skeleton, foretelling the demise of the English reign. It was perfect.

He was stirred from his thoughts by another round of shots from the watching helicopters and the noise of an approaching boat. The job was done. It was time to get out before they were caught.

"C'mon over the side!" he ordered.

Gail and Brian were already in dry suits and ready to go. Almost before Dougie spoke they stepped out over the side of the tug and disappeared into the black watery depths. Alex was still fussing with his scuba tank. He'd been driving the boat and hadn't had time to get the suit on properly. Dougie started to cross the deck to help him when more shots rang out from the chopper and Alex fell forward onto the deck. The earlier shooting had been mostly for show but as it became clear their quarry was escaping the police were now aiming closer to the mark. The tank slipped from his hands and Dougie could see a large pool of blood rapidly forming on the metal deck under Alex. He did not get up.

"You, on the boat. Put your hands in the air," came the voice over the police megaphone.

Without another thought Dougie, grabbed his Dive Propulsion Vehicle and threw himself over the side of the tug and into the cold dark waters of the Firth.

The DPV was a long cylinder with handles and a propeller. Like a creature from the depths, it pulled him along underwater. He was quickly swallowed by the darkness of the Firth unseen and unfollowable.

It was about twenty minutes later that he reached the slipway on the South shore. He squatted in the shallows near the concrete slope staying in the shadow of the pier as he waited for the others. Above him, the orange glow of nearby streetlights lit up the night. One of the seals in the wrist of the dry suit had started to leak and the cold water had found its way into his clothes. He had barely noticed though, his heart still burned with the sweet joy of success.

The boat blazed in the distance, although by the looks of things, there were now fireboats on hand trying to douse the flames.

The only blot on an otherwise perfect mission was the loss of Alex. The guy had been a burden; there was no mistake about that. He'd been more than a little slow on the uptake, but he had been well meaning and he'd done his job. Of course, there were bound to be casualties. This was a war. You can't make omelettes an' all that. But there was something else, *she* had said it quite explicitly: "You do not need to be afraid. Their bullets will not hit you." As disturbing as it was to find her detailed predictions come out exactly as foretold, Dougie decided that it was even more disturbing when they came out dead wrong, particularly when the ones that were wrong concerned his personal safety.

The helicopters now split up. One patroled the area around the boat while the other scanned the waters and banks with its search light. Dougie had come up to the surface twice to get his bearings but he knew they hadn't seen him. While they were still in the water, they were pretty safe, but as soon as they got out, they were exposed.

He was beginning to wonder about the others. They had left the boat before him. They should be here by now. Kneeling in the shallows he stuck his head out of the water and let out a low whistle. All the while he was keeping careful hold of the DPV, it would be a bugger to find in the dark waters if he let it fall.

The escape had, like everything else, been planned to the last detail. The slipway in South Queensferry was sheltered from view on one side by a pier. It was unlit and was not overlooked by the local houses. The car was parked near the top in a public car park.

Dougie waited. There was no response to his call all he could hear was the lapping of the water against the pier wall and the distant drone of the helicopters. The others should be here, he thought again. What if they had been picked up by the police? Or maybe they had got here ahead of him and taken the car already? He forcibly tried to calm himself, staying low in the water. He waited.

The wait went on. The adrenaline high from the operation

was wearing off now. The leak in his suit left him cold and wet and the distant buzz of the helicopters made him anxious. Another ten minutes, he decided. If there was still no sign of the others, he'd start for the car by himself.

The sound of a whistle off interrupted his thoughts. He turned and saw the shape of a dark, dry-suit, head pushing out of the water. An arm came up and waved at him.

He was so relieved that without thinking, he waved back, but then rapidly pulled his hand down and gently cursed his own lack of professionalism. It was Brian and behind him he could just make out the wake of what must be Gail's DPV, just beneath the surface. In a few moments they joined him in the shallows and started hauling the DPVs out onto the slipway.

"Pleased to see us?" asked Gail, seeing the expression on Dougie's face as she approached.

"Let's just get out of here," replied Dougie, through clench-ed teeth.

"Wha abou' the big man? Where's he at?" asked Brian, re-ferring to Alex.

Dougie looked away. "He got shot in the chest, just as we were leavin',"

"No way!" exclaimed Brian, raising his voice considerably more than was safe. "The bastards! It's only an old boat. I canne believe they'd shoot him over a knackered old boat. How is he? Is he hurt bad, like?"

"I don't know if he's going to make it. He fell. There was loads o' blood."

They were all silent for a moment.

"We have to go. Now!" said Dougie, finally.

As quickly as they could, they pulled their diving equipment out of the water and piled it on the slipway, in the shadow of the pier. Then they stripped off their dry suits and Dougie and Brian went to get the car.

They climbed the broken concrete slipway and stepped over the low barrier that marked the edge of the Pay-and-Display car park.

Dougie's car was well chosen, an old blue Ford Mondeo;

it looked like a dozen others in the car park and was instantly forgettable.

"You've still got the keys?" asked Dougie, as they drew near.

"Wha' da ya mean hav' I got the keys?" asked Brian.

"Wha' da ya mean: wha' da *I* mean? You had the keys. You were supposed to bring 'em sos we could *get away*, ken!"

Dougie had had a long night and he was starting to loose patience. His eyes kept drifting toward the sky, which was filled with the distant sound of whirring rotors.

"Nah," said Brian, the realisation slowly dawning on him. "Alex had the keys. Remember? He drove it here."

"Och, shite," said Dougie, realising that Brian was right, and with that the fact that the night had taken a distinct turn for the worse. "Wha' do we do now?"

Suddenly they both noticed the sound of the rotors getting louder, as one of the police helicopters approached.

*****

Mari noticed the silence. The roar of the bike's engine had been replaced with...nothing, empty sound. For a moment she lay still listening to the silence. She could taste earth, and blood. She put a hand to her face. It was numb, but it seemed like the blood she was tasting came from no more than a cut lip. She rolled over and tried to sit up. Pain shot through her body. It felt like every limb was competing to declare itself the most damaged.

She looked around. She sat on the grass verge on the side of the main road. A thin frail moon had just risen above the horizon. In its pale light, it seemed as if there were hundreds of suspicious dark shapes in the distance on all sides. Trees and gorse bushes, she told herself.

She examined herself carefully, gently prodding her aching flesh. The final assessment was not too bad, just several bruises and scrapes. Nothing seemed to be broken as far as she could tell, but her left knee hurt like crazy, the leg of her jeans had been ripped and in the half-light she could see dark blood staining the blue denim.

She took a deep breath and tried to stand up, ignoring the complaints from her battered body. She succeeded, finding she was able to walk, with a bit of a limp. The rear wheel of her bike protruded awkwardly from the ditch. It was in a bad way. The impact had bent the front forks so badly that the front wheel was jammed up against the petrol tank. It was probably a write-off — certainly there was no way it was going anywhere tonight.

She sat down again on the grass and started to consider her options. The strange events of the evening began to wash over her like the memories of a bad dream. Perhaps it was a dream? Maybe she had just fallen off her bike on the way home and hit her head? She looked again at the bike. The tire marks in the soft turf on the far side of the ditch indicated that she had been riding across the field when she hit it. The uncomfortable reality of her memories reasserted itself forcefully. There was no getting out of it, there had been something chasing her, something nasty and whatever it was, it could still be out there. She was less than a mile away from when that light (whatever that was) had struck that creature. Was it dead, she wondered, or just wounded, like her. She could not stay here, that was clear, but where could she go? With her damaged leg she wouldn't get very far, nor could she move quickly and she certainly would leave a great trail for any pursuing dogs (or insane-monster-dog-beasts).

She desperately wanted to go home. She should be helping her father – but the Thornley's would do that and *they* would be waiting for her to come back. She shuddered at the thought. Perhaps that's where they were right now. *Katie*! She had to do something to help Katie; these things had taken her little cousin. She could at least get to a phone and call the police.

She had to admit, all of a sudden, Connor's strange babbling was to be seen in a new light. He clearly knew something, if only she had had the sense to listen to him when she had the chance. From here, she could probably make it to his boat. It was usually moored on the old whaler's pier. He might be able to answer some of her questions and he had said he could protect her.

She chewed on this idea for a moment. She could use a friend right now. On the other hand, what could Connor possibly do to protect her? The scrawny folk singer was not exactly her picture of a body-guard, and a stirring rendition of "The Merry Oak" was not really going to help against these attackers. And there would be no phone on his boat.

God, why were these beasts pursuing her? Attacking her family? Was her father going to be okay? Her eyes flicked warily over the dark hillside again, unsuccessfully searching for movement.

The distant sound of a car roused her from her thoughts. Away at the top of the road, the blank stare of a pair of headlights swept around a corner and turned to meet her gaze. The car was still over half a mile away but it was coming rapidly this way.

Mari waved her aching arms wildly to flag it down. It was a lucky break, there would not be much traffic coming down this road at this time of night.

As it got nearer it started to slow and Mari could begin to make out its shape. It was some sort of two-seater sports car.

Mari knew most of the people in this part of the island pretty well, and she also knew their cars. This was low, fast and mean-looking. She didn't know anyone who drove a sports car. It was not the sort of vehicle people associated with island life. She began to wonder about the wisdom of flagging down the first car she saw, but it was too late now.

The car drew to a halt beside her and the passenger-side window wound itself down with electrical smoothness.

Mari peered apprehensively inside.

"Hello!" said the driver. His voice was smooth, well-spoken and very English. It set Mari's teeth on edge to hear it. "Gosh! Fancy meeting you here."

*****

The police helicopter flew low and fast, its powerful search-light scanning the ground along the banks of the Firth as it went.

Dougie and Brian ducked down between the cars as it drew near. They saw the bright beam of its searchlight sweep through the car park. Hardly daring to breath, they kept their heads low. Then, almost as suddenly as it had arrived, the helicopter banked away and headed out across the water.

"Bugger me! Tha' was close," said Brian under his breath. "Now how are we gonna get oot' a here?"

"Stay here," replied Dougie, "and keep out 'a sight. I'll get us out a here."

Cursing his luck, he crossed the street, and started casting about on the ground for something. Things had been going so well and then Alex had to go and get himself shot — useless bastard! There, he saw what he was looking for, an old house brick. He hopped over a low garden wall and grabbed it.

He strode deliberately back to the car with his trophy and then, without pausing, swung it hard and fast at the driver-side window. There was a loud smashing of glass and the window shattered inwards in a million glass chips. A dog started barking in a nearby yard but there was no other response to the noise.

Dougie reached inside and opened the door. With the end of his jacket pulled over his hand, he swept the worst of the broken glass from the colourless fabric seat and reached across to unlock the passenger door for Brian.

"Aye, that's all very well but how are we gonna go any-where..." Brian was saying.

Dougie ignored him. He'd done this once before, in training — it was tricky to get it to work though. He pulled out a pocket knife and placed it, point first, into the ignition lock. Then, using the brick as a hammer, he bashed its handle until the thin knife was driven deep into the lock. Then grasping the knife handle, he tried to turn it. At first it refused to budge but after a moment or two of jiggling and forcing, the knife twisted and the car started.

"Rock On!" exclaimed Brian, with enthusiasm as the engine sprang to life.

It took less than five minutes to get the car round to the slipway and load up the diving gear. Ten minutes later they were doing 85 miles an hour down the A90 towards Edinburgh.

Brian sprawled out as best as his lanky form would allow the cramped back seat, his head lolling backwards and his eyes closed as he tried to sleep. Gail sat next to him, huddling her arms around her knees as the freezing night air roared through the broken window.

Dougie watched the flicker of the white markings as they passed under the car on the empty road in front of him. His thoughts spun as he tried to make sense of the night's events. It was tough to loose someone, even someone like Alex. It shouldn't have happened, but what was worse than the guilt and the sense of loss was the fear; Dougie knew very well that one of those bullets could have hit him.

*****

Mari stared at the driver of the car. It was the Englishman from the pub that evening. He smiled at her gently, even hopefully. It was a nice smile, warm and kind.

"Look, I didn't get a chance to thank you earlier. For what you did. It was very brave of you."

"You need to watch yerself. You could get yourself seriously hurt," said Mari, reproachfully as she limped towards the car. "We don't like the English around here."

"Er, no."

There was a pause as suddenly neither could think what to say next.

"Having trouble with your motorcycle?" he asked, finally.

"Ah, it's nothin'. It just slid out on the corner," she replied, as casually as she could. She gestured at the road ahead, which, she realised belatedly, was embarrassingly straight.

The Englishman did not seem to notice.

"Can I give you a lift somewhere?" he offered.

"No. Look, I'm just fine," Mari replied and started to hobble off down the road. She had only gone a few steps before she had to stop. Her knee was protesting wildly in pain. Tears came to her eyes and she desperately tried to blink them away, keeping her face turned away from the Englishman.

"Are you really sure?" he persisted, earnestly. "I mean, it's no trouble."

"Well, okay, then" said Mari, reluctantly. She really did not want to get in a car with an Englishman and most of all not *this* Englishman; but there seemed to be no choice.

She opened the long door and got into the low leather seat. She felt the precision-engineered German upholstery softly deforming to support her weight. The car smelled expensive.

"Heavens, you're hurt," he said, seeing her ripped, blood-stained jeans.

"Look, I'll be fine. It's just a scratch, *really*." She looked over and saw his honest face full of heartfelt concern. Perhaps he wasn't actually that bad after all, she thought. Suddenly, she realised she was being an idiot. After all, he was only trying to help. She started to blush. Hopefully, in the dim light, he wouldn't be able to see.

"Are you OK?" he asked.

"I'm honestly no' sure," replied Mari, almost to herself. "It's been a bloody *weird* night."

*****

He crept quietly up behind her.

It was a chill night. A spectacular canopy of stars twinkled brightly and a golden harvest moon reflected off the rippling waves of the sea. She looked down at the waves from the low cliff. It was a most beautiful place indeed. But cold, she had never known such cold. This was too far from Ra's path for her. But she was not unhappy.

He readied his hands to cover her eyes.

"Pamphilos, I know you're there," she said without turning around.

"Scotia, my dear, some day you should let me take you by surprise, just for my own satisfaction," he pouted.

To further confound any pursuers they had assumed new names. Aristos took the name Pamphilos which meant "friend of all" in his tongue. Neferubity took the name Scotia that meant "mother" in her own. It had been more than a little strange at first but now they stuck to their aliases even when they were alone.

Scotia laughed and turned to kiss him. She ran her hands through his thick dark hair. His hands rested on her belly that was round and full with their child.

"Why do you always come here? It's so cold" he asked.

"I like to watch the waves," she lied. "They are soothing."

They stood together for a moment, his arm about her shoulder watching the sea.

They'd been in Alba for more than two years. They had landed on an island in the northeast, home to a powerful thane by the name of Gregorian. His clan, the McLeods, controlled not just the island itself but a large part of the mainland as well. If that were not enough Thane Gregorian was also High Clansman, which in effect, made him king of all Alba.

His reign had been long and peaceful but he was getting old now and trouble was beginning to stir. Gregorian had no heir and there were many pretenders awaiting their chance to seize a share of his power.

He had welcomed Scotia and Pamphilos warmly. These rich regal strangers had a mysterious past that they were clearly unwilling to share, but they had been generous and, over time, Gregorian had come to trust them.

Pamphilos found his skills as a merchant could keep them well fed. He ran his boat up and down the coast trading furs from the north for grain and cattle from the south. He made far less than when he had traded spices and precious metals, back in the civilized world, but it was an honest living.

Scotia spent her time in the politics of the thane's court. Although it was not considered a woman's place in this land, Gregorian had, on occasion, even invited her to attend court itself. Having grown up in one of the most powerful royal houses of the time, she was well schooled in politics, both practically and academically.

She could easily see through the simple games of these more

primitive people. Gregorian had found her advice valuable on more than one occasion.

"Pamphilos, my dear, I have to ask a favour of you," she said, turning away from the sea at last and bringing her dark eyes to meet his.

"Of course," he replied, concerned by the seriousness of her tone.

"Gregorian will be attacked tonight in his sleep."

He frowned and looked away for a moment. "Those are grave tidings. The old Thane has been kind to us. Is there anything we can do?"

"You must save him. Our safety, as well as his, lies in the balance here. Were he to die, we would be like an open purse to an incoming thane in need of gold to help fight his enemies."

"Very well, what needs to be done?" he asked, grimly.

"Just after the third bell as the sky is beginning to light, you must walk past Gregorian's dwelling as if unable to sleep. His guards will be lying dead at the door. You will notice this and rush straight in. Do not pause. Once you are inside, you will find the Thane already wounded, but still alive. You must kill his attacker. Do not leave until you are sure the assassin is dead, when you do no one must see you go."

"I understand," said Pamphilos, as bravely as he could manage. Another man might have asked his wife how she knew these things. Pamphilos knew better. His wife had always had the ability to see things others did not, but since she had had the Stone, she was able to see not only what would happen, but what they should do to prevent it. She could tell him when he should sail to find the most favourable prices, when not to sail to avoid the most dangerous storms. She called it a "speaking stone"; it spoke no word to him, but he trusted her.

"Pamphilos, remember, be sure that the attacker is dead before you leave."

*****

The Englishman put the car in gear and pulled smoothly away.

Mari glanced at him out of the corner of her eye. He didn't suit the car — he was too tall and lanky for it. His blond curls brushed the roof and she got the impression that his knees could get stuck under the small leather bound steering wheel. Then again, he was the sort of person who looked like he would appear out of place in his own front room.

"I need to use a phone," said Mari. "It's very important. Do you have a mobile?"

"Sorry," he said with a shrug. "The reception up here is so bad, I don't even bring it out with me. I could drive you to a telephone box, if you tell me where to go?"

Where was the nearest phone? The only public phone box on this side of the island had been out of order for the last six months. Someone had ripped the handset off and scrawled: "Bugger off English Tourists" on the wall.

There would be no shops or even pubs open at this time.

"I could take you home?" he offered, after what Mari suddenly realised must have been a long pause. "Do you live around here?"

"No, I can't go home right now," she said at once. It was a statement that sort of needed an explanation she realised. Snapshots filled her mind: her father lying beaten on the ground, Katie's bed empty, the window smashing as that creature leaped into the room. What could she tell him that would make sense?

"Someone broke in — I have to call the police," she blurted.

Another realisation was gently dawning on Mari. There was no way she was going back to her house tonight. Where was she going to spend the night? She had about ten pounds in cash on her — not enough money for a hotel or a B&B. Her gran lived nearly an hour's drive away on the mainland.

"That sounds terrible," said the Englishman. Mari looked at him. He was being sincere.

"Do you need somewhere to spend the night?" he asked. "Only I'm renting this cottage. It's got two extra bedrooms, even an extra bathroom. You could get a good night's rest and sort yourself out tomorrow."

Mari thought about it for a minute. It seemed like a genuine offer, god knows she could use a decent night's rest and the monsters that were after her would be unlikely to be able to find her there.

"It's the least I can do after the way you helped me," he pressed.

"Alright," she said finally, "you have a phone there, right?"

"Ah, well, um, no, not really. You see the phones on the estate are all being repaired at the moment."

"The estate?"

"Oh, yes, I'm staying in one of the cottages in the grounds of Dunvegan Castle. Very pretty, trees, ocean view, beautiful sunsets."

"But no telephones?"

"Well, yes, or rather, no. I mean, there is a phone but it's buggered right now. The whole place is closed to the public at the moment. They are rewiring everything. The Clan Chief and his family are in France. The only phone on the site that works at the moment is in the estate manager's house."

"Have you stayed there long?"

"About a month, I'm a friend of the family, you see. Frankly I'm rather glad to get away from telephones, they seem to ring all the time and it's never anyone you want to talk to...

"She's been terribly nice about it ... the estate manager that is, lovely woman ... Cynthia Farrow ... she said I can come by and use her phone anytime."

The mention of that name suddenly set Mari's mind reeling. *Cynthia Farrow,* the name her father had used before he lost consciousness. The unreal scene visited Mari's thoughts again.

She returned to the present and noticed that the Englishman was still talking.

"...never bothered, of course, never really had need..."

"I need to go there tonight. I need to use her phone."

"Oh, well, she did say anytime, but it's rather late. I could take you round there in the morning perhaps?"

"We have to go there *now!* This is important."

"Well, um, okay, whatever you say."

They drove on a little in silence. The car was smooth and

quiet on the winding road. Mari started to relax a little. Her leg throbbed gently but was soothed by the warm air from the car's interior heater that swirled cosily around her feet. With some effort, she took off her heavy leather biker's jacket and folded it into the footwell under her legs.

"My name is William," said the Englishman, awkwardly trying to offer his hand for a handshake that was not reciprocated.

"Mari, I'm Mari," she replied, eventually, folding her arms.

"I know, Mari McLeod," he said. "They told me in The Plough — up the street from The Bonnie Prince Charlie."

"Well, they should mind their own bloody business," exclaimed Mari angrily.

"I'm sorry. I only wanted to say, thank you," said William.

"Right. Well, now ya have," she replied abruptly, but her manner was really more reflex than anything else. She was actually starting to feel a little more positive. She had found somewhere to sleep, access to a telephone and perhaps she could find out a little more about how Cynthia Farrow fitted into the picture. It seemed that the gods were finally smiling on her.

*****

"I don't know," grumped Laphroaig with a deep scowl. "It makes no sense to me."

"Do *you* think they are well-matched, Dalwhinnie?" asked Jura calmly, as they peered at the image of Mari and William in the car.

"My dear, they are perfect for each other," replied the love-goddess with a smirk.

"I have no idea wha' you gals are talkin' aboot. She hates him. It's in her eyes," declared Laphroaig "There's no way those two will get it together. She'd sooner punch him in the face as kiss him."

"Exactly," replied Dalwhinnie, winking at him, "True love."

"I must be missing something," remarked Lagavulin, looking over her knitting. "Mortal love is a beautiful thing, certainly, but why do we care about these two?"

"It's the prophesy, Nan" explained Dalwhinnie. "You remember that monk."

"St. Farole," inserted Ardbeg.

"Now, he was a few drams short of a keg, that one," said Laphroaig.

"He had to be," croaked Dufftown, from the end of the table. "No mortal can see the paths of the distant future and hold on to the reality of the present."

"'*And it will come to pass that the Flower will loose her heart to an enemy,*'"Quoted Talisker with a flourish.

"Are we sure that she is the Flower, though?" Asked Arbeg sharply. "She has still to prove herself."

All of the gods started talking at once, all except Talisker and Oban, who for a few moments seemed somewhat distant at the table, if anyone had been paying attention. In fact, this was literally the case. Oban and Talisker were about a mile distant: standing on a grassy bank under a broad oak tree on the far side of the loch from the council chamber. As gods, it was relatively straightforward for them to be in many places at the same time, although difficult for them to pay attention to what was happening in more than one.

"What is it, my liege?" asked Talisker, looking across the rippling waters of the loch at the torch-lit chamber as his otherself nodded absently to a remark someone had just made. "Why do you bring us apart from the others?"

"Talisker, something is amiss here,"began Oban. "The girl's fate is being twisted against us, and I fear that the conflicting influence is not coming from outside."

"My Lord, you believe we have a traitor in our midst?"asked Talisker, with genuine concern.

"Let's just say I believe we must prepare ourselves against that possibility,"replied Oban.

They fell grimly silent as they both looked back to the distant scene of the arguing gods in the council chamber.

*****

Mari stared into the darkness beyond the glare of the headlights as William drove the sports car with infuriating caution.

She glanced over at him. He had an ugly bruise forming on his left cheek and over his eye. It'd probably be a real shiner in the morning. Pity really, now that she actually looked at his face, he was actually kind of, well, nice-looking in a soppy, useless sort of way. Idly she found herself wondering how it would feel to run her fingers through that curly mop of hair...

"What are you doing here?" she asked, mostly to distract her train of thought.

"What are any of us doing here?"

"No, I mean here, on Skye. We don't get many English here these days — with troubles an' all."

"I'm just visiting friends."

"But how can you have friends here? I mean, you're English." She said the words before realising how stupid they must sound. Still, who around here would have English friends? No one who came drinking in the Bonnie Prince that's for sure.

"Why not? We are all the same."

"Speak fea yerself."

"Look, I'm sorry, but would you even know where the border was if there wasn't a sign post on the A1?"

"That's easy for you to say. You didn't grow up in a land ruled by foreigners for the last four centuries."

"What about the Scottish Parliament?"

"What about it? A pointless talking shop in an overpriced building. How does that help?"

"But isn't it strange how it didn't used to be such a problem for people. Why is it that in the last five years it has suddenly started to matter so much that it's worth dying for? Worth *killing* for?"

He had a point. Why did it suddenly seem so important? Hating the English had gone from jokes about clueless tourists to knife fights. Watching an England-Scotland game in a Scottish pub with on was like a return to the days of warring clanchiefs where anger and hatred flowed almost as fast as lager and eighty-shilling. Why did she hate the English so much? It was all very well to say that they were bastards when they were so far away, but when actually sitting next to one. It seemed a bit — odd.

"Perhaps, we just woke up," she answered. "We finally got it together."

"But let me ask you a question," he said, looking over at her. "Are you united around your love of Scotland, or around your hatred of the English?"

"It doesn't matter. We are fighting together for the first time."

"But what happens when you win?"

"Sorry?"

"When you throw the English out, once and for all, who will be the people in power in the new Scotland? Who is behind all the attacks? Who is the Scottish Separatist Army? What sort of country will it be with them running the place?"

"It's a grass roots organization, ordinary people rising up because they can take no more."

William shook his head.

"I don't think so: fourteen attacks in the last 2 years — every one well-planned and executed. They use military weapons and explosives. They are well-trained, well-organized and well-funded."

"Wha' are you suggestin'?"

"I'm saying that maybe there's more going on than meets the eye. Maybe there is another organization or another country that is behind all this duping the Scottish people."

"Look, I don't want to talk about it, alright," she replied, dismissively and turned away to look out of her window again. They drove on in silence. Mari thoughts returned to Katie and the terrible things that might be happening to her. Perhaps the Englishman had a point. No one knew who was behind the SSA. But right now, she really didn't care.

*****

The phone box was cold and smelled of urine. The light had broken but the phone seemed to work. Dougie stood there in the dark, shivering, waiting for the call, his clothes still wet. In the dim orange glow of a distant streetlight he could just make out the marker-pen scrawls of graffiti on the scratched perspex windows.

Outside, two girls walked past in short skirts and high heels. They were wearing too much make-up and too few clothes. They passed the phone box without even noticing Dougie. He watched them go. It must be a little after three o'clock, he thought to himself, when all the clubs shut. A couple of years ago, he'd have been out there too, partying every weekend. It was strange to see people still doing that. His world had changed a lot since them.

The ringing phone made him start. He grabbed the heavy plastic handset.

"Yes?"

"It's me."

The woman's voice gave him a chill that he felt even above the cold of the night. He had never met her, and hoped very much that he never would.

"The party went according to plan," reported Dougie.

"Good."

"Except," he said slowly, "we suffered a loss."

"I know," replied the voice. "Was there anything else?"

Dougie paused. Suddenly all the anger, frustration and fear that had been festering all night welled up inside him.

"You said the bullets wouldn't hit us. It was on the brief. I read it," he blurted out, forgetting his carefully prepared coded-speak.

"I said that they would not hit *you*. Your colleague had served his purpose." The voice was cold and unfeeling, even impatient. "Be ready. We strike again tomorrow night."

She hung up.

Dougie slammed the receiver back down onto its cradle, swearing silently at his lack of self-control. This was war, he reminded himself again. There was no room for feelings or sentimentality here. She was right; Alex had done what they needed him to do. He was just being soft. Nevertheless he couldn't help asking the question: What was going to happen to him when his purpose had been served?

*****

Pamphilos heard the last chime of the third bell fall away as he walked through the village. He hurried through the streets, not wanting to be late, glad that there was no one watching.

The Thane's house was easy to spot, on the far side of the village square. It was the only two-story building in the village. It was built, as they all were, from uncut stones and roofed with thatch. The Thane was very proud of his upper floor that gave him a commanding view over the village to the woods beyond.

As Pamphilos approached, he saw the bodies of the two guards lying in pools of their own blood at the foot of the wide front door. The door itself was slightly ajar.

Pamphilos drew his sword, stepping over the bodies as quietly as he could. His sword was short and curved, designed for fighting at close quarters on a ship. Training in swordsmanship was a necessary skill for a merchant who wanted to keep his cargo (and his life). Pamphilos was a fair swordsman, but not much of a killer. The closest he had come to killing a man was when he once badly wounded a thief who had sneaked on board his ship while docked, looking for valuables. He may have died eventually, but he was still alive when Pamphilos handed him over to the city guard. Not exactly a warrior's tale.

He heard a noise, a shout from inside.

Quickly he crossed the entryway and into the throne room. There were sounds of fighting coming from the antechamber. His mouth went dry.

Breaking into a run Pamphilos crossed the room in a few strides and burst open the door on the far side. The Thane lay sprawled unconscious on the floor. He had an obvious wound in his shoulder, a red stain creeping across his nightshirt. A man stood over him, poised for a killing blow.

The attacker turned and Pamphilos recognized him at once. His name was Daran of the MacDonald's, son of one of Gregorian's more powerful but least-trusted nobles.

Pamphilos did not pause. Propelled by fear. He rushed up to Daran and plunged his sword into his stomach. Daran fell, his blood pouring over the furs covering the floor. Pamphilos could see that the wound was fatal, but Daran was not yet dead. He hesitated and the heat of the battle was draining from him. Should he finish it? His heart beat as he watched the dying man. Somehow he lacked the brutality to end his life.

Behind him, he heard the sound of footsteps in the throne room. Quickly, he left by the far door of the anti-chamber and found a corridor that led to an outer door. From the town square he could hear shouts of alarm as news was spread and guards and men-at-arms were roused.

Quietly, he slipped away into the darkness of the night, unseen.

*****

The car purred down the dark tree-lined road as they finally approached the edge of the Dunvegan estate. William pointed out the turn off to his cottage as they drove past it and Mari caught a glimpse of a white walled building set in the trees.

"Ms. Farrow's place is just up here," he said, indicating the continuation of the road that ultimately led to the castle itself.

Moments later, he pulled up outside a single story stone building. It was fronted with a black iron fence topped with ornate spikes. Behind the fence was a row of impossibly neat, flowerless rose trees, trimmed with military precision and bristling with thorns. The house itself had huge many-paned front windows and a large gloss-black front door with a heavy-looking brass knocker. There was a light on in the front room.

"Here we are. Looks like she's still up," said William, with a trace of relief.

The hinges on the gate screamed in rusty protest at Mari's touch. As they walked up the short path to the front door, she could hear the sound of a television inside. She reached up and grasped the cold brass of the knocker and swung it down with a squeak. It responded with a loud and satisfying thud on the heavy wood of the door.

After a pause, a light came on in the hall. The door opened slowly and a woman peered out with a suspicious scowl. She looked to be in her mid to late forties, with short dark hair, a narrow face and piercing gray eyes. She wore pyjamas covered with a black corduroy dressing gown. When she saw the two, her face shifted visibly. She smiled warmly.

"Viscount," she said to William, in a very proper Scottish accent. "What brings you to my door at this time and who is your friend?"

Viscount? Mari, thought. There she was thinking that he was just a regular English bastard and he turns out to be an effing aristo! She looked at William feeling betrayed. She had actually started to like him, she realised — ugh!

"Ms. Farrow, I'm sorry to trouble you. This is Mari; she had some trouble at her home and needs to use a phone."

"Mari?" Ms. Farrow thought for a moment. "Not Mari McLeod?"

"Yes," replied Mari, a little suspiciously, looking pointedly at William. "Seems a lot of people know my name tonight."

"Oh, my dear, I just heard about what happened on the news. Your house was burgled, and your father was attacked. Terrible, terrible. I'm so sorry. They said he was taken to hospital."

"Is he alright? Did they mention my cousin?"

"Well, they didn't say. Perhaps you should come in and take a look, do you have somewhere to stay tonight? You'd be welcome to use my spare room?"

"Ms. Farrow, that won't be necessary. Mari will be staying in the cottage with me," William inserted.

Mari glanced at the young English aristocrat. For a moment, she felt more drawn to the honest-faced young man, but reason prevailed. How could she even think of spending a night under the roof of an English aristo? Besides, how dare he tell her or anyone else where she was spending the night?

"Ms. Farrow, that's terribly generous of you. I'd *love* to stay."

"Well, that's settled then. Come on in," said Ms. Farrow, then turning to William. "You can stop by and see how she's doing in the morning. I'm sure she'd be pleased to see you. Goodnight."

"Goodnight, Ms. Farrow," he replied, looking a little surprised by his abrupt dismissal, "Mari, thank you again for your help tonight. I *will* stop by and check on you in the morning. Goodnight."

Ms. Farrow opened the door a little to let Mari in and then closed it abruptly.

"Well my dear, the bathroom is at the end of the hall, if you'd like to take a moment to clean up. Is your leg all right?"

"Just a scratch," said Mari, bravely, "Ms. Farrow, I really need to use your phone."

"Of course, dear. You can use the one in the spare bedroom. It's the next door past the bathroom and when you're ready, come in and have a look at the television with me. We'll see if there's any more news about your family."

Frantic to talk to the police, Mari headed straight for the spare bedroom and the phone. The room was very tidy, containing a neatly made bed with crisp white lace turn-downs. On the bedside table was an old black phone with a rotary dialler.

Mari sat down on the bed, conscious that her filthy clothes would probably leave their mark on the white bedding, but too tired to care.

She lifted the heavy handset and put it to her ear. She heard a few crackles and then silence — no dial tone. She tried again hanging up and lifting the handset. She tried dialling a number — nothing.

Frustrated, Mari headed back down the hall to the sitting room.

"Ms. Farrow," she said, walking in. "I think that phone is broken, do you have another I could try?"

"Oh dear, the lines must be down again, they're working on

them all over the estate, you know."

"Oh, yes. William mentioned it," she managed.

Mari was crushed. Whatever she tried, it seemed that she was not going to get to a phone tonight. The one thing that she thought she could do to help her poor cousin was to call the police. The sense of purpose left her and with it, the fear, exhaustion and stress of the night began to register. In a daze, she sat down on the austere powder-blue couch, across from her host, trying desperately to swallow the tears that were welling up inside her.

"Here, Mari," said Ms. Farrow, pouring tea from a delicate china pot. "This will make you feel better."

She passed Mari one of the fine, gilt-edged floral teacups. Mari sipped at the tea. It was good, hot and strong.

The TV was on in the corner of the room, the sound was turned down but the picture showed the BBC news with pictures of a burning boat.

"It seems that someone pulled the Royal Yacht Britannia into the middle of the Firth and set it on fire," explained Ms. Farrow, indicating the TV pictures. "Another piece of senseless vandalism from the Separatist Army, I imagine. Such pointless violence..."

Mari nodded, staring at the moving pictures but not really seeing them.

"You poor thing," said Ms. Farrow, "You must've had such a terrible night. Can you talk about it? What happened?"

Mari stirred, returning to the present and turned to meet the surprisingly intent gaze of her host who sat across from her in an armchair. She did not want to talk about it. She really did not. She wanted to retreat to the privacy of the spare room and cry herself to sleep. However, courtesy required that she make some sort of effort before she excused herself.

"Our house was broken into," she said, as if retelling some distant event. "I got back after my shift at the pub. Dad was hurt — badly and my cousin was gone – he said they'd taken her."

"How terrible. Have you an idea who could have done

this?"

"No," said Mari, blankly. "They didn't seem to take any-thing – except my cousin."

"But your leg, the scratches on your face? Were you at-tacked?"

"They chased me," said Mari, and then instantly regretted it. "I escaped on my motorbike but I hit a drainage ditch and came off."

"Oh, my! How dreadful," said Ms. Farrow, delicately sip-ping her tea. "Did you get a look at them?"

"I'm not sure," said Mari. "I'm confused about it. I know they had dogs with them — big dogs."

"But you really have no idea why they came after you?"

Mari hesitated for a moment. She thought of Connor, of his warning, perhaps he understood the reason.

"No," she said, quietly. "I have no idea why."

"Well, you must be exhausted. Why don't you get some rest?"

"Ms. Farrow, I have to tell the police about my cousin, and my father, I have to find out how he is."

"Mari, you have had an awful time. There is nothing more you can do for your family tonight. Tomorrow I will drive you to Portree. We can visit the hospital, see your father and you can tell the police about poor Katie. Why don't you get some rest now?"

Resigned to the fact that she could do nothing more tonight and grateful for the excuse to get to bed, Mari drank up the last of her tea. She got out of her seat and started to make her way to the door. Suddenly she stopped; something Ms. Farrow said had been out of place.

"Ms. Farrow," she said turning. "How do you know my cousin's name?"

"Oh, I'm not sure my dear," said Ms. Farrow smoothly, "You must've mentioned it."

"But I'm sure I didn't," said Mari defiantly. Ms. Farrow seemed suddenly too composed.

"Well, that is strange, perhaps they mentioned it on the

news?" she said.

"How could they have?" asked Mari, suddenly no longer feeling tired. She was sure that Ms. Farrow knew something she wasn't saying. "There's no way that the TV news could have shown this story. I was there just over an hour ago and not even the police knew about it then."

It was Mari's turn to look intently at Ms. Farrow.

"You know, just before he lost consciousness, the last thing my father said to me, Ms. Farrow, was your name. Why would he do that? What do you know about all this?"

For a long time Ms. Farrow held Mari's gaze. Ms. Farrow stared back coolly.

"Perhaps it was a warning," she said, slowly.

"What?"

"Perhaps your father was warning you."

"Warning me?" asked Mari, still not comprehending.

"Sean McLeod is a drunken old fool but when he saw the Shadow Beasts he understood at last. He understood that I sent them out and that I sent them out for you; the only the daughter of Tara McLeod."

Had anyone else uttered these words, they would by now be nursing a broken nose, but Ms. Farrow spoke them with so much matter of fact composure that Mari did not know how to react. Was she facing the person responsible for having her father beaten and her cousin kidnapped? Anger filled her, a cold, white anger.

"Why?" she asked, bitterly. "Why would you do that?"

"You really have no idea do you?" replied Ms. Farrow, smiling. "It's like taking candy from a baby."

It was not a nice smile. She paused to sip her tea. Mari waited. She wanted to punch her, but she also wanted to hear what she had to say.

"Power," said Ms. Farrow, finally. "A lot of power. You see, my dear, you are the key to a change in the order of things on this planet, a return to the powers that have not held sway for thousands of years. You have a great deal to learn about your heritage, but it's getting late and I really need to bring this charming conversation to a conclusion."

She carefully set down her teacup on the low table.

"I'm afraid you have forced me to reveal my motives rather earlier than I had anticipated. Unfortunately, this means I can no longer offer you my spare room for the night. I'm sure you understand. But you will be pleased to hear that you will be spending the night with your dear cousin — in Dunvegan dungeon. Perhaps we will talk more about this before you die."

Ms. Farrow looked straight at Mari, her smile still on her lips.

"You see, my dear, Mari, I am going to kill you."

"Like hell you are!" said Mari. "I'm not going to sit around listening to any more of your crap."

Mari started at Ms. Farrow but Ms. Farrow was ready for her. Mari got no further than a step. She was suddenly overwhelmed with fear, a blanket of panic that completely smothered her. A cold chill froze her spine, she could feel sweat suddenly trickling down her back. She found herself unable to move.

Out of the corner of her eye she could see Ms. Farrow holding a black rod in her hand, ornately carved with an animal head at the top. It was the head of a dog.

The fear she felt came from that rod, gushing out, like water from a hose. She sank to the floor and landed roughly on her bruised knee. As the blood drained from her limbs, she lost control of her bladder. She was vaguely aware of the warm urine soaking her jeans and pooling around her on the floor.

"Oh, I do hate it when that happens," said Ms. Farrow. "It's such a mess to have to clean up."

Suddenly there was a loud knock at the front door.

"My goodness it's all go this evening, isn't it? Don't go away dear," she said to Mari.

Mari, still paralysed, watched her captor's fluffy pink slippers walk past her, inches from her nose. She heard the front door open and the sound of Ms. Farrow's voice.

"Viscount, it is very late, you know... no I'm afraid Mari has gone to bed..."

Lying on the floor and no longer exposed to the draining power of the black rod, Mari found she was able to move a little. Her body was numb and unresponsive. She could not get up but she could move her arms. Her hand went to the pocket of her jeans and reached inside. As it closed around the hard metal and brushed the smooth surface of that giant pearl, she started to feel a warmth spread up her arm and through her body.

Still shaken and nauseous, she got to her feet uncertainly. There was another door from the sitting room, leading, she guessed, to the kitchen. She staggered across to it.

"... I am sure Mari can last the night without her jacket. Why don't you bring it back in the morning..." said Ms. Farrow impatiently. "Yes I will tell her you were here... now, it's terribly late, I really must go to bed...goodnight."

Mari could hear the front door closing as she crossed the kitchen. There was a back door leading to a garden partially illuminated by the light spilling from the house.

Mari reached the back door and tried the handle — it was unlocked. She threw open the door and ran wildly across the garden. Adrenalin fuelled her legs and masked the pain of her knee. She scrambled over a low dry-stone wall that marked the edge of the garden, crossed a driveway and climbed over a gate on the other side. Beyond the gate was a wood. Gratefully, she plunged into the shadowy cover of the trees, crashing through the undergrowth as rapidly as her tired legs would allow.

"I know you're out there somewhere, Mari," shouted Ms. Farrow from her back door. She peered angrily into the darkness in the direction Mari had fled. "You won't get far. My daughters will bring you back."

*****

"This is not going very well," remarked Ardbeg, turning in disgust from the scene in the mirror that filled the table before them.

"Our influence here is weak," said Jura, "weaker than I have ever known it."

"It's Anput," declared MacAllan in a low voice. "She's working against us. She is indeed, still powerful." He took a sip from a pewter goblet in his hand, set it down on the rough oak table and stared deeply into the scene before them, trying to penetrate the reality and feel the paths forward.

"I, too, feel the touch of Anput and she has been long in preparation for this, but she is not alone in influencing this drama," said Oban, carefully. He scratched his white beard for a moment, in thought. "Fate cuts deeply into the paths being woven. It will take more than whisperings to bring things back on course now."

"Oh, I do love it when the boys get serious," said Dalwhinnie, saucily. "What have you got in mind chief?"

"The time has come for us to risk a more direct intervention."

"But the cost," said Ardbeg, sharply. "If we intervene, so can *she*. This will escalate."

"Ardbeg has a point, Oban," offered Lagavulin, gently. "It could well turn to Anput's advantage if we open up the field."

"Perhaps, but I believe we have no choice," declared Oban, decisively. "Look at the paths before us. There are very few that lead to our victory. It is our only way forward." He looked carefully around the table. No one offered any more opinions. The decision had been made.

"Talisker, listen carefully. Here is what you must do."

*****

"Did you kill him?" she asked directly. Her gaze was fierce.

"I left him with a fatal wound," he replied.

"But, Pamphilos, you did not check that he was dead?" she persisted.

"I was disturbed. I barely got away without being seen."

Scotia looked away, staring at the ground for a moment lost in thought. Her brow was deeply furrowed.

"What is it?" he asked, suddenly afraid.

"Pamphilos, this is most serious," she said. "Daran will die, but before he does, he will have the opportunity to tell his brother who it was that killed him. His brother will come after us."

"Do you know when, how it will come to pass? Surely we can defend ourselves?"

"I do not know these things. I only know that we are in grave danger. We must flee, now, tonight."

"What?"

"We must gather what we can, get on your ship and sail away. We can leave some of your men. They will be safe. In a few weeks, or months, it may be safe for us to return."

"Scotia... Neferubity, my wife, I am finished with running. This is our home now. If this man comes for me, we must face him."

"If we do, we will die."

*****

Mari scrambled desperately through the woods. Branches whipped at her face, brambles tore at her legs and ankles. She could think of nothing else but to put as much distance between her and that crazy witch as she could. The prospect of the giant dogs coming after her only spurred her further. Mari was confident that she could out-run Cynthia Farrow in her carpet slippers, but she had barely been able to out distance those creatures on a motorbike.

It was tough going through the undergrowth, and it was not long before Mari's strength started to flag. It had been a hard night. Her body was tired and damaged. Her breathing became more and more laboured; her leg ached and her jeans became damp from the blood trickling out of the reopened wound. She could ignore the pain for a while but, more disturbing, was the deep fatigue in her limbs. Her legs just didn't seem to be moving as fast as she asked them to.

The game trail that she followed was choked with weeds and grasses that whipped at her legs. Her foot stepped on something hidden in the brush, a rock or a tree root. She stumbled and her ankle caught on a bramble that had grown across the path. All of a sudden she found herself face down in the mud.

She started to rise but noticed there was someone standing right in front of her. The man switched on an electric lantern that gave off a pale halogen light. The first thing she saw were the heavy leather walking boots. He peered at her for a moment from beneath his bushy brows that were so prominent Mari could make out their shape in his silhouette.

Without a word, he offered his hand and helped her to her feet. He had a remarkably strong grip and, despite his size, seemed to lift her to her feet with little effort. He was smaller than her and looked old, really old. He had an infeasibly large bulbous nose that dominated his face. Everything else about him was small by comparison. He moved with an unexpected lightness.

"I'm the game-keeper 'ere," he said gruffly. "Who are ya? And what are ya doing on ma land?"

His voice was heavy with suspicion and his dark eyes stared at her intently. Although, Mari thought she saw a twinkle of mirth behind the gaze.

"I'm sorry, I wasn't doin' any damage," said Mari, frantically. She didn't have time for this, but the old man blocked her only way forward. He seemed harmless enough but she had to keep moving.

"D'ya have a name, girl?" he demanded.

"Mari," she gasped. "Mari McLeod"

"Oh, a McLeod. I've always time for a McLeod," he replied, relaxing a little. "But what are ya doin' running through my woods in the middle o' the night."

"There's somebody after me," blurted Mari. "I have to get away from here, get to the police. Do you have a car?"

"Hmmph!" grunted the old man, unimpressed. "I have no car — I've no need of one neither, cars are fea towns-folk."

"Aye, right," said Mari, searching for common ground. "I don't have a car either. I've just an old dirt bike I use to cross the fields to get to work."

"Oh a motorcycle! Now you're talking, I used te have a 1959 Triumph TR-6. Best off-road bike ever built by man. The Desert Sled they called it – probably still have it somewhere."

There was a misty look in the man's eyes. "If I need a motor these days, o' course, I use the tractor."

"I need your help...," began Mari again.

"So what kind of bike do you have?"

"What? Err it's a Yamaha, 250cc," she replied, taken by surprise.

"Ah, Japanese. I can't say I ever rated them foreign bikes."

"I'm being chased!" Mari exclaimed.

"What's it like?"

"It's bloody terrifying – what do you think it's like?" said Mari, in frustration.

"No, no, the bike. What's it like?"

"Well, it was great until about an hour ago when I drove it into a ditch and twisted the forks."

"Och, what a shame. Why did you do that?"

"There's a crazy woman chasing me with wild dogs," said Mari, finally regaining control of the conversation. "I barely got away. She is still after me. Her name is Cynthia Farrow. She has dogs. She'll be sending them after me any minute. I need help."

The man looked at her steadily. In the light of the pale lantern she briefly saw his eyes twinkling again from beneath his enormous eyebrows, as if somewhere deep inside he were really enjoying this. His face showed no signs of amusement, however.

"Cynthia Farrow, now, she's a bad 'un. She's the new estate manager here. I never liked her from the moment we met. She's a townie ya know, but I've seen her out in the woods wi' her weirdo friends — all black robes, candles and sheep's bones."

Mari nodded, encouragingly.

"Dogs you say?"

"Big, savage, black dogs," she replied.

Then, at that moment, as if on cue, a loud howl could be heard from the direction Mari had come.

The old man seemed to reach a decision.

"Alright, you'd better come with me," he muttered. "See these woods? I know 'em like no one else. I've been Groundsman and Game Keeper here all ma life. Now, there's a cave I'll show you. They'll no be able ta find ya there. It's a special place ma father showed me, it's been a hiding place fer whisky-makers, rogue clan chiefs and even kings!"

"Thank you," said Mari. She was a little unsure, but could see no other options.

"The name's Ally. C'mon, follow me, Mari *McLeod*. We'd better move quickly."

He set off into the trees so rapidly that Mari found herself struggling to keep up.

*****

"You don't think he might be laying it on a bit thick?" asked Dalwhinnie, gently.

"Tal's always one for a bit 'o theatre," said Laphroaig, with a grin. He caught her eye for a moment, and she smiled back, her favourite winsome smile. Inwardly, he groaned slightly. He knew well where that smile could lead, but somehow he found himself grinning back and staring into those big brown eyes.

"She believes him, dear, and that is what matters," pointed out Lagavulin, without looking up. Her fingers still worked busily on her knitting. Despite the fact she had been working at it all night, the ball of wool that sat beside her on the chair did not seem to have diminished, nor, for that matter, had the garment she was making increased noticeably in size.

"We are taking a big risk here, Oban," said Ardbeg. "They'll be a price to pay for this."

"Do not think we have taken this action lightly," replied Oban, with more than a hint of frustration. "We clearly had no other choice. There were no credible paths without intervention in which she lasted the night."

*****

Ally, may have looked old, but he moved through the woods with a speed and grace that Mari could not match. The dim light from his lantern bobbed ahead of her like an electric firefly as he darted swiftly between the twisted shadows of the trees. He followed a series of game trails that would have been barely visible to Mari in the daylight. Every now and again he got so far ahead that the light became obscured by some tree or bush and Mari would have to rush forward so as not to lose him. On every occasion she found him waiting for her and as she approached to within a few yards, he took off again through the undergrowth with barely a rustle.

The erratic bouncing lantern ahead finally stopped and Mari caught up with the old man on the banks of a small brook. He wasn't even out of breath.

"Keep t' water. They'll no be able to follow yer scent" was all he said and before she could reply, he took off again wading into the middle of the stream.

Mari was more than a little apprehensive about the old man who seemed such an unlikely rescuer but she saw little else that she could do but follow him. His lantern was already growing distant. With a deep breath Mari stepped into the stream and started splashing after him.

The water was bitterly cold and soaked through her trainers instantly; within a few minutes, Mari's feet were numb. She lost her footing on the slippery rocks several times staggering and landing awkwardly in the water. Before long she was thoroughly drenched and freezing cold. All this time the old man kept up his determined pace.

Eventually they came to a gorge where the flow had cut a deep crack between two large rocks; it just wide enough for a person to enter. Without pausing, Ally continued in and disappeared out of sight. Mari watched him go. She was nearing the end of her strength. Her leg was hurting badly and most of all she was *so* cold.

She reached the mouth of the gorge and leaned against the rock wall for a moment peering into the gloom for a sign of the little lantern. To her surprise, she saw the little light shining out of a small opening in the rock wall a few feet in front of her just above the waterline.

"Here it is," he announced brightly. "Come along Mari

McLeod, in here."

He disappeared back into the opening in the rock. It was well hidden beneath a broad outcrop. Had she not been shown the entrance, there was no way she would have noticed it.

Mari watched the little light disappear inside, leaving her in darkness again. There was nothing for it, she knew, but to follow the crazy old man into the cave.

Past the entrance, it opened up into a small chamber just big enough for Mari to stand up in. Ally lit a candle that cast a warm yellow glow on the walls.

It was dry inside and fairly clean. In one corner was a heap of dried leaves and grass, perhaps washed in here by the brook. They smelled unexpectedly fresh, of wood-sap and pine needles. Optimistically, Mari sat down on them and actually found them soft and fairly comfortable. She thought about taking her sodden trainers off but her fingers were too cold.

"You say that kings hid here?" she asked, doubtfully looking around the small cave.

"Aye, do ya no ken the story of Robert the Bruce?"

"You mean how he hid in a cave and saw a spider and it convinced him to go and beat back the English army?"

"Six times the spider threw her web and six times it fell short, just as King Robert's armies had been beaten back six times, but on the seventh time the thread caught. The king was inspired and led his armies back into the field and victory."

"Yeah, I heard the story."

"Well, this is the very cave."

"You're kidding me!"

"No fer real. Robert the Bruce lay down just where you're sitting now and the web was just over there." He pointed into the corner.

"So, this cave has spiders in it?" asked Mari, uncertainly.

Ally didn't seem to hear her he was fumbling for something in his coat. Eventually, he pulled out a small silver hip flask and a cloth pouch tied with a cord. He handed them to Mari.

"Help yourself," he said. "They'll make you feel better. You can keep 'em."

She opened the flask and sniffed. It smelled of whisky. Not the rough smell of a cheap blend but the complex rich aroma of a single malt. Ally, it seemed, had taste.

She took a small swig. It was amazing. Mari knew her whiskies, but it was like nothing she had ever tasted. Smooth and rich it burned down her throat with a warm fire that extended to her toes. She took another swig this time with a little more enthusiasm.

"Easy does it lass, that is strong stuff, and you may be needing it again before you're done. If you're hungry, try the barley. A couple of grains should see you right."

A couple of grains of barley? Mari opened the pouch that contained a handful of whole barley seeds. Not expecting much, she pulled a couple out and started to chew them. They were delicious, nutty and full of flavour. The husks crunched crisply between her teeth, revealing the soft sweet meat. It was the most delicious thing she had ever tasted, not only that but it filled her up like a bowl-full of pasta. Two more grains was all she could manage.

"I'll leave ya now. Don't worry about Cynthia Farrow for tonight. She'll no find you here."

With that, the mysterious old man left the cave.

Mari took one last small swig from the hip flask, noticing the vessel as if for the first time. It was very small and neat, made from antique silver. It had various Celtic patterns engraved in it and in one corner the letter 'T'.

Suddenly, she noticed just how tired she was. Carefully noting where the candle and matches were, she blew out the flame and sank down on the soft leafy mattress. Within minutes, she was asleep.

*****

The Stone of Scone, also known as the Stone of Destiny, The Speaking Stone or, in Gaelic, simply "An Clach" ("The Stone") has been a symbol of Scotland for centuries. Cambray, in his "Monuments Celtiques," claims to have seen the Stone when it bore the inscription: "Ni fallat fatum, Scoti quocumque locatum Invenient lapidiem, regnasse tenetur ibidem," which means: *If the Destiny prove true, then the Scots are known to have been Kings where'er men find this Stone.*

It is said that An Clach was Jacob's pillow upon which his head rested when he dreamed his ladder to heaven. It is also said that it was the pedestal upon which the Arc of the Covenant was set.

For many years the Stone rested in the Historic Abbey at Scone, once the capital of Scotland. The Stone of Destiny was "reverently kept for the consecration of the kings of Alba" and, according to an old chronicler, "no king was ever wont to reign in Scotland unless he had first [..] sat upon this Stone at Scone."

Although the Stone now rests in the castle at Edinburgh, it remains the property of the British Royal Family who have generously loaned it to the people of Scotland.

> — *"The Stone of Destiny"*
> *Tourist Trust Scotland Pamphlet.*

*****

In the dream, the moth was lucky. For, though she had flown right into the web, it was not yet finished. The spider, sleek and black, was still working on it but she needed to cast each strand seven times before it would hold and it was taking a long time.

With a wrench and a twist, the moth was able to break the bonds holding her but just as she fluttered free, she noticed that another creature, a small fly, had not shared her luck and had become trapped in the sticky strands.

The moth was not alone in noticing the fly. The spider, angry at the interruption and damage to her work had abandoned the laborious construction to advance menacingly on the struggling insect.

The moth did not like the fly, or maybe she did, because for some reason she was overcome with a deep need to help it. It seemed to be important, more important than she was herself.

Summoning all her courage, she dived headlong with into the very centre of the web. She felt the sticky strands wrapping themselves around her soft wings. She was trapped.

The spider turned furiously. Ignoring the smaller prey, she advanced instead on the moth. A quick bite, an injection of poison and she would have food there for weeks.

The moth saw the advancing predator and she knew her time was up. With her fleeting moment of heroism, she had thrown away her life for nothing. The fly was not free and she was stuck fast, now they would both die.

As the spider came within biting distance, the moth gave one last desperate bid for freedom. She struggled against the sticky bonds holding her and all of a sudden they gave way. The web was torn to shreds. The moth flew free and the fly fell away. The spider was left hanging on a small, broken fragment, glaring at the retreating insects with bitter fury in all eight eyes.

*****

"Are you absolutely sure about this?" asked Connor, seemingly to the air around him. "These Egyptian rituals never seem *right* somehow. I've never quite got the hang of them." He stood alone in the centre of the ruined chapel, surrounded by a forest of tall candles that lit the open area before him with a soft yellow light. The air was still with a crisp autumn chill. Over his head, the stars were resplendent in the dark night sky.

"Just get on with it," replied the voice in his head. "Four turns about staff, then look to the west and throw the saffron into the brazier."

Connor sighed.

"If this works, you're gonna owe me, big time. This is above and beyond the call ya know."

"Try to focus would you?" replied the voice, stiffly.

On the flagstone and packed earth floor was a circle of blood-red powder surrounded by a series of a dozen or more hieroglyphic-like figures and stylized images. Some were recognizable as images of people or animals, one looked like an eye weeping, another a key, and a third was a triangle surrounded by arrows on all three sides.

Inside the circle, lay the paraphernalia of an Egyptian High Ritual. Connor's staff lay in the centre and across it lay an old knife with a long curved blade. On the west side of the circle, smouldered a small portable charcoal barbeque. Off to one side was a wooden crate that contained a small, scraggly-looking chicken. Every now and again, the chicken would punctuate the proceedings with an occasional, comically sad, little 'cluck.'

Connor moved with what he hoped was appropriate mystic reverence around the staff and then tossed his handful of spice onto the glowing coals on the west side of the circle. A pungent grey cloud billowed upwards from the burning powder. The caustic fumes caught in his throat and he coughed hard, abandoning all pretence to being either mystical or reverent.

On the edge of the candlelight, crumbling stonewalls could be seen. The place of the ritual was Trumpan Chapel, an old, ruined church in the North East of Skye. Over four hundred years ago, the chapel had been the scene of a brutal and bloody massacre. A MacDonald raiding party had barred the doors, trapping the McLeod congregation inside and burned the building to the ground. All, but one, of the McLeods had been killed. There was little left of the building now; just a few tumbling walls that marked the sorrowful sight.

Hundreds of years later the presence of terror and death still filled the place – for those who could sense it. That is why it was chosen for this particular ritual. It was also among the reasons why Connor was more than somewhat reluctant to go through with it.

"Now the sacrifice, and the final incantation," pressed the voice.

Connor took a deep breath and crossed to the small crate. He had carried out countless rituals in his time, but very few had involved a live sacrifice. The gods he followed were not so blood-thirsty, thank goodness. He had lived on farms and killed his share of chickens for food but he could not get past the feeling that it was distasteful to take a life in this way. However, there was nothing else for it. In this case, the sacrifice was necessary.

"Cluck?" asked the chicken, hopefully, as Connor opened the crate.

Connor pulled the bird out and held it aloft over the fire.

"C'tha Qathn Nmor," he called out in a loud clear voice and snapped its neck.

"C'tha Qathn Nmor," he said again as he held the wriggling carcase over the flames and slit its chest open with the knife. Blood and entrails poured out, hissing as they hit the coals.

"C'tha Qathn Nmor Anubis," he called out and dropped the still twitching remains of the bird into the flames.

He waited. Still. Silent. Anxious. His attention focused on the chalk triangle that lay just beyond the fire, outside the circle. He could hear the distant sound of the waves washing up against the shore, a breeze gently stirring the leaves in a nearby tree. He could hear his heart thumping.

The smell of burning feathers and charred chicken filled the air. He tried not to choke.

A minute passed. Still, he waited.

Another minute went by. Smoke continued to pour from the fire.

"Do ya know, I don't think it worked," he said finally with more than a trace of relief in his voice.

He turned, still looking for some sign to indicate the outcome. He knew well enough not to step out of the circle yet, that fragile line of powdered chalk presented a powerful barrier between him and anything that might have been summoned. Even if the ritual did not succeed in its intent, this dark magic had the potential to summon all kinds of other unexpected and unpleasant things.

It would be dawn soon. The sky was starting to grow lighter in the east. He rubbed his eyes. They were sore from all the smoke and watering slightly, making his vision a little blurred.

He looked again at the chalk triangle. For a moment he thought he saw a shape forming within it but then again maybe it was just a curl of smoke. No, there was definitely something forming.

The hairs rose up on the back of his neck and he gradually became aware of a sound in the air. It was quiet at first like the distant rumble of thunder, barely registering. But it built rapidly to a roar like a giant waterfall and his clothes were vibrating with the deep heavy sound that smashed over him.

As the sound swelled, the form within the triangle became more and more substantial. Connor felt fear rising within his chest. He was breathing hard and sweat was breaking out on his neck. The curls of smoke and vapour before him seemed to thicken and condense. Swirls and wisps became limbs and torso. Gradually, the shapes coalesced, becoming denser, more substantial, until eventually they became solid in appearance.

Sitting before him in the triangle, on a grand high-backed throne, was the elegant and terrifying dog-faced Egyptian God of Death, Anubis. He was clothed in shimmering black ornamental armour that left his slender black human arms bare. Atop his long neck was the distinctive and memorable face with its sharply pointed ears and thin canine muzzle.

A strange thing was happening to Connors perspective. He knew that the form of the god had to stay within the two-foot wide triangle he had laid out and when he looked down and checked he could see that the base of the throne was indeed within the dusty lines. Nevertheless, it was, somehow, simultaneously several times this size and the figure of the seated god that should have come up to his chest was towering imperiously over him, despite the fact he could clearly see over its head to the crumbling walls beyond. It was as if the presence of the god was so strong that reality itself was twisting to accommodate.

The roaring fell silent.

The god sniffed gently at the air. The movement was barely perceptible and yet it felt tectonic to Connor.

Anubis began to move slowly, looking around. His gaze scanned the surroundings, the chapel, the man before him, the candles and the charred chicken bones. Then he spoke in a voice that was deep and rich, that was barely a whisper and yet almost deafening. It came from the figure and from everywhere at the same time.

"It has been many years since I was last called to this realm," he said, slowly. "The last time I was summoned, it took the combined will of seventy two priests and acolytes and the sacrifice of seven white oxen and a human virgin.

"And yet, you, mortal, have summoned me to this pitiful place single-handedly with the death, of a small fowl. You must truly be very powerful, and very brave."

Connor suddenly realised that he was prostrate on the floor before the god. He was not sure how he got there. He lifted his head slightly.

"O great Anubis, Lord of the underworld, Jackal-Ruler of the Nine Bows, Shadow of Darkness and Master of the Ultimate Truth, I summon you to..."

"Wait," said the god, sniffing the air again. "You are not alone. I sense a presence with you. Let us dispense with these trappings. I would know who it is I am dealing with."

Anubis straightened the fingers of his left hand that had been curled around the arm of his throne. The wind began to stir in the trees. It was no longer the careless breeze that had been playing earlier. This was a different wind, a forceful current of air with a purpose. It grew rapidly, starting to snatch at Connor's hair and jacket as he knelt on the ground. Hardly daring to move, he frantically tried to see out of the corners of his eyes what was going on, all the while wondering what was coming. Then, with horror, he realised what was happening. The carefully drawn chalk lines were being lifted into the air and disbursed across the countryside. Without those lines he was defenceless, and yet there was nothing he could do.

Eventually, the wind dropped and with great trepidation Connor looked up. No trace was left of the hieroglyphs or the precious circle of protection. Somehow the candles were still lighted but the walls of the chapel were less visible than they had been before. Connor could also see around him the torch-lit walls of Anubis' throne room. It was as if he were looking at a double-exposed photograph. Anubis towered over him, splendid and terrifying. His fingers had curled once again around the arm of his throne and he had barely moved. He sniffed the air again.

"Show yourself, *Talisker*," he said directly.

The Scottish God was suddenly there next to Connor. He

was dressed in full highland battle regalia with a great kilt in McLeod tartan, complete with a fly-plaid, a broad swath of tartan cloth worn over his shoulder and a broad leather belt. On his back he wore a two handed broadsword in an ornate leather scabbard. He appeared on one knee next to Connor.

Connor was rather glad that Talisker had been found out. It was comforting to have a god next to him although he knew that there was probably very little Talisker could do to protect him if the situation turned nasty. The weapon, he knew, was just for show. It was considered "bad form" for gods to summon each other and strained the rules of conduct and engagement by which they lived. This was why Talisker had involved Connor. Technically, Talisker would claim, this kept him in the clear. Unfortunately, Anubis may not see it the same way and might consider Talisker to be guilty of a very significant divine faux pas.

"Anubis," said Talisker, keeping his eyes on the ground in front of him. "I must beg your forgiveness at my rudeness in calling on you in this way. I humbly seek your great wisdom. Matters of great import are pressing, the usual signs would have been too slow."

The dog-face regarded him impassively.

"What is it Talisker?" The deep voice rumbled with the hint of a Middle-Eastern accent.

"O great Anubis, you know my companion gods and I are facing a grave time. Dark powers are gathering near this very place, and we are approaching a bifurcation that could destabilise the entire realm. Our very existence may be at stake."

"This is not of my concern, Talisker. You dare to trouble me with such trivialities?"

"Anubis, hear me," said Talisker, standing and raising his gaze for the first time. "It is your wife, Anput, who is behind this."

"Ah, I understand," said Anubis. Connor noted with considerable relief that his tone had lost its anger. The Egyptian god was silent for a moment as he gazed off into the distance.

"Yes, I feel her touch here," he said, finally.

"Can you use your influence to aid us?" prompted Talisker, hopefully.

"Why is it that you think I would help you? Perhaps I should be assisting my wife. Your annihilation would prevent these tedious meetings, would it not?"

"Great Anubis, you intervened before."

"That was different, Talisker, and you know it. She made an unholy pact with the Pharaoh's priest. I could not allow that to be fulfilled. This time, no such deal has been made. She simply thirsts for the old times when she had worshippers in the thousands who would lay down their lives at her whim. She craves the power the old gods used to have. If she succeeds, it will mean the end of this realm as it is today. Chaos will reign and millions will die."

"Is that not reason enough to intervene."

"Talisker, you are naïve: you ask a god of death to spare lives? I care not for these mortals and their fleeting lives. Would you stoop to save an anthill from being crushed? These mortals are nothing to me."

"But she would become powerful – too powerful. It will upset the balance. It could lead to a war among the gods."

"Perhaps. I, too, miss the old power, but I see farther than she does. I can see the turning of the wheel and I know that this is not the time."

"Then you will help us?"

"No, I will not. However, the terms I set in place when last I intervened are still in force – while the line of the Pharaoh's daughter survives, Anput may not destroy your land – not directly anyway."

"But she has poisoned its people with hate, she means to raise the Leviathan and bring about a new age of fear and cruelty to the earth," implored Talisker.

"This is of little concern to me. If she succeeds and brings about an imbalance, it will restore itself, in time."

"Can we stop her?" asked Talisker.

"Perhaps, but I see that the scales are tipped in her favour. Hatred anger and fear are rife here. I can smell it. This land is thick with their odour. The Leviathan would truly feast were it to be raised. You must either prevent the summoning or bring peace to the people of this land."

"How could that be achieved mighty Anubis?"

"No more questions Talisker, I have given you more than you deserve already. I will leave you now," and, for a moment, the tone of threat returned to the voice of the great god. "You risked a great deal in calling me forth in this way, Talisker. Do not presume I would be so lenient if you were foolish enough to try it again."

When Connor looked up, he was alone. The rosy glow of the sunrise was visible in the east. He was shaking, partly from cold but mostly from fear and exhaustion.

Moving slowly he began to collect his things and tidy up the site. He packed up the candlesticks into an old, worn rucksack. He was not sure what he should have expected from that meeting and, in many ways, he was glad simply to still be alive and in possession of his soul. However, he was fairly sure that Talisker had hoped for more. Anubis had the power to turn the tide in their favour had he so wished, but it seemed that they were on their own. The prospects were not looking so good, he thought glumly, as he tossed the charred chicken bones into a bush.

*****

Mari woke on her bed of leaves. For a moment she had difficulty remembering who she was, let alone where. She had had a strange dream involving spiders. A small orange flicker of daylight came from the cave opening. She resisted the urge to try and flutter over to it.

She had slept well and felt refreshed and invigorated. Her leg was much better and amazingly her feet were even dry – though how her trainers and socks had managed to dry on her feet, she had no idea.

She collected her things and then crawled through the small opening and back out into the world. The brook trickled playfully down the gorge. The trees beyond were fresh and green.

Bathed as it was in the orange dawn light, the scene was idyllic. Certainly, it was a far cry from the grotesque twisted shapes that had populated the dark shadows in this very spot last night.

Careful to avoid getting her feet wet this time, she started retracing her steps down the hill. Through gaps in the trees she could see glimpses of Dunvegan castle, and the sunrise behind it. She must have only slept for a few hours. It felt like days.

It was clear to her now what she knew what she had to do. She had to rescue Katie. She could not face the long walk to Portree, and the inevitable disbelief of the police. The only way to do it was to get into the castle and get Katie out herself.

Of course, doing so meant avoiding Cynthia Farrow and her creatures. The terror of the night before had not left Mari but in the warm sunlight, it seemed like a long way away. Quietly pleased that she had woken so early, she marched down the hill, full of determination.

And then suddenly, she realised, that could not be a sunrise. She had to be looking west; that was the setting sun ahead. She had slept all day! Thinking of Katie in that dreadful dungeon, she picked up her pace.

*****

The fishing rod blurred as it whipped rhythmically back and forth, sending waves playing gracefully down the huge length of line. At the end of the line, a small hook carefully adorned with a twist of twine skipped tantalisingly over the surface of the pool just above the heads of a trio of brown trout. MacAllan was absolutely focussed as he played the long flexible rod back and forth in great arcs. At last, he threw the line forward and let the fly rest on the surface for a moment.

"Impressive, Uncle, but isn't it a bit of a waste of time? If you want to catch fish, use a net," exclaimed a voice from behind him. It was Talisker. They were standing on the bank of a mountain brook at a point where the small waterway bounced over a rocky outcropping and fell a good thirty feet. The little waterfall had worn a deep pool into the soft loam beneath. It was a perfect place for trout.

"Shouldn't you be back at the council?" asked MacAllan without turning around.

"I am still there," smiled Talisker. "There's nothing much going on and I just felt like a break." He held up a fine clay pipe that suddenly appeared in his hand already filled and lit. "But what's your excuse? Looks like you've been here a while."

"Oban pretty much has things covered in there. He knows I'm here if he needs me." He whipped up his line and started casting the fly again.

Talisker sucked on his pipe and sat down on the root of a nearby tree. "I still don't understand, though," he said, watching the other god. "It's like that confounded sweater Lagavulin's been knitting for the last three centuries. You're the god of seas and rivers. You could just tell those fish to jump out of the water."

"Talisker, it is not about catching fish," explained MacAllan, patiently. "You will come to realise someday that that which is most important comes from *how* we do something, not *what* we do, or even its outcome. The rod, the line, the movement of the fly; it's a way to become part of the river itself, to let go of everything else and be right here, right now."

"But you're a god, you *can* become part of the river if you want to," argued Talisker.

"Come, we should return. My brother will be missing us soon," said MacAllan, starting to reel in his line. "It is not about the river, Talisker. It is about being: being here and being part of the world around. It is about the simplicity, grace and beauty of the moment."

*****

"C'mon, Gail, stick that big arse 'o yer's oot," sniggered Brian, from the bushes. "At least *try* an' gi' it a bit o' sex."

Dougie silently rolled his eyes.

They were about five miles outside Edinburgh city on a quiet road a little way from the A90. It was early evening; the sun was low in the sky casting long shadows. It was warm and birds were twittering in the hedgerows that lined the road.

"Bugger off!" she called back, without looking up.

Gail leaned over the engine of Dougie's Mondeo with an air of desperate helplessness. The bonnet was up and the hazard warning lights flashed. To any passer-by on the quiet side road, she was clearly a damsel-driver in mechanical distress.

She wore tight black jeans, high heels and a camisole top and looked as if she was heading into the city for a Saturday night out. On her head she wore a log dark wig. She hadn't wanted to but Dougie had insisted. It would make her harder to recognise later.

Of course, there was nothing really wrong with the old blue Ford, aside from a broken drivers-side window. Hitched to the back of the car was a large, fibreglass trailer, the size of a horse-box.

A white transit van appeared down the road heading in her direction.

"Here they are," hissed Dougie. "Get ready everyone."

Gail stepped out into the road as the van approached, and waived her arms so wildly that Dougie was expecting the wig to go flying. Fortunately, it did not. The van pulled up in front of her. The driver had no choice, as there was no way he could get around.

He rolled down his window.

"Wha's wrong hen?" he asked.

"Oh, thanks so much for stoppin'. I don't know what I was goin' ta do," exclaimed Gail flapping here eyelashes. "The motor just cut oot. I've no phone and a can'ae walk into town in these. Could ya take a look? Please!"

"Well...ahem, I could take a quick shuftie, but we're sup-posed ta be somewhere, mind. I havene' got long."

The driver, a stocky balding man with a neatly trimmed moustache, got out of the car; leaving his passenger, a younger man with red hair and glasses, watching with an amused smile.

"Right now, lass," said the driver, peering into the engine compartment. "Go and turn her over."

As he leaned over the engine, Dougie came out from the bushes to the side of the car and clamped a chloroform-soaked cloth over his face. At the same time, Brian sneaked around the side of the van and jammed a rag in the passenger's face. Both victims struggled. This time Dougie was ready for it and since the driver had been bent over anyway, he had nowhere to go. He banged his head on the underside of the open bonnet but then, after a moment, sank limply over the engine. Dougie slid him off the car and onto the road.

Brian had more difficulty with the passenger, who managed to elbow his attacker in the face before he finally succumbed to the fumes.

"Oh, would you look at that," said Gail, turning the key and starting the engine of the car. "There doesn't seem to be a problem after all."

"That bastard hit me," complained Brian, holding his nose.

"Ya were druggin' him unconscious," said Gail, leaning out of the window. "What do you expect?"

"Well, I'm just sayin'. It hurts, alright?" he whined, checking his hand for any blood.

"So when you kids are through, perhaps we could turn our attention to the job at hand?" cut in Dougie. Their banter was really starting to get on his nerves.

Dougie and Brian unhitched a trailer from the car and attached it to the back of the van. They stripped the overalls off the two men, taking care to ensure that they took their identity cards. Then they tied up their hands and feet with duct tape, gagged them and dumped them behind a couple of bushes beside the road. They would be asleep for hours and, by the time they woke up, it would all be over.

"Oh man," said Brian as he started pulling on the younger man's blue overalls "B-O or wha'?"

"I don't care if he crapped himself. Get it on and let's get out of here," said Dougie, sharply, pulling on his own borrowed outfit. "Keep your gloves on. We don't want to leave any fingerprints."

Dougie and Brian took their seats in the van. Dougie took a moment with the driver's mirror to stick a false moustache to his upper lip. Then he started up the van and they set off.

Gail pulled her own set of blue overalls out of the boot of the car and pulled them on, discarding the wig. After closing the bonnet, she got back in the driver's seat and pulled out to follow the van.

As the van drove passed, she could just make out a sign written on the side in simple black letters. It read, "Extreme Display Services – The Firework Professionals."

*****

The sunset scorched the sky; rose-pink turned slowly to lavender as Mari strode purposefully down the wooded hillside. A soft breeze stirred the treetops gently as the woodland birds called out their evensong tributes.

The brush and brambles that last night had seemed almost insurmountable did not trouble her today. Her feet seemed to find a path of their own accord. She was going to find Katie and get her out of that place and there was nothing that old witch-bitch could do to even slow her down.

The sky darkened to purple as Mari reached the edge of the trees. Before her was a narrow gravel path which led between the rocks and gorse to the bridge over the moat and the castle entrance.

Mari did not pause as she left the cover of the trees and continued along the path.

In front of her, the yellow-brown sandstone walls of the castle looked stark and impressive in silhouette. Many of the so-called castles in Scotland were just large houses with the odd turret or decorative crenulations. Dunvegan was different. It had been a real defensive structure and it showed; the small windows and strong high walls were built to repel attack. A moat encircled the castle on three sides. On the fourth side the walls were built to the edge of a small cliff beneath which was a sea loch. There had been a stronghold on this ground for at least two-and-a-half thousand years.

The gravel crunched beneath her feet as Mari marched over the narrow stonewalled bridge that crossed the moat. A pair of octagonal watchtowers flanked the stone porch that contained the front door. Archers on these towers would have been able to control an approach to the castle very effectively. Mari noticed there were lights on in a couple of the windows to the left of the entry. Curious, from what William had said, the McLeod's were in France, no one was supposed to be home.

She climbed the steps onto the porch and stopped before the large wooden doors. They were twelve feet high and made of solid oak, impressively grand and unimpregnable. She took hold of one of the huge brass handles and tried to turn it. It moved a little, as if drawing back a catch but when she pulled, the doors held fast. It was locked.

Mari left the porch and started to survey the rest of the building in the fading light. Each of the watchtowers had a narrow ground floor window. It should be fairly straightforward to knock out some of the glass panes and crawl through.

She was just starting to search for a rock when a light came on in the entryway and she heard sounds from inside – footsteps and voices – and they were coming closer.

Mari turned, desperately looking for somewhere to hide. There was nothing by the door and the nearest cover was a good thirty yards away on the other side of the bridge.

There was a sound of keys jangling and the scrape of metal on metal. Then the door started to open.

"Mr. Jessop, I have to tell you that Lord McLeod will not be pleased to hear this."

"I'm sorry Ms. Farrow, but you'll have to tell that to the people who claimed to do the wiring overhaul two years ago. The cables are just nae te regulation for the number of fittings. It needs to be redone - it's a serious fire haz'rd."

Cynthia Farrow emerged into the twilight followed by a short, broad man with balding grey hair and a bristly ginger moustache.

"Surely, there's a way to fix it."

"Aye – ya rip it all out and start again."

"Mr. Jessop, there is no question of ripping it out. It was very expensive to install. We have to find a way to make it work."

"I can nae rewire the fittings if the supply won't take the load. I'd loose ma license."

The crunch of Ms. Farrow's boots on the gravel rang out in the quiet evening, a sound Mari could hear with terrifying clarity as she clung desperately to the outside of the bridge parapet. The low wall had a lip a few inches wide at about ground level, which Mari stood on. Her head was out of sight but her fingers clung to the top of the stonewall. The dark stagnant water of the moat was 20 feet beneath her. If her fingers slipped, it would be a nasty drop.

The crisp footsteps stopped in the middle of the bridge only a few feet from where Mari hid. Ms. Farrow turned and walked to the edge, to look out for a moment at the dimming sunset. Mari could just see the top of her head as she looked out. If she were to look down now it would all be over. Mari crouched as low as she could, her heart beating wildly.

"Mr. Jessop, do you know how I got where I am today?" Ms. Farrow paused for effect. "Let me tell you. I am extremely good at making problems resolve themselves so that things can proceed smoothly and efficiently. So, allow me make this very clear." She turned back to the electrician. Her tone had moved from business-like distraction to ruthless and menacing. "You will finish this job and get it working by the end of next week, as we agreed, or you will have more to worry about than your license."

Even without the boots, Ms. Farrow stood a good six inches taller than Mr Jessop. He made the mistake of catching her eye and suddenly felt the full force of her gaze.

"Well, I'm sure we can, er...fix somethin' up," he managed, meekly.

"That's the way, Mr. Jessop," replied Ms. Farrow, merrily, all trace of menace gone.

The footsteps resumed, to Mari's relief. Painfully slowly, the voices receded as the pair made their way to the car park, their discussion moving on to the details of the work itself.

Sure that she would end up in the moat if she waited any longer, Mari clambered from her perch back over the parapet and onto the path. There was no one in sight as she emerged.

She went up to the door and once again reached out and turned the big brass handle. Once again there was the click of a catch, only this time when she pulled, the door gave a low creak and swung open. Ms. Farrow had forgotten to lock it.

*****

A plume of fire flared into the air from the mouth of the unicyclist as he wobbled back and forth. The crowd cheered enthusiastically grudgingly parting to let the white van through.

Dougie edged the vehicle through the throng as they turned the corner at the top of the royal mile. The traffic had been terrible, half the city was closed off and there were people everywhere, and now they were running late. He drove as quickly as he dared across the expansive esplanade of Edinburgh castle and pulled up in front of the red-and-white-striped barrier at the entrance to the imposing fortress. His false moustache itched. He hoped it was still straight; too late to fix it now, he thought, as he wound down the driver's window.

They had left the car carefully placed half way up Johnston Terrace in the shadow of the South side of the castle and Gail was now huddled down in the rear of the van hidden from sight behind a large box marked "DANGER – HIGH EXPLOSIVES."

The soldier at the gate checked the registration of the van against a clipboard, then he came to the window and examined Dougie and Brian's passes briefly.

"Okay," he said, returning them. He leant on the counterweight and the barrier swung upward to let them through.

Dougie revved the engine and drove sharply through the gatehouse and up the cobbled road that led into the castle. The tires squeaked as they bounced over the damp cobblestones, rattling through Argyle Tower and under the heavy iron portcullis.

He brought the van to a halt at the top of the hill, by the castle wall where the one o'clock gun sat overlooking Princes Street Gardens.

"Alright, people," called Dougie, "You know what to do. We're behind schedule so let's be quick."

"People?" asked Brian. "There's only the two of us, ken."

Dougie sighed, "Let's just get to work."

The three dismounted the van and opened up the trailer. The trailer was filled with several large plastic canisters, like oil drums, which had to be set in place along the top of the battlements. It took two of them just to tip each one so that it could be wheeled on its rim down the ramp and off the trailer.

The battlements afforded a magnificent view over Princess Street Gardens, through the lights of the old town, across the inky black of the Firth of Forth to the winking lights of Fife on the far bank.

As they rolled the second barrel into place, Dougie, mopped his brow on the sleeve of his borrowed blue overalls and allowed himself a moment of triumph. Looking out past the city, against the dark waters of the Firth, he could just make out the shape of the Royal yacht now beached and blackened. He grinned. Tonight was going to be even more spectacular. Below him on Princes Street he could see the crowd starting to gather, those with tickets to the Gardens finding their seats or laying out picnic blankets on the grass. Tonight was certainly going to be different from the usual festival fireworks concert.

Dougie's reverie was rudely interrupted by the sound of heavy boots on stone. He looked up, apprehensively. There were two soldiers walking towards them. They were not moving with any great urgency, but Dougie found his gaze drawn inexorably to the semi-automatic rifles that were hanging casually from their shoulders.

*****

Mari crept quietly into the dark wood panelled hallway. It smelled of bee's wax and wood polish and it reminded her of school trips here – hiding in alcoves from the teacher, eating chips from the cafe and sandwiches wrapped in tin foil by her mother. They were soft, happy memories that felt out of place now.

As a McLeod, Dunvegan was technically her ancestral home and she had always felt a distant sense of ownership over the old castle. Tonight, however, it felt eerie. The only sound was the deep throaty tick of a giant clock somewhere down the hall. In the gloom, she could just make out the flagstones on the floor and the broad, steep wooden staircase that led up to the museum level.

Mari closed the door behind her and started cautiously up the stairs. The staircase had always felt to Mari like something out of the Sound of Music or The Addams Family. The first broad flight of steps ended in a landing. Then on each side, the stairs doubled back in twin narrower flights that ran up to the top.

At the top of the first flight was a stained glass window showing the McLeod coat of arms in blue and red, topped by a black bull's head and the family motto: "Hold Fast." On the sidewalls was another coat-of-arms, and a tapestry of Robert-the-Bruce with his spider. Behind it, she remembered with a smile, was the concealed door where Billy Bracken had tried to kiss her – more fool him.

Mari pushed open the wide door at the top of the stairs that led to the private museum. The trophy room held the prize possessions of the McLeod clan. It was lit now only by the soulless green and white florescent glow of the Exit sign above the door. In this ugly light she could make out the glass-topped cabinets that held the assorted McLeod bric-a-brac, a small collection of eclectic but interesting exhibits. Each one had a story. There was Rory Mor's Horn, a lock of Bonnie Prince Charlie's hair, the pincushion embroidered by Flora MacDonald, the Dunvegan cup and several weapons, including a large rusting claymore – sword of the clan's first chief.

On the far wall by the window in a large glass fronted case was the prize of the collection: the Fairy Flag. Its origins were lost in time, it was thought by some to have been once the robe of a saint. It was said that a McLeod, who was true of heart, that carried the flag into battle could not be defeated.

Mari glanced scornfully at the worn greying tatters of silk

cloth. Quite honestly it didn't look fit to mop the floor with. It was a funny thing how something being old suddenly made it special.

Crossing the room quickly, she pulled open the heavy door on the far side. She knew Katie was here, she could feel it. She was so close now that she abandoned caution and ran down the short corridor and burst into the guardroom above the dungeon.

The dungeon at Dunvegan is simple and brutally practical: a sealed stone-walled room with no windows or doors, accessible only from the guardroom above by a trapdoor in the ceiling.

Mari dashed to the trapdoor and then heaved it open with the cold iron ring at its centre. Inside, it was dark as pitch; she could make out nothing below, neither walls nor floor.

"Katie!" she shouted, unable to contain herself any longer. "Are you there? Katie?"

"Mari?" the voice was quiet and hoarse from crying. "Is that you? Mari!"

Mari's heart leapt. "It's me Katie." To one side of the opening in the floor, leaning against the wall, was an old wooden ladder. Mari grabbed it and started lowering it into the dark space below. "Watch out, I'm puttin' the ladder down."

*****

Dougie watched the soldiers approach with mounting apprehension. Play it cool, he told himself, but his palms were sweating.

"You're cutting it a bit fine ain't ya, mate?" asked one of them. He had a thick London accent.

Dougie stared blankly at him for a moment or two. "I'm sorry?" he said.

He could feel Gail and Brian tensing up beside him. Despite himself, he kept looking at the weapons the soldiers were carrying. He felt sure the others were doing the same.

"The concert's about to start, mate," he explained. "Isn't it a bit late to be addin' stuff?"

"Yer tellin' me," said Dougie, regaining his wits "There was last-minute cock-up with the inventory. If we don't get these set on the top of the walls, the big finale will be ... och, well ... small."

The two soldiers considered this for a moment. Dougie held his breath but tried to look casual.

"Well, we shouldn't keep you then," said one of them eventually.

"Do you want a hand?" offered the other.

"Do I ever!" replied Dougie with immense relief. "We have to get these along the battlements. Right up on top of the walls."

"What are they?" he asked.

"Oh, something very special, like you've never seen before. They'll be talking about this one for years," replied Dougie, grinning despite himself.

With the soldiers help, they got the plastic drums in place on the very top of the walls. Each drum had an elaborate set of tubular fixtures that had to be applied. Brian set to work making the final assembly and checks on the devices.

Dougie thanked the soldiers, who continued on their round, and he and Gail headed quickly back to the van. There was more to do and, even with the unexpected help, they were running out of time.

*****

Without thinking, Mari rushed down the ladder as fast as she could. It was so dark at the bottom, she could see nothing. The world was black on black with just a faint patch of slightly paler black in the ceiling where the trapdoor lay open.

"Katie?" she whispered, trying not to sound afraid. "Where are you?"

"Mari," sobbed Katie. "I'm here."

Flailing through the dark in the direction of her cousin's voice, Mari finally found her and grabbed her in her arms, hugging her so tight that Mari was barely able to breathe.

"Mari," she said, between sobs. "I knew you would come for me." She was shaking. "They were like dogs, Mari, but with hands. They grabbed me."

"I know. Katie. It's alright now."

"Do you believe me?"

"I saw them. When I went home they were waiting for me."

"What about Uncle Sean? He tried to stop them. They attacked him. Is he OK?"

"Dad was badly hurt Katie, I don't know how he is. He'll be in hospital by now."

"Did you bring the police?"

"No, it's just me."

"Oh," Katie sounded a little disappointed but said no more.

Kneeling on the hard stone floor in the dark, they held each other in silence.

"Katie, are you hungry?"

"Starving!"

"Try some of this." Mari passed her the bag of barley, pushing it into her hands.

"Wow!" exclaimed Katie as she chewed on a handful. "What *is* this stuff, it tastes *amazing.*"

"I don't really know," answered Mari, honestly, "It's a kind of barley, but it's not like the stuff that grows in the Thornley's north field, that's for sure. Now, try drinkin' this, but just a sip now."

Katie felt for her hand and took the flask. Then Mari heard a sharp cough.

"Gee Wilikers, Mari!" said Katie. "That's whisky, that is. What would ma mum say?"

Even in the dark, Mari could tell she was grinning broadly.

"C'mon, give it back. We need to get out of here while we still can."

Mari shoved the hip flask and the empty bag back into her pocket and helped Katie to her feet. They climbed the ladder. Katie went first ponderous and slow.

At the top of the ladder, Mari could see Katie for the first time. She was still wearing her pyjamas – white with small yellow ducks on them and a towelling pink dressing gown. The clothes were grubby, soiled with mud and grease. She looked fragile and vulnerable, like a favourite doll that had been left out in the rain.

Taking Katie by the hand, Mari started to retrace her steps towards the front door.

She reached the trophy room and started to lead the way between the cabinets when they heard something. The sound made Mari's blood freeze in her veins and she felt Katie's hand tightening on hers. They stood motionless, hardly daring to breathe.

Behind the door ahead of them they both heard the snarling growl of a large angry dog.

*****

Edinburgh Festival Fireworks Concert is a spectacular evening of live music with a choreographed firework display set against the stunning backdrop of Edinburgh Castle. It is the biggest annual event of its kind in Europe, providing the grand finale to the Edinburgh International Festival of the Arts.

Upwards of ten thousand people line the one-mile length of Prince's Street to watch the fireworks as music from the orchestra in the Garden's pavilion stage is relayed to them through a rock-concert sized PA system. Several times this number watch from other vantage points in the city and listen to the music being simultaneously broadcast on local radio.

This year's program is provided, as usual, by the Scottish Chamber Orchestra and begins with Grieg's 'In the Hall of the Mountain King' from Peer Gynt.

— *Weekender's Scotland,*
Edinburgh City

*****

Dougie and Gail could just hear the opening bars of the music from the orchestra in the Gardens below as they got back into the van. Dougie had a small FM radio strapped to his belt.

He flipped it on. It was tuned to Fourth FM, the local radio station that always covered the fireworks concert live.

They were behind schedule. There was a lot they needed to do in the next seven minutes and twenty-four seconds before this piece came to an end.

Dougie drove the van up through the next level of defences known as Foog's Gate and into the very heart of the castle, bringing it to a squealing halt in Crown Square.

Crown Square was a courtyard at the top of the castle, bordered on all four sides by grey stone buildings. The one on the east was the Royal Palace, their target.

Dougie's first task was to go around and disable the two closed circuit TV cameras trained on the courtyard. He had a long stick with a can of black spray paint taped to the end of it. It was rigged with a string that he could use to operate the spray. With the lenses blackened it would probably be assumed that the cameras were faulty. They had been told that the pictures from the cameras were usually not watched when the castle was closed, but they didn't want to take the chance.

While he blacked out the cameras, Gail started hurriedly unloading equipment from the van and dumping it by the wall of the Royal Palace.

*****

Upon his coronation, James VI had commissioned a remodelling of the Royal Palace that had included the construction of a strong room on the first floor. Today the strong room is the highlight of the castle's museum experience. Visitors, equipped with the ubiquitous audio headsets, pass through a long twisting passage that contains a series of life-sized montages depicting momentous scenes from Scottish history. At the end of this passageway, though four-and-a-half-inch-thick solid steel doors, is the strong room. Inside its dimly lit interior, on a plinth covered in rich black velvet, lies Edinburgh Castle's most prized and valuable treasures, the "Honours of Scotland": the Crown, Sceptre and Sword of State, first used for the crowning of Mary Queen of Scots.

Seemingly out of place amid the jewel-studded regalia is a very plain-looking block of sand stone, chipped and worn with several missing corners. On its top are set two iron rings. This is "An Clach", the Stone of Destiny.

— *Tourists Guide to Historic Scotland*

*****

Once he finished with the cameras, Dougie grabbed a crowbar from the back of the truck and strode over to where Gail arranged the other equipment. He marched up to a door marked "Private" and forced one end of the crowbar into the doorjamb just by the lock. After a few seconds of careful prying, there was a deep splintering sound and the lock gave way. Dougie gave it a final kick and it swung wildly inwards.

The room inside was a storeroom. There was an untidy thicket of brooms and mops in one corner, and a long table with a couple of empty teacups and a tattered clipboard. On the far wall was another door that led to the Royal Chambers.

Without a word, Gail set to work on the explosives. She erected a set of folding steps from the van, climbed up them, and started drilling holes in the wooden beams on the ceiling. Into each hole she carefully inserted a pencil-sized metal rod.

Directly above her was the strong room and in it the object of their mission, the Stone of Destiny.

As Gail worked, Dougie could hear the music of the Scottish Chamber Orchestra coming from his little radio. It was a constant reminder of how little time they had left. Brian should be here by now. He glanced out of the door and saw the lanky Scott hurrying across the courtyard.

"See they call tha' the 'Lang Stair'" gasped Brain, fighting for breath, as he drew near. "Well, they're no bloody kiddin'!"

Dougie said nothing, but quietly rolled his eyes, pushing the door open to let him in. Gail was almost finished with the charges.

From the small radio at his belt he could hear the music starting to build to a climax. There was only a few seconds left.

Gail leaped down from the steps and ducked into the corner of the room beckoning wildly for the others to join her.

Dougie and Brian rushed in and crouched beside her. They looked up apprehensively at the rectangle of explosive charges mounted on the ceiling. A pair of curly wires ran between the charges. Gail's eyes were wild as she held the trigger in her hand.

The final chords of the music were being drawn out.

"Aren't we a bit close, like?" asked Brian, apprehensively.

Gail looked at him sharply, "what do ya mean?"

"Ta the explosives, we're a bit close..."

"Nah," replied Gail, but with less certainty than any of them would have liked. "It'll just blow out the wee section – you'll see."

"Are ya sure?"

Dougie looked from one to the other.

"Outside, quick!" he yelled, indicating the door that led to the royal apartments.

They grabbed the remaining equipment and dashed for the door as the final cadence from *The Hall of the Mountain King* started to fade. Brian was there first. He burst into the royal apartments with Dougie hard on his heels. Gail came last. Her lips were moving as she ran from the room, counting silently to herself.

"One... two... three..."

*****

Mari looked wildly around the trophy room. There was nowhere to hide and no time. The door was opening. The creature would be on them in moments.

In desperation, she grabbed for the old claymore, ripping the rusty sword unceremoniously from its mountings. As the shadow beast crashed through the door, she brought the sword around with both hands, holding it at arm's length, so that the tip of the four-foot-long blade pointed directly, if a little unsteadily, between its eyes.

Katie let out a small gasp of fear and cowered behind Mari.

For a moment, the beast stared at Mari, assessing the situation. Then it feigned an attack, snarling loudly and snapping at her. Mari drew rapidly back, her guard faltering, as the sword point wavered uncertainly. Her attacker immediately sensed her inexperience with the weapon and got ready to pounce forward.

Seeing the inevitable, Mari desperately changed tactics. She swung the sword in wide arcs and advanced, forcing the surprised creature briefly backwards. Gaining a little confidence, Mari hefted the sword back over her head, ready to bring it down in a killing blow. Unfortunately, she misjudged the considerable weight of the weapon and found herself pulled off balance. The sword swept backward into the display cabinet holding the Faerie Flag. The glass shattered with a glorious explosion that sent razor sharp shards raining down across the room.

*****

The boom was deafening. Over a hundred thousand people felt Prince's Street shudder with the force as the seven hundred pound firework exploded over their heads...

"...*five*" mouthed Gail to herself and she pushed down on the trigger under her thumb.

The explosion shook the door on its hinges and in the darkness of the royal chambers, Dougie, Gail and Brian could see the bright white flash around the edges of the door as the charges went off. The initial bang was followed by a roar of falling masonry and a loud smashing of glass as the large display case fell fifteen feet from the floor above and hit the flag stones below.

Two hundred thousand eyes watched the shower of sparkles open up across the sky like a giant multicoloured chrysanthemum of flame almost four hundred feet across...

Dougie opened the door. Plaster dust billowed out from the darkened room, making it impossible to see anything inside for a few moments. He pulled a torch from his belt and shone it through the doorway to survey the devastation.

"Wow," said Gail with awe in her voice.

The storeroom they had been in only moments before had changed beyond all recognition. The beam of white light from the torch cut through the dusty air. As it moved about, they could see the whole space covered with rubble and splintered wooden beams.

Looking upwards, the torch shone straight into the museum vault above and Dougie could see that the vault doors were still very firmly in place.

A heavy oak beam had fallen across the area they'd been crouching in only moments before, crushing the aluminium stepladder.

"Bloody hell!" exclaimed Brain, when he saw it. "Ya were only supposed ta blow a hole in the floor."

"Well, a cannae help it if the floors all knackered," responded Gail, quickly. "It's over four hundred years old, ken!"

Dougie moved quickly into the room, his torch scanning the ground. The Honours of Scotland had been thrown across the floor. The sword looked as if it was in one piece but the crown had been badly bent out of shape. He ignored them. No doubt they were well insured and could be fixed or quietly replaced. To their left was what he was looking for. The Stone was sitting on the remains of the shattered display case, seemingly unscathed by the fall.

He started to move carefully over the rubble, holding the specially made padded harness that they had built for the purpose. It was made from a very tough canvas tarpaulin lined with a couple of furniture blankets. There was still a rather bumpy ride ahead and this should protect it from a lot of knocks and scrapes.

"C'mon, you two," he said without looking round. "I cannae lift it on ma own."

They were still on a clock. They estimated that they had around two minutes before the first military security got there. It would probably be another seven to ten before the police arrived.

Their hope was that the guards would think that the firework had triggered the motion sensors and set off the alarms. They probably wouldn't be hurrying and when they arrived they would find the vault doors intact and it would take a little while to get them open. Of course, when the doors were opened, all hell would truly break loose and, by then, Dougie and his team needed to be long gone.

*****

The last shards of glass fell to the floor of the trophy room with a gentle tinkle. Mari regained her footing, but the creature saw its opening and leapt.

Mari, saw at once that she could never complete the sword stroke in time and instead threw the heavy weapon, handle first, at her attacker. Then she grabbed Katie and pulled her aside.

The sword miraculously found its target, the heavy pommel striking the long muzzle of the beast with a satisfying crack. It let out a yelp and landed awkwardly where Mari and Katie had been moments earlier.

They drew back into the corner of the room, putting a display cabinet between them and the beast. The creature brought its head around slowly and glowered at them. There was pure hatred in its dark black eyes it was making an impossibly low menacing growl in its throat like the rumble of thunder.

"Looks like we've pissed it off," said Mari, trying to sound brave in front of her cousin.

"Aye," said Katie, unable to take her fear filled eyes off the beast.

"Well, let's see what it makes of this," said Mari, suddenly remembering the brooch. She pulled it out of her pocket and brandished it at the creature like a vampire-hunter with a crucifix.

There was a moment of hesitation, a brief look of uncertainty from the creature. The growl faltered.

Then, without warning, it pounced with a bellow like an angry bear. It leaped over the display case, its teeth bared and its arms outstretched.

Mari watched the attack as if in slow motion. Three hundred pounds of muscle and teeth flew through the air toward her. For a moment, the world seemed to slow to a stop and she felt as if she could almost step out of it, like waking out of a dream.

From somewhere inside her she felt an energy building, a sort of tingling sensation, like pins and needles on steroids. It shot down her arm to the brooch and then all of a sudden it felt as if a switch had been thrown and she had been hooked up to the electrical mains.

The world returned to its natural and alarming speed. The enormous creature was still hurtling toward them in mid-air and in moments, literally fractions of a second, it would be tearing them to pieces but at that moment the energy discharged. There was a blinding flash of blue-white light that came from the brooch and Mari watched with elation as the enormous bulk of the startled shadow-beast changed its direction in mid-air and was thrown forcefully against the far wall.

It bounced off the wood panelling and smashed through a display case, shattering it to broken splinters, finally landing heavily on the floor next to Rory Mor's Horn. It did not get up.

The room fell suddenly quiet as the last pieces of broken furniture clattered to the floor.

"Bloody hell-fire, Mari! How the hell did you do that?" exclaimed Katie.

"You watch yer language, Katie McGrieg!" said Mari, reflexively. "Come on, let's get out of here before it wakes up."

They crossed the room, carefully avoiding the prone body.

On impulse, as she passed, Mari reached up between the broken shards of the display case and grabbed the Faerie Flag. There was a slight tearing sound and the tattered silk cloth came away from its mountings.

"What did you do that for?" asked Katie, puzzled and a little shocked at the desecration Mari's action represented.

"I don't know," answered Mari, honestly, stuffing the folded rag into the top of her jeans, "but it feels important. Come on, let's go."

*****

"Did I not tell you: she is, indeed, The Flower," boasted Talisker, flashing a grin down the table to the assembled gods.

"Oh, Tal, you were right all along!" exclaimed Dalwhinnie, with big wide eyes and an impish smile that brought out her dimples. Talisker knew he was being teased, of course, but there was something about those dimples that just made him smile back all the same.

"She's certainly starting to do a lot better, dear," agreed Jura. There were murmurs of agreement from around the table.

"At least we've got some fire-power," declared Laphroaig, emphatically. "Now we can hit back!"

"I agree," said Oban, sounding pleased. "If she can keep this up, perhaps we can turn the tables. Nice touch getting her to pick up the Flag, Talisker, very subtle I barely felt your influence there."

"That wasn't me, father," admitted Talisker. "She did that herself."

Oban, raised his eyebrows in surprise. "Impressive," he muttered.

"Gentlemen," interrupted Ardbeg, with a scowl. "This self-congratulation is all very heart-warming, but I suspect it may be a little premature. Little Mari has a long way to go and she still has no idea of the burden she must carry."

*****

Dougie knew that the Stone of Scone weighs one hundred and fifty-two kilograms and he felt every one of them as they rolled it into the harness. Using a pair of poles that slipped through handles, they were then able to carry it out, stretcher-like, into the royal apartments. They moved as quickly as they could through the empty hallway to a little room in the back known as the birthing chamber, where King James was born. Here they set the Stone down.

The tall window looked out to the South of the castle. It was composed of tiny diamond shaped panels held together with lead strips. Immediately below, was the cliff of Castle Rock, at the foot of which was Johnson Terrace and their parked car.

Hardly pausing in his stride, Dougie picked up the ancient varnished log by the fireplace that came from Queen Anne's thorn tree, and hurled it through the window. Dozens of small diamond shaped panes shattered. With gloved hands, he quickly tore away at the soft lead supports that had held the rest in place until he had a wide hole.

The grassy banks on the slopes of castle rock beneath the window were off limits to the public, as was the rock itself. They were, however, kept carefully trimmed by a large warren of rabbits that grazed there. Although well camouflaged against the rocky slope, to this day, the careful observer can see dozens of them peacefully eating the grass at most times of day or night, lit as it is by the powerful castle floodlights. For the most part, the rabbits are left to themselves, but every now and again something will startle them and you will see dozens of little white tails suddenly bob up and down as they run for cover.

Thus it was that anyone who had been watching the castle rock at that moment would have seen fifty or so small bunnies take flight as the Stone of Scone, carefully wrapped in its protective padding, came bouncing inelegantly down the side of the rock and roll across the grass to come to a jarring halt at the railings.

"You bloody idiot!" yelled Dougie at Brian.

"What do ya mean? *I'm* an idiot? You were the one who was supposed to be lowering it down."

"Aye, but you were s'posd ta be helping!'"

"Well, I slipped, alright? It's bloody' heavy."

Dougie took a deep breath and glanced at his watch. They really didn't have time for this.

From the small radio at his belt the next piece of music from the firework's concert began. It was Wagner's "Ride of the Valkyries."

"Alright, they'll be here any minute," He said as the music started to build. "If we're not away in the car by the time they figure out how we got oot, we're dead. Brian, you go first. Gail, your next."

As soon as Gail was free of the rope, Dougie clipped on his harness and swung out of the window.

If there had been any rabbits left on the slopes they would have been even more startled to see three humans abseiling out of the castle accompanied by the stirring tones from the brass section of the Scottish Chamber Orchestra.

*****

Mari started down the wooden stairs to the main doors. She held Katie's small hand in hers. She still shook from the encounter with the beast in the trophy room but was filled with a feeling of exultation at their escape. Maybe, they could get away after all. They were almost out of the castle and it was not far to William's cottage. Then he could drive them to Portree, or even as far as the mainland.

A thin sliver of a moon had risen and could just be seen glinting through the large stained-glass window as they rushed down the stairs. But they only got as far as the landing before a terrifying sound behind them dashed her hopes of an easy escape. It was a piercing howl that cut the air and seemed to echo long after the voice making it had stopped. It was coming from the trophy room. The beast she had knocked out had just recovered.

Katie grabbed at Mari's arm and looked at her with fear in her eyes. Mari looked down at Katie and realised what she had to do.

"Go on, Katie. Get out," whispered Mari, quickly. "I'll meet you around by the boat houses."

"But Mari..." Katie started.

"Look, I went to a lot of trouble to get you out. I'm not having them take you back. It's me they're after. If I'm not out in ten minutes, walk to Kilmuir and knock on the first door you come to and call the police. Understand?"

"Mari, come with me!" whispered Katie, desperately pulling at her cousin's hand. "I'm no goin' without ya."

"Katie, listen, if we try to run, we won't even get across the moat. These things are fast. The only way is for me to face them. Now go! Quickly!"

Reluctantly, Katie turned, made her way down the stairs and out of the front door. Mari watched her go with relief. She turned her attention back to the top of the stairs where the door was opening and an angry snout peered out with slow menace.

Mari held up the brooch bravely. However, it was starting to dawn on her that she didn't really know how it worked. She had blasted this monster once, she reminded herself, but, when it came down to it, she had no idea how she had done it, or whether she could do it again.

The creature eyed her wearily but did not advance. It was as if it was waiting for something. Waiting for what? Then, suddenly it struck her – backup!

She looked down and there, in the shadows, appeared a second beast, summoned by the howl of its sister.

Mari regarded the two creatures. The one at the top continued to hold its distance, but its stance changed. It was no longer waiting. It was now alert, expectant. It was probably not possible for the black dog lips to curl into a smile, but if they could, Mari knew she would be seeing a cruel, sneering look of triumph on its dark face.

The creature at the bottom of the stairs started advancing.

Mari swung the brooch around helplessly. Fear began rising within her. She pointed the brooch first up and then down the stairs, trying hard to work out what she had done to trigger it. She tried changing her grip on it, touching the pearl at its centre but it just sat in her hand, cold and inert.

Think! Mari, think! This would be a really good time for an idea. She started edging back from the advancing beasts into the corner of the landing. Both of them moved now; their eyes glittering with the knowledge that they had won, although their movements were still slow and careful.

Then, unbidden, the memory of an old school trip flashed

into her mind. Five years earlier she had stood on this landing with Billy Bracken, trying to find a place to hide to skip out of the museum tour. Billy had shown her a secret door, hidden behind the tapestry of Robert the Bruce. He had tried to kiss her while they hid in the dark and got a scorching slap on the face for his efforts.

With one swift, fluid motion, she ducked behind Robert. She slipped through the hidden door and slammed it closed behind her. It was dark but she vaguely remembered a bolt on this side. Her fingers flew over the wood until she found it and threw it into place.

Mari knew she had to move. As quickly as she dared, she started climbing. It was very steep, and the steps were irregular. Her left hand slid up the central pillar and her right brushed against the rough stonewall. Below her, she could hear the loud banging of the shadow beasts battering at the secret door. Under her right hand she felt the stonewall give way to wood – a door. She fumbled for a door handle and turned it. She pushed and pulled. It was locked. Crap!

Below her came a splintering crack as the bolt on the door gave way. With howls of delight, the creatures started up the dark stairs.

She abandoned the locked door and went back to the dark scramble up the twisting stairs. The higher she went, the steeper and more irregular the stairs became.

The growls and snarls echoed up the stairwell beneath her so that it sounded as if they were coming from all around.

At last, her lungs burning, she reached the top. The stairs ended in a small wooden door. She tried the handle, after a brief struggle, it opened and she ran out onto the flat roof of the castle.

The slender moon half-lit the scene that greeted her. This part of the roof was broad and covered in gravel. There were a few chimney-like vents poking up and several square-framed skylights.

Past the skylights was the wall of another part of the building, hidden in shadow. Along the edges of the roof she could make out the crenulations that formed a low barrier and beyond them she could see out to the sea loch on one side and the dark woods on the other. Where now?

She ran to the sea loch side and looked over the edge. The drop looked dizzying, ending in the rocky shallows of the loch. There was no way to climb down. She scanned the roof again, but at that moment, a figure stepped out from the shadows of the far wall. Mari recognised her at once.

"Mari, my dear," said Ms. Farrow, menacingly. "How nice of you to drop by."

*****

"Where the hell did she slither out from!" cried Laphroaig, staring at the image in the giant glass on the table.

"She has help too, remember?" pointed out MacAllan. "We are now paying the price of our earlier intervention."

"We have to blast her, now!" exclaimed the war god. "Have Mari use the brooch. She won't be expectin' it."

"She can't control it yet," said Ardbeg, peering at him down her sharp nose. "Who knows what would happen if she tried again."

"Well, we bloody-well know what'll happen if she doesn't," exclaimed Laphroaig, leaping to his feet. "We should take control and open fire."

"No, Laphroaig," retorted Talisker, sharply. "She has to learn. She has to do this herself."

"What are you talkin' about?"

"The closer we get to the confluence, the less we can influence events. If we help her now, where will she find the strength when the final test comes?"

"If we don't help her, she's nae gonna make it to the final test."

"Laphroaig," croaked Dufftown, "your brother is right, we may have helped her too much already. This challenge she must face alone. Do not intervene."

"I don't like it," declared Laphroaig, watching the image of Ms. Farrow advancing menacingly on Mari.

*****

There was a cold breeze blowing off the sea loch that carried with it a salt tang and the brackish whiff of rotting seaweed. Katie pulled the grubby pink dressing gown more tightly around her as she leant against the wall of the boathouse. As the minutes ticked by, she became more and more anxious about Mari. The prospect of having to walk to Kilmuir in the dark in bare feet was troubling her, but more than that she was worried about her cousin and what those dreadful creatures might do to her.

She heard the sound of footsteps approaching. With relief, she stepped out of the shadows. She expected to see Mari walking towards her, but it was not. The footsteps belonged to a tall ungainly looking man with curly hair. He was carrying a small leather jacket. It was clearly too small for him. There was something about that jacket – it looked like Mari's.

"My goodness you nearly scared me to death," said the man in the most English of English accents. "What are you doing back there?"

Katie said nothing. She was gently cursing under her breath for revealing herself, but it was too late now.

"It's alright, you can come out, I'm not going to bite, you know. You look a bit young to be out on your own at night. Do you live around here?"

"Where did you get that jacket?" asked Katie.

"It belongs to a friend of mine," replied the man. "I was trying to return it, but it seems she's not around." He looked wistful. Then he turned back to Katie. "Listen, you're going to catch your death in those pyjamas. Why don't you put it on until she comes back."

Katie took the heavy jacket from the man. She recognised it at once. There was a Celtic knot design running up one arm. It was hand drawn in silver marker pen but it was very well done. To the casual observer it looked like a print on the jacket, but Katie knew better – she helped do it.

"This is Mari's jacket. What are you doing with it?" she asked suspiciously.

"You know Mari? Oh, that's splendid!" said the man, with genuine enthusiasm. "My name is William. I met Mari in the pub last night. She sort of helped me out and I gave her a lift. She was going to stay the night with the estate manager, Cynthia Farrow. I dropped by a couple of times but there's no sign of her. How do you know her?"

Katie regarded William intently. He certainly seemed honest enough but he was clearly English and she didn't like the English. Eventually, she replied, "She's ma cousin."

"Cousin, good, that's good. Do you know where she is?"

"She's in there," Katie nodded towards the castle. "I'm waiting for her to come out."

He looked forlornly towards the castle, his curly hair bobbing in the breeze. He was actually quite good looking, she noticed, when you couldn't hear his accent. Then, a thought occurred to her.

"Do you like Mari?" she asked, with the sort of innocent directness that only a child could use.

"Erm, well, yes, of course, she's a very nice girl," blustered William.

"No I mean do you *like* her?" persisted Katie.

"Oh, you mean like that? Er, well, no doubt she has a boyfriend so..." He let it hang.

Katie was enjoying this but she was careful to stifle all but the smallest hint of a smile. "No, actually, she doesn't."

"Oh, really? That's very interesting," said William and then looked as if he wished he hadn't.

"I don't think she'd want to go out with an Englishman, though."

"Oh, no, of course." He was still gazing absently at the distant building.

Katie was disappointed; he didn't really seem to be listening.

He pointed up at the parapet. "Look, up there on the roof. Can you see something moving?"

"Mari?" gasped Katie.

*****

At the bottom of the Castle rock, just by Johnson Terrace, with not a rabbit in sight, Dougie put his foot against the top of a section of the spiked fence. He had been up here the day before and had taken out the bolts at the top. As he pushed, the fixings on the bottom started to bend and the whole section pivoted down to the ground.

He and Brian half lifted, half dragged the Stone over the horizontal section of railings and dumped it into the boot of the car. Dougie took the keys from Gail and sat behind the wheel. Brian took the passenger seat and Gail sat in the back. Dougie started the engine and they pulled away. Once they managed to get away from the immediate vicinity of the castle, he could breathe again.

His palms were wet with sweat as he turned the car up toward Toll Cross, forcing himself to drive slowly and carefully. He switched on the car radio. They could hear the last bars of the Valkyries fading to applause from the crowd.

"Okay, Gail," he said, "let's do it!"

He deliberately ignored the smirk the statement brought to Brian's face.

"Right, y'are, chief," said Gail. On the back seat next to her was a small metal briefcase. It was open, and inside, it had what looked like a radio control unit with several switches and a large red button, protected by a safety key.

The radio announcer started the usual banal filler between pieces:

"The applause for the Scottish Chamber Orchestra, tonight conducted by Geraldine Fisher. That was Wagner's *Ride of the Valkyries*. The orchestra is now preparing for the final piece in tonight's concert. This is a surprise piece..."

Gail flipped a switch. The commentator fell silent as a new and unexpected voice addressed the ten-thousand people packed onto Prince's Street.

"*There will be no more lies, no more talk, no more delays. The English occupation of Scotland must end tonight. The Stone of Destiny has just been reclaimed for the Scottish people. This night will go down in history as the night the Scots reclaim their honour and reclaim their nation.*"

This short impassioned speech was followed by the sound of a lone piper playing The Flower of Scotland, the country's unofficial national anthem.

As the sombre tune started, Gail flipped two more switches. A series of floodlights and showers of clear fireworks suddenly lit up the walls of the castle. Finally, Gail turned the safety key to the "armed" position on the control and reached for the red button.

*****

The bitter wind swept across the castle rooftop but Mari didn't notice. She was still staring at Ms. Farrow in shock. How could she possibly have known that Mari would end up here?

The door from the stairs that Mari had come through moments before suddenly burst open and the two creatures pursuing her dashed out onto the roof. Seeing their mistress, they hastened to take up positions on each side of her. They dropped to all fours, resting on their knuckles like apes, and growling menacingly as they stared at Mari with black featureless eyes.

Ms. Farrow smiled coldly. "My dear, Mari, you have nowhere to run."

She was right. There was no way past the monsters and behind her was the sheer drop into the sea loch. Mari's mind raced – there had to be a way out.

Ms. Farrow brought up her hand; in it she held the dreaded black rod. Suddenly remembering the brooch, Mari ripped it out of her jeans pocket and held it out before her.

Ms. Farrow watched carefully for a moment. "Ah, so that is how you escaped me before, but you don't actually know what that is or how to use it, do you?"

"I know it kills your monsters."

"My dear, you cannot bring death to those that come from the Land of Dead."

"P'raps not," answered Mari, bravely, "but *you're* not from there are ya?"

"No, but this is." She raised the black rod and again Mari felt the fear strike her like a physical blow. She gasped; suddenly just standing took an effort of will, but she had not fallen...yet. The brooch seemed to be offering her some protection. If only she could figure out how to make it do that zapping thing again.

She focused her attention on it, trying to remember what it felt like when the energy had surged through her, trying to imagine that feeling now. She felt something — not a blast like before, but this time a flow that swept down her arm and though the brooch. It streamed out toward Ms. Farrow, pushing back the projected fear like a jet of water forcing back a flame. Mari felt her strength start to return.

Ms. Farrow scowled and retaliated by pushing harder; driving the dark energy back toward Mari. The fear returned and the weakness with it but she had started to understand something about how the brooch worked. Reaching inside herself, Mari summoned all her energy and forced it out through the brooch. It flowed down her arm, washing away the fear and driving the brooch's energy back at the estate manager.

Ms. Farrow let out a sharp cry; she had been hurt. Mari gasped with the effort but at the same time broke into a quiet grin. She'd been hurt, which meant she could be beaten.

However, her newfound optimism was short lived. At that moment one of the beasts pounced at her. With her focus on the duelling energies, this physical attack took her completely by surprise. Mari saw the movement out of the corner of her eye and staggered awkwardly out of the way. She reached out to save herself and her forearm hit the edge of the stone parapet. A jolt of pain shot along her arm and the brooch slipped from her fingers and went skittering across the rooftop.

Ms. Farrow watched with satisfaction, the confident smile returning to her face. "Don't worry, Mari. We aren't going to kill you today. I need you alive." Then her voice became harsh, "But I don't need you to be sane. Before we lock you up, I am going to teach you a lesson in what fear really is. By the time I've finished, you won't even know your own name."

She raised the rod once again. Mari stood there defenceless

as the fear started to grow insider her. It was not sudden this time but built gradually, relentlessly. Without the brooch, there was no way to stop it.

Desperately, she sought for an escape, but there was nowhere to go. It was hopeless. A scream rose unbidden within her and burst forth into the night, tearing at the quiet darkness. The sense of terror was overwhelming. It blocked all thought and strangled her will. She felt her knees starting to give way. She was losing control of her body. Panic overcame her and she found herself almost wishing for an end to her sanity, wishing for any release from the crushing fear. In a moment, she would fall to the floor and then it would just be a matter of time until her mind could take no more and finally break like a clockwork toy that had been wound too far.

But there was a corner of Mari's consciousness that was untouched. Beneath the fear that filled her mind was a deeper sense of self. From here, she saw what was happening to her body and mind and she knew with a quiet acceptance, that this could be the end of Mari McLeod. She saw the only thing left for her to do.

She made a choice, a final act of defiance. Summoning all her will, she forced a last action out of her overwhelmed body. Instead of collapsing forwards onto the roof, she let fall backwards so that she over the low parapet and down... down... down... towards the icy black waters of the loch.

*****

In the back seat of the moving car, Gail pushed the red button on the control unit. In response, hundreds of gallons of red paint started pouring from the carefully placed barrels along the castle battlements.

The effect was chilling. Ten thousand people on Princess Street watched as the brightly lit walls of Edinburgh Castle bled. Red rivers of blood cascaded from the top of the walls, half pouring, half oozing down towards the castle rock.

Then, one by one, the crowd started singing along with the lone piper that could still be heard over the P.A. system.

The lyrics of The Flower of Scotland tell the story of the defeat of the English army at Bannockburn in 1314. It's a song of independence and defiance of English rule. They were into the second verse before someone managed to pull the plug on the recorded piper but, by then, the song had its own momentum and the voices of the crowd carried it.

Back in the car, the mood was ecstatic. They knew the feed would be cut but they never expected the crowd to take up the song.

"Och, I wish we could see it," said Brian, choking with excitement and blinking back tears.

The radio commentator had found his voice and was completely beside himself:

"The walls of Edinburgh Castle are *bleeding*! There's *blood* running down walls! I've never seen anything like it."

Despite his professional airs, Dougie was grinning uncontrollably. Two down, one to go, he thought, with satisfaction. Although, he had to admit, tomorrow night's attack was troubling him.

*****

It happened in the late afternoon, a few weeks after the attempt on Gregorian's life. Pamphilos was not expecting it. He had all but forgotten the dire warning of his wife.

The sun was warm and the gentle breeze brought Pamphilos the smell of the sea. The preparations for his next trip were going well. It should be a profitable venture and give him opportunity to set some money aside. He thought often of his impending fatherhood and the mix of joy and responsibility it represented. His trips, he told himself, would have to be shorter and less frequent in just a few months.

The walk from the pier where he kept his boat to their home was not long but it involved taking a path that climbed steeply up the cliff. It was not a dangerous route in good weather but there were points at which the path became narrow and the drop on one side sheer.

Pamphilos was approaching such a section when he thought he heard something behind him. He looked back, but saw nothing. The wind or one of the sea birds, he told himself, but as he turned the next corner, he found himself face to face with Daran's brother, Carther MacDonald. The tall clansman was fully armed and stood blocking the path forward.

There were no words exchanged. Both men knew why he was there. Pamphilos looked back only to see another of Gordar's crew blocking his retreat.

When they found the body the next day, dashed on the rocks below, it was assumed by most that he had simply lost his footing.

Scotia had been expecting it. There are some turns of the wheel of fortune that cannot be avoided. But her knowledge did little to lessen the sense of shock and loss. On that day, she lost what mattered to her most; Pamphilos, Aristos. He was the reason she had come here. The reason she had left her home, her life, her family. Their unborn daughter, still to set foot in this cruel world, was the only reason that they did not find her body on those rocks that day, next to his.

*****

Katie stared up at the rooftop. From this angle, she couldn't see much but there was definitely someone or something moving up there.

Katie pointed. "That's Mari." She just knew it had to be her cousin.

"Are you sure?" William asked. "It's a long way away."

Then came the scream, a raw and desperate sound that rang out and echoed around the hills.

"It's Mari, alright!"

At that moment, the figure collapsed, falling backwards over the low parapet. Her limp body tumbled over the edge and plummeted towards the loch.

"Mari!" screamed Katie, unable to believe what she was seeing.

"Hold this!" William tossed his coat at Katie, and dashed headlong towards the castle. Nearby, a short pier jutted out into the loch. William reached it as Mari hit the water. He cleared its length in three long strides and dived in after her sinking body.

The cold, salty water soaked through William's clothes dragging him down, but he was a strong swimmer and covered the distance to where she had hit the water in under a dozen strokes. He plunged down under the surface of the inky black water and found it deeper than he expected. William groped around until his lungs burned like fire, then he swam back up. He held his head up just long enough to take another gulp of air and then dive back down.

Katie watched from the pier in horror.

On his third attempt he found Mari. He brought her body back up to the surface, limp and lifeless. He righted her and placed his arm around her chin and towed her back towards the pier, swimming sidestroke.

There was a ladder on the side and, taking Mari over his shoulder, he lifted her out of the water and laid her down gently on the rough wooden planks. Katie flew to Mari's side but drew back when she saw how she looked.

Mari's skin was blue-white, her eyes were closed and there were no signs of life – no breathing. Desperately, William laid her out on her front, put her head on one side and pressed down firmly on her back. Water gushed out of her mouth and dripped between the wooden planks.

For a long moment, nothing happened, and then suddenly, Mari coughed and took a huge gasp of air.

It was startling to see the life return to her body as if some giant puppet master had just picked up the strings again. All of a sudden the lifeless piece of meat he hauled out of the water was, once again, Mari. She coughed, bringing up more muddy loch water from her lungs. Then, she vomited, hard.

Katie hugged her, tears streaming down her face. "I thought you were dead Mari. I thought you were dead!" Too weak to protest, Mari sagged in her young cousin's arms and for a moment she just clung there, breathing.

"We need to get her inside and into some dry clothes," said William. He was shivering with cold himself.

From the direction of the castle, they heard a piercing howl. Mari looked up; there was movement visible on the roof. "I'm too tired," she mumbled, "too tired to run."

William looked out across the loch. "I say, there's a boat!"

Mari struggled to raise her head. A small sailing boat had just rounded a spit in the loch. It tacked gracefully and turned toward them. The sails filled and the bow rose as it cut through the water, shedding white foam on either side. It seemed to be moving incredibly fast in such a light wind. She could just make out the man at the controls. It was Connor.

In a few moments the boat drew near. Connor turned her in a tight arc and pulled up alongside the pier.

He reached out to help lift Mari into the cockpit. "Quickly now, they'll be here any minute." As he laid her out on the bench, he noticed the hip flask protruding from the back pocket of her jeans and pulled it out. Noting the 'T' monograph, he opened it and gave it a sniff. "Ah, Mari, this is the good stuff. This will make you feel a little better."

He opened the flask and helped her bring it to her lips.

She coughed at first, but then swallowed. He fed her a little more. This time it went down more smoothly.

"How's she doing?" asked William, clambering aboard.

"She's gonna be fine," said Connor with a smile and stuffed a life jacket under Mari's head. He offered William his hand.

"Connor McColl," he said.

"William Davenport."

"Hey, don't you twos get friendly," said Mari, looking up at them weakly. "He's a scoundrel," she said, nodding at Connor, "and he's a English aristo'," she continued, indicating William.

"How are you feeling?" asked William.

"Like the worst hangover of ma life," said Mari. "Where's that whisky gone Conner?"

Connor handed her the flask and returned his attention to the boat. There was another howl. His eyes scanned the shadows around the castle. It sounded much closer. "We haven't much time. William can you shove us off?" Connor set the sails as William pushed the boat away from the pier.

At that moment, the first of the dog-beasts appeared. It emerged from the shadows of the boathouses running flat out on all fours down the pier. It reached the end and leaped for the boat. The creature could easily clear the widening six-foot gap, but Connor was ready for it. Before it reached the boat, he turned swiftly and swung his staff so that it struck the beast full in the face.

The staff flared a brilliant blue-white for a moment and the beast howled pitifully before falling heavily into the water.

"It is a little known fact," remarked Connor, casually watching it flounder, "that the dogs-of-death are very poor swimmers."

"What the bloody hell was that?" exclaimed William. "And what did you just do to it?"

Connor looked at him wearily for a moment. "Let's get underway. I'll explain it as we go."

The boat started to pick up speed, as Connor headed North up the sea loch, towards the Atlantic. The others watched the bank warily. Two more beasts appeared on the shore, but they did not attempt to swim after the retreating boat. Instead, they ran up the shore, snarling and howling. Their companion managed eventually to drag itself from the loch and stood watching the retreating boat with hatred in her eyes.

"We've lost them!" exclaimed Katie.

"For now," said Connor, his eyes scanning the shoreline for signs of their pursuers as he sheeted in the sail and adjusted their course.

Mari tried to sit up. She felt dreadful, every part of her body ached. She tasted vomit in her mouth and she was freezing cold. Her clothes were drenched and her lips and fingers were numb.

Katie came over and sat next to her. "Here, I've got your jacket."

She handed Mari the heavy leather jacket. William sat on a bench on the opposite side of the little cockpit. She reached across and handed him his heavy wool coat. "There you go, hero!"

"Thanks Katie, and thank you, William," said Mari, sincerely, "for saving me, I mean." She looked long and hard at the Englishman.

"Well, let's just say we're quits," he mumbled after an awkward pause.

As Mari pulled her jacket on, she noticed that she was sitting on something. She tugged at the thick folds of cloth that had somehow become stuffed down the back of her jeans. Then she remembered it was the faerie flag except, it felt very different. She pulled it out and held it up.

What had been an old stained rag was now long flowing folds of the most beautiful white material. And it got worse. As it unfurled, she saw it was not just a length of cloth but a dress of pure silver-white silk. It reflected the dim moonlight so perfectly that it almost seemed to glow with a light of its own and, unlike the rest of her clothing, it was dry as if the waters of the loch had just run off it. Speechless, she just stared at it for a while, turning it over in her hands.

"That's like an unlikely thing to find in your back pocket, Mari," said Connor.

"It was the flag, the Faerie Flag of the McLeods. I stuffed it into my jeans as we were running from that creature and now – well I don't know what happened."

"The flag is a mystery," said Connor. "It is powerful, but no one knows for sure where it came from, nor what it really does. It seems to have taken a liking to you though and it looks like your size. You'd be smart to put it on and get out of those wet clothes."

He indicated the cabin. Gratefully, she opened the little door and disappeared down the steps inside.

Mari had never been on Connor's boat, but she had seen it from a distance. It was a wide, 30-foot sloop that bulged in the middle in a sort of sensual, feminine way. The paint was peeling in several places and the sails looked worn and stained, but it had a feeling of solidity and togetherness. It seemed to have been taken care of where it really counted, as if the shabbiness was more a sort of stylistic choice, like ripped jeans.

After drawing the curtains over the little windows, Mari stripped out of her wet clothes and pulled on the white dress.

*****

The rush started to wear off by the time Dougie dropped the others off in the outskirts of the City. He was still enjoying the afterglow of tonight's success, but he was tired now and still had a long night ahead of him. His instructions, detailed and explicit as always, required that he hide the stone down some farm track deep in the Perthshire countryside. He had a lot of ground to cover if he was to get home and get some sleep before tomorrow night's attack.

As he drove through the night, chilled to the bone by the unrelenting blast of cold air that rushed in through the broken window, his thoughts wandered. The plan for tomorrow night troubled him.

So far, the SSA "attacks" had been big stunts. They had desecrated a few national monuments, smashed a few shop windows, pissed people off and drawn attention to themselves and the cause, but no one had really got hurt.

Well, a few people had been hurt, a few even killed, but only incidentally — as a sort of side effect: those two policemen by the petrol bomb some idiot had tossed into the police cordon. No one had really meant for them to die; they had just been... unlucky. Dougie felt all right about that, anonymous people died all the time in accidents of one kind or another. Most of the deaths had been due to the trigger-happy police. Tomorrow all that was going to change. People would die, lots of people. He'd have real blood on his hands.

He'd been told that they were all English lackeys under the influence of their English masters; they deserved to die; they had betrayed Scotland. It sounded good at the time, but now he was questioning it.

Why should all those people die? Could he take responsibility for hundreds of deaths?

There were other things that were bothering him too. There must be a thousand and one places this bloody great rock could be hidden. It was, after all, a piece of cut sandstone. Edinburgh was built from pieces of cut sandstone! Why did he have to drive it all this way? Why the urgency?

Above all, the biggest question on his mind was about who was behind all this? Was it that crazy woman on the phone that gave him the instructions? How could she know what was *going* to happen? She used all the right words but, as he drove through the dark night, Dougie had to admit that he found himself wondering: what was the real motivation of his posh-spoken superior.

*****

The boat flew across the loch. Its full sails roared loudly in the wind and its bow cut sharply through the water. They were nearing the end of the loch where it opened out into the Atlantic and the swell was starting to pick up. Every now and again they would hit a crest, throwing salty spray across the deck.

Connor stood at the helm, constantly adjusting their heading whilst keeping a wary eye open for signs of pursuit along the shore. Mari was below getting changed. He glanced at the others who were sitting on the side benches of the cockpit. William was huddled up shivering slightly. His clothes were still sopping wet and dripping on the deck. Katie was wearing the pyjamas and dressing gown that she had been taken in and also looked cold. "I'll have some clothes you can borrow down below, William. There might even be something for you, Katie. I've a friend with a boy about your age who stays on the boat now and then. I think there are some o' his things in there. It's all in the wee closet in the bows."

"Thank you," said Katie, quietly and slipped down below to join Mari.

"Yeah, thanks," said William, through chattering teeth. He was watching the grim look on Connor's face as he scanned the shoreline. "So, what were those things that attacked us?"

"They are called the Dogs of the Dead, or Shadow Beasts," replied Connor, matter-of-factly. "They are summoned from the realm of the dead as guards or servants."

"Do you mean to say they're some sort of ghost?" William shrugged helplessly, "I'm afraid I don't believe in that sort of thing."

"It is said by some that they are the souls of humans who have failed to keep their promises to the gods of death. It's foolish to believe children's tales of ghosts and magic, but even more foolish to deny the evidence of your own experience. This is real William. You are taking a step into a bigger world."

"And I suppose you're also going to tell me that's a magical staff?" asked William, sceptically, eying the six feet of willow that was lying once again on the floor of the boat.

"Since you ask, yes, it is."

Connor glanced at him again. William obviously didn't believe what he had just said, but then few people these days would. It was always hard for other people to come to terms with the world he lived in. William actually seemed to be taking it fairly well. There was something odd about the Englishman though; that he should be there at just the right time to save Mari, could not have been a coincidence. Fate *had* to be involved and he wanted to understand how William fitted in to all of this.

"So," he began casually, "how do you come to be out at Dunvegan?"

"Oh, just taking a break from the office."

"I see. We don't get many English tourists up here these days, what with the Troubles. You're not put off by that?"

"Well, I'm a relative of the McLeods. They let me use the holiday cottage from time to time."

"Ah, I see," said Connor, quietly. "I noticed you've visited most of the pubs on the island while you've been here."

"Just getting the feel of the place."

"Right, right," responded Connor, "and askin' a lot of questions too. Interesting way to spend your holiday, no?"

William looked awkward for a moment but before he could

respond, they were interrupted. The cabin door opened and Mari came out onto the deck.

She was wearing the Faerie Flag.

It fitted her perfectly. The white silk shone in the moonlight and somehow it made Mari shine too, despite her bedraggled hair.

"What do you think?" asked Mari, self-consciously. "It's no really ma style."

For a moment the two men just looked at her.

"What?" exclaimed Mari.

"You look beautiful," said William.

"It's only a dress," said Mari, quickly and she sat down. She was still wearing her wet, grubby trainers and, as she sat, she pulled her black leather bikers jacket over her exposed arms, completing the picture of incongruity.

Katie followed her out of the cabin wearing a pair of jeans and a sweater that looked two sizes too big for her. Though, somehow her pajamas still hung out around the edges. She sat down next to her cousin and William disappeared below to look for some dry clothes.

They were leaving the loch now, heading out into the open sea. The boat was still making good speed and, if anything, the going had become easier. Connor's eyes watched the dark outline of the shore. "They're still out there." He muttered almost to himself.

"We're safe here, though, right?" asked Katie, the fear evident in her eyes.

"We're safe from them," replied Connor, cautiously.

Mari was starting to feel herself again and with it she felt a thirst for answers. She was still a bit groggy but here was the man who had warned her yesterday that she faced danger, before any of this had started. Here was a man who might have some answers. She felt questions bubbling up inside her, bursting for attention. "What's going on Connor? What is all this? And why is it happening to me?"

"I'm sorry, Mari, I should've told you about it before, years ago but, well, I didn't think you'd believe me and your father...

let's just say your father didn't want me to have anything to do with ya, after what happened to your mother."

Mari felt a chill go down her spine at the mention of her mother, but she said nothing, eager to hear what Connor could tell her – not that she'd necessarily believe it.

"Let's see, Mari. You ever heard of Scotia?"

"You mean the Egyptian princess that Scotland is s'posed to be named after?"

"Aye, that's her. Well, you are her last direct descendant, through the female line."

"You wha'?"

"She is your great, great, great grandmother, many times over. She saved this land, nearly five thousand years ago, saved it from a dreadful curse. And she won the hearts of the people.

"That's your legacy, Mari. You are the Heart of Scotland. The heart of the Scottish people today."

"Connor, I don't understand what you're talking about."

"Five thousand years ago, a terrible curse was placed on this land by Anput, the Egyptian goddess of death. Now, Scotia was not just a princess but she was also a powerful sorceress and she made a bargain with Anubis, Anput's husband. He would not lift the curse, but he modified it, qualified it, if you like, at the cost of her life. Through her sacrifice, Scotland would be safe, so long as the Heart of Scotland lived. Scotia held this title first. Then it passed to her daughter and so on down the female line. When your mother died it passed to you."

"Are you telling me that that crazy old bitch believes that killing me will bring down a five thousand year old curse on Scotland?"

"I'm sure she does," said Connor, "but there's more. There's an old prophecy called the Manuscript of Saint Farole that was found amongst the texts in the monastery on Holy Island. It talks of an apocalypse, the return to the earth of an ancient evil to be brought about by the 'Keeper' at Dunvegan..."

"The estate manager?"

"The text rambles a great deal – lots of death and fire and brimstone, brother fighting brother, mother fighting daughter, rising up of the dead, all that sort of thing – however, one passage seems clear: There is only one person who can stop the Keeper. In the numerous copies of the scroll this individual, praised for both courage and beauty, is described as the "Fleur d'Ecosse" — the Flower of Scotland and that title has been given to many who have changed the course of the history of this country.

"However, it is a mis-transcription. If you look carefully at the original, and you know what you are looking for, you can see that the prophets was actually referring to the "Cœur d'Écosse" — the Heart of Scotland; the direct female descendant of Scotia herself. Given the context of the piece, that is clearly a reference to you, Mari, or your mother."

"What are ya talkin' about? Ma mother was a hairdresser."

"Your mother, Mari, was one of the most powerful witches I have ever met. I will never understand how she let Cynthia Farrow get the better of her."

Mari stared out over the waves. She was expecting Connor to give her some half-hearted tale that sounded plausible but didn't ring true. What Connor was giving her was clearly not scoring high on her plausibility scale. Unfortunately, she reluctantly found herself conceding that that probably made it more likely to be true.

The connection to her mother was difficult to process. Every time Connor brought it up, it twanged some random heartstring inside, sending her thoughts shooting off in a different direction. Was this really what was behind her mother's death? She looked directly up at Connor, "Are you telling me that Cynthia Farrow killed my mother?"

"Well, probably not with her own hands. She's smarter than that, but I'm pretty sure she arranged for it to happen."

A picture flashed into Mari's head, her poor beaten father lying on the floor by his chair. "That must've been what my father was trying to tell me."

"Your father's a good man, Mari, but he never understood about Tara's powers or her role. Then, when she died, well, he sort o' went into denial about it all. He never wanted to face up to it."

"Do you believe these prophesies?"

Connor sat still for a moment, his eyes fixed on the sea.

"Mari, right now, what I believe is beside the point. The problem is that Cynthia Farrow believes it. She believes that she is destined to bring about a new world order and the only person who can stop her is you.

"She's going to carry out a ritual. It will be on the next moonless night...tomorrow."

"Do you know what she is going to do?"

"I believe she plans to awaken the Leviathan, an ancient and terrible beast. Its coming is said to mark the end of each epoch of human history signalling the fall of civilization. It feeds on hate and violence – very nasty. If she can do it, it would be ... well, bad."

Mari wanted to scream about how unfair this was. It was not her problem! She wanted to stamp her foot and refuse to do anything, to go any further, even to believe what Connor was telling her. But she did not. Somehow, his words rang true, though she was no longer sure what truths remained that she could hold on to.

Connor paused for a moment and scratched his beard.

"One more thing, Mari," he said, reluctantly, "you need to hear this. The manuscript also says that you will die."

*****

Leviathan was one of the early gods of the Ancient Egyptians, rather like Titans for Romans and Greeks – the early gods who preceded Osiris and Ra. Leviathan was a devourer of souls who spread fear, hate and destruction. She was believed, to be sleeping in the deepest depths of the ocean and to awake once every few thousand years to reign down terror and destruction

In her fully corporeal form, Leviathan is said, according to one ancient Sanskrit account, to stand four hundred cubits in height and resembles a giant squid with hundreds of tentacles.

Leviathan is most feared and revered, not for her physical destructive ability, but by her incitement of violence in others. The appearance of the Leviathan is associated with the collapse of many, if not all, of the major civilisations of the world.

Some accounts identify Leviathan with the Babylonian goddess, Tiamat. She is also connected with accounts of the powerful Saron Priesthood and, in particular, their practice of human sacrifice.

> — *Gimwald's Cyclopedic*
> *Daemons and Demi-gods*
> *of the Ancients.*

*****

Following her husband's death, Scotia found herself getting more and more drawn into the politics of Gregorian's court. It was, at first, a distraction from the pain of her loss, but increasingly, as her role grew, she saw the value she might bring to the people of Alba who stood poised on the brink of a brutal civil war.

She found herself spending increasing amounts of time with Gregorian. The old man was weak after the attack from which he never really recovered. Scotia was able to use herbs and, although she hid it, magic, to help with his maladies. She was also able to give him clarity and wise council in this difficult time.

A few short months after Pamphilos' death, the gods intruded once more in Scotia's affairs; this time to bring life rather than to take it. Scotia was blessed with a beautiful baby daughter, an image of her mother. She named the child Scandia.

Shortly after this Gregorian came to her with a proposal that would change the course, not only of her life and that of her new baby, but of the country of Alba itself.

"Scotia, my dear," said Gregorian, weakly from his bed. "It has been too long since your last visit. How is Scandia?"

"Why she is well, my liege. She grows in size and in mischief as any good child should."

The old man smiled. As they talked, Scotia busied herself around the room – opening drapes across the windows to let in the light, stoking the fire in the grate.

"Tell me, what news at court?"

"My liege, the chiefs come to you every day; surely you do not need my reports as well. Why would you hear everything twice?"

"The chiefs are getting more and more selective in their reporting. I fear it is only you that I can really trust."

"You flatter me," said Scotia, and she described the latest twists in plots at the Thane's court. Between her skill, intuition, and the power of the Stone, there was very little that passed her by.

When she had finished, the Thane had her sit by his bedside and take his hand.

"I have been giving a lot of thought Scotia, to what should happen when I am gone."

"My liege, you should not speak of such things. You will see many summers yet."

"Scotia, we both know that is a lie. Now, listen to what I have to say. I have reached a decision. When I die, I want you to take over as High Thane of Alba in my place."

"Once again, my liege, I am flattered by your faith in me, but I fear that it is surely not that simple. The other clan chiefs would never swear allegiance to a foreigner and a woman."

"Perhaps not to any woman, but I suspect that they might ... to my wife. Scotia, would you consider marrying me and taking care of my country when I am gone?"

Those who are blessed with foresight are usually aware of the twists and turns that fate throws at them. This had been the way with Scotia for many years. Pamphilos' death was all the more painful because she knew it could not be avoided. It was unusual therefore for her to be caught out and yet destiny sometimes plays a close hand. It can be difficult to predict your own fate. Scotia knew that she might play an important role in the country's future, but the Thane's proposal took her by surprise. She almost blushed and was, for a moment, lost for words.

"You can think about it, of course," said the old man, sensing her discomfort. "I know..."

"I accept," she interrupted. It made sense. She could not, of course, say that she loved the old Thane, not romantically, anyway; but he was kind, respected and respectable. More importantly, he might just be right. If the wedding was staged properly and if the Thane were to be clear in his wish for her to follow him, perhaps the other chiefs might accept her succession.

Silently, as she looked into the Thane's smiling eyes, she made herself a promise. Alba had been good to her. It had taken her in when she had nowhere to go and it would be the place her daughter would call home. She promised herself to do what she could to take care of it, to keep it from civil war and to make it a safe place for her child to grow up, just as Pamphilos would have wanted.

*****

"Oh, right, that's just effing brilliant, that is!" exclaimed Mari, standing up. The news of her prophesied demise had really been the last straw, "I've heard enough of this crap, Connor. Just let me off somewhere. I'm not gonna listen to any more of this."

"No," said Connor, simply.

"What?"

"No. I'm not letting you off. Last time I let you out of ma sight, I lost you for forty-eight hours and, by the time I'd found you again, you'd nearly drowned. It's ma job to protect you and I'm gonna do it if a have to tie you up. Now, sit down."

Mari opened her mouth. Then she shut it again. Finally, she sat back down next to Katie. Connor might be right, but she didn't have to like it. She folded her arms and scowled blackly.

"So, what are we going to do?" she asked, sulkily

"We're going to stop her," he replied.

"Oh, yeah? How?"

"We'll have to see."

"Oh great! That's great! Great plan that..."

They sailed on without a word for several minutes. The only sounds were the crack of the sails and splash of the water against the hull. Finally Mari spoke again. "Connor, do you really think I am going to die."

"Not if I can help it, Mari. See, the thing about ancient prophesies is you always have to take them with a pinch o' salt; even the really good ones. There's always a different angle on them, a different way of thinking about them."

"Right," said Mari unconvinced.

"But, Mari!" said Katie, seriously. "You already have died."

"What?"

"When you fell into the loch there. You stopped breathing for a while."

"I s'pose."

"So it's already happened and you survived it."

They both looked at Connor for assurance.

"Could be," he offered but did not sound convinced.

William reappeared from below. He was wearing a pair of saggy worn cords and a matted wool sweater, both were too small for him, enhancing his gangliness. Mari had to stifle a grin. Katie elbowed her sharply in the ribs and Mari could feel a giggle building up inside.

"Where are we going?" she asked Connor, desperate to shift her attention.

"I've a friend on the mainland who can help us. We should be able to get there in about three hours if the wind holds."

The time passed slowly. Katie dozed on Mari's arm as the boat rode through the waves, waking fitfully every time the boat rocked unexpectedly. Mari's mind was racing as she tried to understand what Connor had told her. William sat across from her in his long coat, Connor's cords rising up over his ankles. He seemed to be dividing his time between trying not to stare at Mari and trying not to look seasick. His gaze drifted out over the back of the boat.

"What's that?" he asked suddenly, pointing up in the sky.

Mari looked up. There, in the sky, were five white shapes barely visible in the starlit sky, almost like seagulls, flying towards them. They grew in size slowly and Mari watched with a strange fascination as it became more and more obvious that they were not birds, their shape was all wrong. They were more like bats, but too big. They were approaching at a great speed and it was only as they came within a few hundred feet that it became clear how big they were. The body of each one was the size of a man and their wingspan was over twenty feet across.

"Oh, crap," muttered Connor, and he recovered his staff from the base of the boat.

"What are they?" asked Katie.

"More conjurings of the Demoness of Dunvegan," replied Connor, grimly. "They're called Parzule, or Angels of Terror. Don't let them get near you. They feed by sucking on your life force – then sometimes they'll bite off your head for dessert."

"Gross!"

"Stay down."

With economical beats of their large leathery wings, the malformed angels gained rapidly on the fleeing boat. Once they had reached a point where they were almost directly overhead, they paused for a moment as if selecting a target. Then sweeping their wings back, one by one they started to dive.

*****

Parzule are a minor demon named after the Sumerian god, Parzuzu, lord of the southwest wind and bringer of disease. Parzule are rather like large white hairless bats in appearance that vary in size between ten and thirty feet in wingspan. Accounts of Parzule are often confused with those of vampires. Like vampires, they feed on the life force of their mortal victims, often through the physical act of drinking their blood.

The touch of the Parzule is said to be deadly. It brings a withering disease. According to one Knight Templar's account the victim's "flesh and bone became as dust and ash".

They were referred to in Medieval Europe as 'Angels of Terror.'

Gimwald's Cyclopedic Daemons and Demi-gods of the Ancients.

*****

Mari stared up in horror as the ghoulish creatures plummeted toward the boat. They had wild, ferocious faces, deformed and misshapen, with large fangs jutting awkwardly from their small mouths and fierce blood-red eyes. Their bodies were bulged with powerful muscles and in place of hands and feet they had vicious-looking talons tipped with sharp, black claws.

The first Parzule dived until it was barely twenty feet above the ocean and then suddenly flared its wings and swung its talon-like feet over the boat, grabbing for Connor's back.

Connor already had his staff raised and, as the creature attacked, a blinding ray of light burst from it bathing the lead Parzule in a corona of intense white. The beast reeled and let out a high-pitched screech, then plunged downward towards the sea. It hit the water with a splash as the other Parzule veered away from the boat on either side, startled by the unexpected counter attack.

"They'll be back any moment," said Connor, breathlessly. "I'm not going to be able to hold them off for long this way. Mari, quickly, do you have the brooch?"

Mari had forgotten all about it.

"I lost it," she admitted, forlornly. "It got knocked out of my hand on the castle roof."

"Oh, Crap! You know, it would have been really bloody useful right about now."

"Sorry, alright! There was a lot goin' on," retorted Mari, angrily.

"Aye, well, I know, I'm just sayin'. We'll have to think of something else."

The Parzule had circled around to regain altitude and looked like they were getting ready for a second attack.

"Watch out. Everyone keep down," yelled Connor, his eyes on the flying beasts as he steered the boat. He pulled out a small silver whistle that was attached to a leather thong round his neck.

"I was hopin' I'd never have to resort to this," he muttered to himself.

He put the whistle to his lips and blew on it so hard his

cheeks puffed out and his face went red with the effort. The whistle made no sound.

"A dog whistle?" asked William, sceptically.

"This is no dog whistle," replied Connor, flatly. "Hold on everyone. It's going to get a bit choppy."

As he said this, there was a sudden, noticeable drop in the air temperature, as if someone had just turned on the air conditioning.

The Parzule had already started on another dive. Connor turned just as the first of them was reaching for him, dark claws outstretched. He wheeled the staff around over his head bringing it into sharp contact with the flying monster.

The staff flared its white light again and the beast shrieked and reeled to the side, knocking into one of its companions as it fell into the sea.

Mari crouched down in the bottom of the boat's cockpit and clutched Katie to her desperately. The remaining two Parzule were hovering inelegantly above the boat trying to find a way to grab her without getting too close to the staff.

William, armed with a boat hook, was jabbing at their outstretched claws, but his futile attempts did little more than anger them.

The wind, meanwhile, started to pick up. The breeze that had carried them this far was growing teeth. The halliards began beating against the mast with loud snaps and the sail started to roar as it filled.

The circling beasts noticed the change in the air currents and cried out their strange, inhuman screech in defiance. It seemed to Mari that they became less steady in their flight.

As the gale grew Connor's boat started to accelerate, gradually at first, then faster and faster until they were tearing across the water and the Parzule were no longer circling but now in pursuit.

The wind was just the start. When they set out, there had been a low rolling swell on the ocean, like rolling tussocks of soft grass. The tussocks became hillocks, and then hills. The hills became mountains and which grew to towering precipices of ragged white water. It seemed that the whole world was moving. Mari could no longer tell water from sky. She clung to a rail as they were tipped through impossible angles. For a moment, they were surrounded by mountains of angry sea, and then suddenly they were lifted up onto a crest and she could look out across the jagged saw-toothed water, only to be plunged dizzyingly back into a trough between the next waves.

The wind screamed, beating against their faces and threatening to tear them from the scant support of the boat and throw them over the sides. Connor frantically worked the controls; sheeting in the sails, letting them out, heaving on the tiller to keep the bow to the waves.

The Parzule were lost from sight. They fell behind, forced to retreat to a higher altitude from wind and waves.

"I think we've seen the last of the Pazule, for now," cried Connor, not taking his eyes off the waves. "There's no way they can make it through this storm."

"Well, that's a relief," Mari screamed back.

"The problem," he continued, without even looking at her, "is whether we will."

"Ya might a thought 'o that earlier!" shouted Mari, finding that yelling at Connor was a welcome distraction from the aquatic onslaught.

"Well, the boat can take it," he responded, sounding hurt. "At least she can out in the open water. It's just we're getting close to shore. If we hit the rocks, we're kindling...wet kindling."

The waves were now terrifying, towering up to sixty feet above the small vessel.

Katie was clinging to Mari and screamed as one came crashing over the boat. Tons of water poured down on top of them. It felt as if they had been sucked to the bottom and then the plucky little boat popped up to the surface spilling gallons of seawater on each side as it came up. It was all they could do to hold on.

William, who had been getting greener and greener, suddenly emptied the contents of his stomach, mostly over the side.

"It'll calm down in a few minutes," yelled Conner, trying to reassure the group.

It was then that the rain started.

Mari had grown up on the West coast of Scotland and she thought she knew about rain, but this rain was different. The raindrops were huge, some the size of golfballs. They came so thick and fast that Mari and her companions could do nothing but cover their faces and duck down as low as they could.

The deluge lasted for only a few minutes, and then, almost as quickly as it had come, the rain abated, the wind dropped and the towering waves calmed to a ripple.

In fact, the storm died away so completely that the surface of the ocean was almost flat as far as they could see, and the sails sagged against the mast, flapping gently one way and then the other.

Connor stood up and lifted the seat behind him. He rooted around in the compartment below for a few seconds until there came a satisfying little roar and a cough of diesel fumes.

"Well, thank goodness I changed out of those wet clothes," said Mari, with glum irony, looking around at the bedraggled group. Katie's wet hair was still dripping and William's woollen coat looked like it might have shrunk. Only Connor seemed unruffled. He was soaked, of course, but his heavy wax jacket repelled the worst of the water and, fundamentally, he looked bedraggled at the best of times.

"How long 'till we reach your friend?" asked Mari.

"It shouldn't be long now," he said. "The storm carried us quite a way. They'll be back in a few hours, but I think we should be safe enough tonight."

"And tomorrow?"

"Tomorrow, Mari, we have to save the world."

*****

Oban frowned. "She has lost the brooch," he said testily.

Tempers were starting to fray in the council of Uisge Beatha. Outside the stone council chambers, the sky had clouded over and a steady thick rain splattered into the loch. This was no ordinary place and no ordinary weather: the elements here reflected the mood of the council, which was as bleak and grey as the clouds overhead.

"She still has the Flag," replied Talisker, defensively.

"Di'ne' start on aboot tha' Faerie dishcloth crap," retorted Laphroaig. "Remember what happened with the MacDonalds that time. We know that what they say aboot that thing is not true. We've seen McLeods tak' it into battle and have their arses whipped!"

"They were not true of heart but driven by greed and sought to plunder. Besides, it still has power, look how it transformed."

"Changing back into a frock is not gonna give us much in the way of fire power."

"How did we come to lose the brooch in the first place?" asked MacAllan, changing the subject. "I thought that protecting that was a primary concern."

"It would appear that our ability to influence these events is more limited than we would expect," said Oban, gravely.

"At the end of the day, we are all subject to the forces of fate," pointed out Talisker, bleakly, "and as we approach the confluence, the currents will get stronger."

"We are doing all we can," exclaimed Lagavulin, soberly. "We must trust in the strength of the powers of balance."

The gods fell silent for a moment, brooding on their troubles.

"Perhaps we should be looking for another hero?" suggested Ardbeg.

"What do you mean?" asked Oban.

"Well, the girl, she is too close to the centre of the confluence already. You said it yourself. We cannot help her. She must find her own destiny."

"But we can't sit back and do nothing."

"So, my Lord, we should find a new champion, someone we *can* influence."

"Ardbeg, it is too late. We cannot groom a new champion in a mere mortal day."

"Perhaps we could find one who is almost ready?"

"Who do you have in mind?"

"How about this one?" she suggested and passed her hand over the glass; the picture on the table before them shifted. For a moment it was hazy and then it cleared to reveal the image of a young man, sitting behind the wheel of a car, driving through the night. His hair was blowing in the wind as the driver's side window had been smashed.

As the image appeared, uproar broke out amongst the gods.

"You have got to be bloody kiddin' me," yelled Laphroaig above the din. "He's on their side!"

*****

Dougie's troubled thoughts wandered as he drove. The dark road and yellow streetlights melted past unnoticed as he rushed through the night to drop off the stone.

It had been much simpler, he thought, when he had first joined the SSA. He had been recruited by this guy about four years ago.

The guy's name was Gary, at least he had called himself Gary. Gary was a hard-ass, short on words and full of anger, although you rarely saw it. It boiled away inside him, hidden behind his thick, black-rimmed glasses.

Dougie had been pretty pissed that night. He was working on a job in Paisley, a couple of weeks of good money to help out on building one of the new estates. He had gone out with some of the others from the job-site. It was a pretty grim pub they went to, full of the local hard drinkers and a few arse-holes looking for fights.

When Dougie got drunk, he talked shite. This night he found himself talking shite about the English. It was getting him lots of attention and a few drinks and so, as the night went on, his ranting became wilder and wilder.

Gary found him, invited him to join him and his friends at a quieter table in the back of the bar, away from the jukebox.

Back then no one had heard of the SSA. If Gary had not been so deadly serious, Dougie would have just laughed at him.

As it was, he was fairly sure it was all a big wind-up and he'd be the laughing stock of the site on Monday morning.

Gary gave him a number to call. It was the first thought Dougie had when he woke up the next morning. Despite his hangover he made the call. It felt important. That was the thing about the SSA; it made him feel important, like he was making a difference.

There were a couple of cars on the road ahead of him. He checked his speed to make sure he was only going a little over the limit and glided slowly past them in the fast lane. He couldn't be certain in the dark, but neither of them looked like police. But he kept a check on them until both sets of headlights had disappeared from his rear-view mirror.

At first, he had just been one of the many foot soldiers. They were brought in to start fights at demonstrations. Dougie had been good at that. He was also smart enough to keep himself from getting arrested. Then, they started to train him, small stuff at first. They taught him about weapons, how to use them, how to make them, how to steal them. Sometimes the trainers would meet him in Scotland, in a barn in the highlands, an old warehouse in Leith, or the back room of a pub in Wester Hales. Several times he went over to Ireland where he went through intensive training weekends with other SSA operatives under the tutelage of ex-IRA specialists. One time, he was actually flown out to a special camp in North Africa – he still didn't know exactly where – for advanced training in portable artillery.

Despite all his time in the organization, he knew very little about how it worked, who actually ran it, who funded it, even how big it was. Of course, they said that this was for security. "Need to know" only. Asking questions was seriously frowned on.

His best guess would be that there were probably hundreds of foot soldiers recruited like he had been to stir up trouble but there might be no more than a dozen trained operatives at the level he was at now. They were split into cells so that no one really knew anyone in the organization outside their cell. All he knew was the posh bitch on the phone with ever more exacting instructions.

The Stone, she had said, was to be left at a clearing in the woods just north of Perth. He had a very specific description (as always) as to where and how to leave the Stone. Once he had made the drop, he was to drive home and prepare for tomorrow night.

As he drove through the dark night Dougie found himself starting to wonder for the first time, about whether to follow his instructions. It was funny really, but he couldn't remember having felt this way before. He'd always kept his mouth shut and done what he was told, but now, all of a sudden, it seemed very important to find out what was going to happen to the Stone, why it was needed so urgently and, most of all, who his superior was and what she was really up to.

*****

News of the wedding redoubled the politics of Gregorian's court. Some were afraid it would lead to a young heir. A few, the more perceptive, recognized or at least suspected the real reason behind the match and, among these, Scotia saw factions forming.

There were those who were clearly against the marriage, although they only spoke such thoughts in dark corners. Who, after all, would deny their beloved Thane a wife? Of more concern were those who went out of their way to demonstrate their support for the union. Of these, it was very clear that more than one was doing so in order to obscure their true allegiance. Finally there were one or two who genuinely welcomed the prospect, not only of the marriage, but also of the new queen.

Scotia, gently worked her new court, as she had started to think of them, carefully weeding and sorting, gently marginalizing the troublemakers and welcoming the helpers. It was all done with such smooth fineness that she gained much respect and admiration.

The wedding itself took place in the open air, in a stone circle on the top of a hill in the northeast of the island; a holy place where much later a chapel was built, and later still razed to the ground.

The day was warm. The pale Alban sun made an effort even this late in the year. The crops had just been gathered and the Thane's storehouses overflowed with food for the days of feasting ahead.

The hillside was full, lined with thousands who had come for this day. Everyone in the local villages was there, and hundreds had come from the mainland, too. All the Thanes in Alba were there – with some politically notable exceptions – and they came with their families and attendants. It was a sight to see, with everyone clad in their finest robes and dozens of clan standards fluttering in the breeze.

Atop the hill, in view of all, Scotia and Gregorian, attended by Gregorian's minister, made their vows. It was a simple ceremony, where they offered each other a cup of wine to symbolize their love, exchanged garlands to honour each other and rings to symbolize their promise. Once Scotia had given Gregorian her ring, they embraced and a roaring cheer went up from the assembled onlookers.

The feasting went on for days. It was almost two weeks before things returned to normal. The farmers went back to their fields, the fishermen to their boats. However, life for Scotia was different; she found herself queen. It was a role she fitted as if it had been tailored for her. It was a role that she had been born to.

*****

The stars shone brightly in the clear sky, and the waves lapped gently against fenders as Mari watched Connor secure the boat to the small pier.

Aside from their sopping wet clothes, there was no sign left of the unnatural storm they had just experienced. All was now calm and still.

Connor pulled out some tarpaulins from under one of the cabin seats and directed the others to tie them in place over the boat.

Everyone shivered with cold and conversation fell to necessities.

Mari felt the sombre mood but was enjoying the quiet. The storm had overwhelmed every sense. The stars, the soft sound of the water against the boat, the hint of a breeze, it all provided a healing peace after the onslaught of the gale. Her numb hands pulled ineffectively at ropes and covers as she mutely followed Connor's instructions.

"Why don't we just leave the sodding boat and get somewhere warm?" complained William, suddenly. He was struggling ineffectively to undo a knot in one of the lines.

"We need to cover out tracks," explained Connor, patiently. "They'll be looking for her." He nodded upwards to the open sky and several pairs of eyes apprehensively followed his gaze. "With the covers on, she'll look like any other boat. It might buy us a few hours."

"It's not far," declared Connor, to the bedraggled group that stood dripping and sneezing on the pier side, once the covers were in place, "about half a mile up the hill."

Katie's teeth were chattering. Mari pulled her close. She was wrapped in the one dry blanket that they had. Mari felt silently grateful for the solid, unshifting pier beneath her feet. She would think hard about getting on another boat.

They set off wordlessly along the narrow lane that twisted up the cliff, their feet squelching in their shoes and their wet clothes pulling at their legs.

The cottage could be seen from about half way up the hill, its windows bright with a warm yellow light. In many ways, it was nothing special. There were many similar stone cottages all over the highlands, but right now, cold and wet as they were, it looked like a palace.

Connor opened the gate and walked up the short path. To either side of him were flowerbeds, packed to bursting with plants of all shapes and sizes. Even in the silver-grey moonlight, the garden was a riot of colours. Purple white and yellow pansies fought for space at the front. Forget-me-nots and Blue Bells had taken over the shady corners. To each side of the door were hanging baskets with ivy trailing little red and white flowers. It was a breath-taking chaos of leaves and petals that seemed to burst with life.

He turned as he drew up to the door and spoke for the first time since they left the boat.

"This is the house of an old, old friend of mine," he said, in a hushed tone. "Some find her a little... well... *unusual.* Most people take to her in time but she can be a little unexpected at first. She takes a bit of getting used to."

He turned to knock at the door but before his knuckles met with the wood, the door opened inwards and there in the doorway stood a large woman in a violently pink dress.

She smiled at them, welcomingly, and her eyes glinted over the top of the half round reading glasses perched on the end of her nose.

Connor lowered his hand.

"I hate it when you do that, Dee," he muttered. "You're just showing off."

"Connor McColl! You're a fine one to talk about showing off," she replied, quickly. "Now come on in, all of you, where it's warm."

She stood aside to allow Connor, William, Mari and Katie to enter.

A log and peat fire glowed brightly in the grate, filling the room with a warm, rich fragrance. Set around it were two worn-looking armchairs and three mismatched dining chairs. Behind them was a kitchen with a large, rough wooden table.

"Here, take a seat." Dee, bustled off toward the stove. "I've some soup on for you. It might be a little burnt on the bottom – I was expecting you earlier."

"Expecting us?" exclaimed Mari, quietly.

"Dee is a *very* gifted seer," said Connor, happily bagging one of the armchairs right in front of the fire. "Anyone who comes to visit here finds that they have been expected."

She returned quickly and passed out mugs of steaming hot soup and heavy, warm, prickly blankets.

"Now, then," she said, finally settling in the other armchair. She turned to peer over her spectacles at Mari. "So you must be Mari? Well, well. It is splendid to have you here, I must say."

Mari shuffled uncomfortably in her seat but did her best to return Dee's warm smile. She had decided she liked the woman but was far from used to the idea that she was in some way famous, even among Connor's weirdy friends.

"Well, Connor McColl," she said, sharply, "where are your manners? You haven't even introduced us yet."

Connor leaped to his feet with a flourish, casually wiping bits of soup from his scraggly beard.

"My friends, allow me to introduce Dedrei McDee, dairy farmer, bee-keeper, wine-maker and the best white-witch North of Jedburgh."

"Aw wha' day a mean *North of Jedburgh*," interrupted Dee. "You've just got the hots for that Nancy Braidburn, who lives in the borders. She's no better than me! ... at least not at witchin.'"

Connor carefully ignored the interruption and continued.

"Dee, may I present Mari McLeod, only daughter of Tara McLeod, direct female descendant of Scotia McLeod and the Heart of Scotland."

Mari was starting to feel very uncomfortable by this point but, thankfully, Connor moved on.

"Her cousin, Katie McGrieg, recently rescued from the terrible clutches of Cynthia Farrow.

"Last but not least, this is William, who fished Mari out of the sea loch at Dunvegan."

"Well, I'm very pleased to meet you all," replied Dee. "You are most welcome. After you have warmed up a bit, we can get you out of those wet clothes. I have some beds made up for you."

Connor turned to William. "While we are on introductions William, I'd like to hear more about you. What is it that you do?"

There was an awkward pause.

"I'm a Systems Operator," he replied.

Connor scratched his beard. "That sounds very technical, William," what kind of systems do you...operate."

"Mainly, um, telephony," replied William, trying and failing to sound casual.

Dee looked at him intently. "I think you should tell the truth William. You know you are among friends."

Mari, watched him carefully. He seemed to be weighing some decision. Then, William's shoulders suddenly slumped.

"I'm a police officer," he said, finally.

"What?" exclaimed Mari.

"I work for Scotland Yard – the anti-terrorist unit."

"English police!" Mari felt the anger rising inside her. "You think we're terrorists? Is that why you're here?"

"No, no," said William, too quickly. "I haven't lied," he added.

"I thought you said you were a 'System's Operator'?" asked Connor, his tone level.

"I *am* a System's Operator." William was starting to get really exasperated. "Surveillance systems. I manage the office that records telephone taps, hidden microphones, SMS and email intercepts, social web – you name it. I listen to the phone calls, read the emails and posts. I look for ways to classify and organize all the information."

"I see. You didn't seem like much of a field agent to me," Connor observed, a little smugly.

"No, I'm not. I haven't even done basic field training."

"Then what are you doin' here, exactly?" asked Mari, clearly unconvinced.

William looked from face to face, his eyes finally falling on Mari. He held her critical gaze for a moment and then his eyes dropped. "Look, it's like this. A few weeks ago we taped a call, almost by accident. It was Farrow making the arrangements for a riot in Glasgow – which streets to barricade, which shop windows to smash. It happened the next day just as she had planned it and I mean *exactly* as she had planned it. I was pretty convinced that it indicated Farrow as the mastermind behind the SSA attacks.

"Well, of course, I took the transcripts straight to my superiors. This was hot stuff. We've been trying to get a handle on the organizers for years and there'd been very little progress made. There was masses of pressure on the department to come up with some promising leads. This one was the one that would blow it open. I knew it." William paused, making a physical effort to reign in his enthusiasm.

"Anyway, I waited, expecting to see more taps, an investigation team, eventually arrests...but there was nothing. Nothing at all! When I followed up, I found there was no sign of the transcripts – they had been lost. I couldn't even find my copy of them which should have been filed in my office with all the other transcripts I have generated. The files were gone from my hard drive, too. I went back to archives to get the original recordings and there was no record of those tapes ever having existed.

"It was clear that someone in the department had read my transcripts and done a very thorough job of removing all the evidence. I tried to convince my superiors that there was something going on here, but they didn't want to know. The implication that someone internal had been destroying critical evidence was too serious. I was told that I might have been working too hard. That I should take a break and I was put on paid medical leave.

"I knew I was on to something. I just had to prove it. I'm a sort of a distant relation to the McLeod Clan; we used to visit Dunvegan when I was a child. Since the cottages were empty for the refit, it was easy to get the use of one. I borrowed my sister's car and drove up here. I've been trying to find out everything I can about Cynthia Farrow ever since.

"That's it. That's why I'm here. That's my story."

*****

"Tell me a story, Mama."

The child rolled over in bed, her eyes expectantly on her mother.

"You may have a story," said Scotia, "but only one and then straight off to sleep."

"Tell me the one about Grandma and the monster."

"Very well. Settle down now."

The girl lay back obediently on the pillows, her face full of anticipation.

"This is a story that happened many, many years ago in a land far, far away, when your great, great, great, many times great, grandmother Nefertari was a beautiful young girl, who lived in the land of Babylon. Her father was rich and powerful and her mother beautiful and virtuous. Nefertari was talented and clever and as she grew up, she shone like a star in that land so that all knew of her gifts.

"Well, at that time in the land was a powerful priesthood that were feared by all, even the king. The people were grateful to the priests for the wealth that they brought to the land but they were also afraid of them for their prosperity was bought at a dreadful price.

"The priests revered a half-god creature called the Tiamat; a hideous dragon-beast that fed off and fuelled the fears and hatred of people. The Tiamat was very powerful and kept the enemies of Babylon at bay and saw that good fortune shone on the kingdom.

"To keep the beast in favour, the priests had to feed it a sacrifice. Once every five years a young girl was chosen, the most beautiful and talented in the land, and she was fed to the beast. If the sacrifice was not made or if the girl was not indeed the most beautiful and talented, then it was well known to all that the beast would rise in anger and the land would fall to ruin. And so it was that they lived.

"Well, when the time came, Nefertari was one of the hundreds of girls summoned to the king's palace from whom the sacrifice was to be selected. The chosen maiden would live there at the palace for a year and a day. She would be waited on by a hundred servants and want for nothing until the sacrifice was to be made. It was a great honour to be invited and many girls found their future husbands at the Selection. Nevertheless, Nefertari's parents were afraid for her.

"At the time of Selection there was a huge party at the palace that went on for days and days. Many important people attended, including a Hittite prince called Urhites. He was dashing and brave and rode up the palace in a golden chariot pulled by two of the biggest horses that have ever lived.

"The Hittites were disdained by the Babylonians who considered them little more than barbarians. However, Urhites' station and the rules of the gathering made it impossible for the priests to refuse to entertain him.

"Despite his origins, Urhites' charms quickly won him the attention of the other guests. Everyone wanted to meet him, but as soon as his eyes fell on Nefertari, he had no time for anyone else. They danced together, ate together, laughed together and then watched the sun go down together.

"At last, came the time of the selection and being the most beautiful and talented girl in the kingdom, sadly, Nefertari was selected for the sacrifice.

"Urhites was incensed. He pleaded with the priests to reconsider their choice. He offered them gold, even threatened to invade their kingdom but they would not listen for they knew the consequences of giving the wrong sacrifice.

"Determined that he would not let his new-found love be taken from him, Urhites decided to steal her away. That night, aided by his slaves, he broke into the sacred chambers of the priesthood and overcame the guards to snatch her away. They fled into the night on his chariot, the great horses tearing across the ground as the dark, moonless sky hid their escape.

"The priests were both furious and terrified. Nothing like this had ever happened before. They sent out an entire army to try and bring back the escaped couple.

"For many days and many nights, the lovers fled. The great horses pulled them tirelessly across the land, over mountains and rivers, through forests and deserts. A few times, they were sighted in the distance by the fastest riders in the Babylonian army but fast as they were, they could not match the speed and endurance of Urhites' great horses.

"Eventually, they found refuge in a small mountain cabin on the shores of a beautiful blue lake and there they stayed. Urhites, the great warrior prince, would spend his days hunting and fishing for food and Nefertari would spend her days picking nuts and berries and wild herbs and cooking the catches her lover brought home. Thus did they live together for a year and a day in harmony with each other and the land around them and they did want for nothing.

"During this special year Nefertari bore a child. That child was your great, great, many times great grandmother, who grew up to become a high priestess in Egypt – but that is another story – for as the year drew to a close, Nefertari grew more and more sad until there came a dreadful day. The day when Nefertari turned to Urhites and told him that he must take her back. Urhites threw himself on the ground and begged Nefertari to reconsider. They would never be found here, he told her. They could hide forever.

"But Nefertari understood that her destiny could not be escaped and eventually, after much persuading, Urhites did her bidding. He hitched his great horses to his war chariot and together with their baby daughter they rode back to Babylon.

"It was night time when they arrived at the cliff top where the sacrifices took place. There was no moon but the path was lit with a thousand torches. Nefertari bade Urhites goodbye, and ask him to take good care of their daughter. Then helplessly, he watched as she walked calmly into the torch-lit night alone.

"Nefertari was graceful and dignified to the end. No hands held her or chains bound her. When the monster came out of the water and reared up its huge, ugly head toward the cliff top, she dived down to meet its gaping jaws like the kiss of a lover."

"Why did she have to die?" asked the little girl, quietly.

"It was her fate." Scotia replied simply. "If she had not, the land and her family and the people that she loved would have been destroyed."

The child lay quietly for a while and then turned her head to look at her mother.

"It's coming, isn't it, Mama?" she asked, matter-of-factly.

"That monster is coming here."

There was no fear in the little child's eyes as she looked up at her mother. For a moment Scotia was taken aback. The girl's perception was so keen, she could already hear the voice from the Stone and she clearly felt what was coming.

"Yes," said Scotia gently, "it is coming. Someone will call it here. Don't you worry about it, though. You will be safe."

She smiled warmly and kissed the little girl's forehead as she tucked her in. It was only when she had turned away and was blowing out the lamp that the frown clouded her face. She had to be more careful what she promised the girl. Scandia was smart enough to see through simple lies and, as well she knew, no one's safety in this land was assured.

*****

Connor broke the silence. "That's an interesting story you have there, William. I was in two minds about you until I heard it but even though it pains me, I have to say, it makes some kind of sense. You see Cynthia Farrow is a black witch and, by the way, the most evil-hearted wee bitch I have ever met." Connors face furrowed deeply as he spat out these last words.

"She has been working with some of the darkest of the ancient powers to bring about a change in the order of this world. She is building a world of hatred using black arts to draw on people's deepest fears. The hatred feeds back on itself, fuelling the spell. The more hatred she can generate, the more it will spread. The SSA would be the perfect way to help drive the process in the physical world.

"And all this at a time when we are approaching a Confluence, a time when a small set of events between a few people can affect the next ten thousand years of human history."

"Aye, she's clever. I'll give her that," said Dee, with a sigh.

"Are you saying that the whole anti-English movement is the result of witchcraft?" asked Mari, a little perplexed by the idea.

"Well, not entirely," admitted Connor. "I mean, the Scots have pretty much hated the English for two thousand years –

at least. But in the last century it was kind a' abstract, at least for most folks. Ya didn't so much hate the English themselves just the idea of them. O' course, there were plenty who'd go out and pick a fight but not like it is now. Now, it's personal. She's done that, she's taken the undercurrents, the black fears and insecurities in the nation and fed them, given them a life of their own. Now people are planting bombs. I never thought that she was behind the bombs, too, but I have to say it makes sense."

Connor fell silent. He stared absently into the flames.

"So, tomorrow night," began Mari, "Ms. Farrow is going to summon some big ugly beastie..."

"The Leviathan," provided Connor.

"...and we have to stop her?"

"Aye."

"And exactly how are we planning to do that?" Mari was watching Connor very carefully.

"Ah, well. See there's going to be a big ceremony probably some variant of a Khasamic summoning rite. You know, priests, drums, candles, incense, pentagrams...the usual stuff. It'll take a while; probably a few hours and it'll come to a climax at the time of the dark moonrise. Our job is to disrupt the ceremony... make it fail."

"OK? Where's it going to be?" asked Mari, not yet satisfied.

"Oh, well, that's obvious – there's only one body of water around here that's deep enough to summon the Leviathan from. The place the ancients called the Great Loch – Loch Ness."

"You tellin' me she's going to summon Nessie?" asked Mari, wondering just how absurd this was going to get.

"There's a truth hidden behind every folk-tale, if you know where to look," replied Connor, "but nah, Nessie is just a bunch of sightings of logs and seals and old bits of boat. We are talking about a creature that would stand over 200 feet high with a writhing mass of tentacled arms over 60 feet long that can grab up flailing victims and hoist them into its ever open mouth. I guarantee no one has seen anything like that on the Loch in the last few thousand years."

"So, how are we going to stop them?" asked Mari.

"Well, the key to summoning a beastie like this is not so much the summoning. That part is relatively easy for a witch like Farrow. She'll need help, of course. I guess they'll be a small group of them, but the summoning itself is fairly straight forward – you see, it *wants* to be summoned. The difficulty is the control. Without the creature being controlled, it would run riot gorging on the fear, hatred and flesh of anyone that it could find. It would seek out the summoner, first, of course as a matter of pride."

"And, how do you control it?"

"Well, it usually comes down to an offering." Connor shot a hasty glance in the direction of Dee who was suddenly very busy with her knitting.

"Offering?" pressed Mari.

"Well, sacrifice to be specific."

"Like a goat?" offered William, helpfully.

"A bit like a goat..."

"It's me!" said Mari suddenly. "I'm the sacrifice, that's what Cynthia Farrow wants me for. She wants to make me into an *offering* for this creature."

For a fleeting moment, Mari hoped that Connor or Dee would step in and correct her. They just looked at her, gauging her reaction.

"It is, isn't it? I'm bloody right. She's planning to slice my throat with some rusty three thousand year old knife and..."

"Actually," interrupted Connor, "she's planning to stab you through the heart with the Sceptre of Gralkaran but the effect is similar."

"Connor!" exclaimed Dee.

"Well, she has to know," said Connor, defensively. Mari was just glowering at him.

"Don't worry Mari it's going to be alright," said Dee, soothingly.

"Bullshit!" screamed Mari. "This is so fucked up!"

*****

Dougie stared blearily at the dark, unchanging bend in the road ahead of him. He was ready for bed. He had almost nodded off twice now and keeping his eyelids open was becoming a serious physical challenge.

In the three and a half hours he had been parked there, three cars had passed. None of them had started down the little track that led to where he had left the Stone.

He was aware that he was breaking with his instructions but somehow it felt important. He sighed deeply and watched his breath condense on the windscreen in front of him. Give it another twenty minutes, he decided, eventually.

*****

The bed was hard but the sheets were soft and the heavy blankets promised warmth. Gratefully, Mari swung her legs under the covers. Katie lay in the bed across from her already tucked in and apparently close to sleep.

"So, do you like him?" asked Katie, who had obviously been waiting for this moment.

"Wha? Who?" Mari replied, knowing exactly what Katie was asking, but trying to buy herself time.

"You know," returned the younger cousin with a knowing grin.

"It's really late. We have to get some sleep," tried Mari.

"Mari, this is *important*. Do...you...like...him?"

"I dunno," said Mari, with a grump. "He's kinna cute sometimes. But he's so English!"

"He likes you, ya know."

"Wha?"

"He does so. I asked 'im."

"Ya never!"

"I did so! He was all 'does she have a boyfriend?' and I'm like, 'no.'"

"Katie!"

"He *really* likes you, Mari."

"Katie McGreig, it is time to go to sleep. I'm turning off the light now."

"Goodnight Mari. I didnae realise you like him tha' much."

Mari was smiling despite herself as she turned out the light. Her sassy young cousin knew her too well. Maybe there was something between her and William – god help her, an English, aristo policeman. She needed her head examined or, at least, a good night's sleep.

*****

"I tell ya he's no gonna stay," said Laphroaig, emphatically. "We're wastin' our time here. Let's get back to the lassie. She's made it this far."

"Laphroaig, Ardbeg may be right," said Jura with a sigh. "There is little that we can do for her, whereas this mortal could well serve our purpose."

"At least, she's on our side!" bellowed Laphroaig. "This guy's working for *her*!"

"Ah, but look how easily he can be influenced." replied Ardbeg. "He can be made to disrupt the ceremony. That is all we need."

"How?" demand Laphroaig.

"He has doubts and fears. He does not know who he serves nor her plans. That can be turned to our end."

"Yer playin' with fire, old lady. Besides, he's gonna be out o' there before they come looking for that ol stone, anyway."

"Just watch," said Ardbeg.

She reached into a pouch at her side and pulled out a pinch of fine grey powder. She held it in her palm, weighing it for a moment, carefully adjusting the quantity and then she blew it across the glass between them.

Several of the gods moved back warily as a small cloud of grey particles formed about the table and then suddenly fell through the glass and into the image of the man in the car.

Suddenly, Dougie was asleep.

*****

Mari awoke with a start; she was drenched in sweat and felt cold. She had only vague memories of the dream from which she had awoken and she wanted to keep it that way. She looked over at her sleeping cousin.

The wee troublemaker looked so innocent and peaceful in her sleep. It must have been horrific to be trapped in that medieval dungeon for a full twenty-four hours and yet lying there she looked so peaceful.

Mari decided to get up and find herself a glass of water. It was not really that she was thirsty but her dream hung over her like a bad smell and she needed to clear her head before trying to get back to sleep.

She pulled on the threadbare dressing gown that Dee had lent her over the top of the huge nightshirt and tiptoed out of the bedroom, back to the kitchen. There was still a light on over the stove, and a warm red glow coming from the fire. In the flickering light, she could make out the rows of clothes now hanging across the room and lain out on the hearth, amongst them, on the far side, the white dress that had been a tattered flag. It seemed to have decided to remain a dress for now, which was just as well since Mari would not have been happy having to go out in something from Dee's wardrobe.

She started opening cupboards in search of a glass.

"Having trouble sleeping?" asked a voice. It was Dee. She was still in her armchair by the fire, partially in shadow.

"Yes," replied Mari. "I didn't see you there."

"I made some cocoa for you, if you'd like it?" offered Dee, indicating a cup on the mantelpiece. She was still holding her knitting.

"You were expecting me to wake up?" Mari, was still having trouble getting used to the idea of a real seer.

"There are very few things that take me by surprise around here," said Dee. "Why don't you come over and sit down? I think you and I need to have a little chat."

Mari walked over, took down the cup of cocoa and sat next to the fire. More out of habit than any real need, she lifted a poker and started pushing the wood around. There was something on her mind and she knew it was important to talk about it. She did not know Dee but somehow she trusted her. She continued to stare into the glowing hearth as she spoke.

"Am I going to die, Dee?"

"Mari," said Dee, softly, "I cannot tell you. I honestly don't know. It's all too messed up around a confluence – nothing is certain. But I can tell you this. I know that you will fight and whatever happens you will not give in."

Mari continued to stare into the fire. A single tear trickled down her face but she choked back on the rest.

"You have your mother's blood, Mari, and her mother's right back to Scotia herself. You will face this, Mari. You can win."

"How?"

"Stay true to your heart. Listen to your feelings, your true feelings, mind, and follow them, follow them completely. That is where your power lies."

Mari sipped her cocoa while she thought about this. It did not feel as if it was particularly useful or comforting advice but Dee did not seem to offer anything else and had returned her attention to her knitting. It was comforting to be here, though. The night was peaceful between the gentle crackle of the fire and the click of the knitting needles.

"It's getting late, Mari," said Dee, eventually. "Enough of this talk of death. You should get back to bed. You are going to need all the sleep you can get."

*****

The old king died quietly in the night. It was not a surprise to anyone. He had lived way past his years. His longevity was due, in large part, to the care and attention that he received from Scotia. She was strict about his diet, ensured he got fresh air and exercise and administered regular herbal infusions that helped his constitution.

There were mutterings from time to time of witchcraft, but somehow the mutterings never festered into rumour. The fact was that the people of Alba had grown to love Scotia almost as much as they loved the old man himself.

It was well understood that Gregorian had largely retired from government and the people attributed the prosperity of the last few years very much to Scotia's rule. Nevertheless, his death represented a political crisis, as Scotia understood better than anyone.

The funeral was held on the beach. A huge pyre was built of logs and tree trunks and the kings pale body placed at its summit.

A great crowd had gathered for the occasion, larger even than that which had gathered for the wedding. Representatives of all the clans across Alba were there, stretching out across the beach and crowded along the cliff-top. Many of the paths that led up and down the cliff were clogged with onlookers.

Scotia herself lit the pyre, thrusting a long torch deep into the base of the logs. The light grasses and twigs at the bottom burst quickly into flame. The branches and logs soon followed until within a few minutes the body of the old king was lost from sight amid the flames and many of those at the base had to move back from the heat and smoke.

Three cheers rose up from the crowd; a salute to a fallen warrior. It was a fitting tribute to the greatest ruler the country had ever known.

For a long time Scotia just watched the flames. She would miss the old man. He had been a good friend.

Her thoughts were broken by the advance of a young red-headed man flanked by two of his clansmen. Scotia recognised him as Gendrig MacDonald, the son of the MacDonald's chief. He was smiling smugly to himself.

"My queen," he began, almost mockingly, "I am sorry to disturb your grieving but I wonder, have you given any thought to who will rule, now that the king is gone?"

Scotia regarded him coolly. She had, of course, been expecting this.

"I have called for a council a fortnight hence to discuss the arrangements. The MacDonald's are invited, of course. In the meantime, I will be handling affairs of state."

"The MacDonalds will not be attending your council, my lady," he replied.

"Gendrig, have we not enjoyed a time of peace and prosperity? Let us build a future together."

"The MacDonalds will never be ruled by a woman – or a witch!"

"Choose your words carefully, my hot-headed friend. I have many supporters here who would strike you down for the way you talk."

For a moment Gendrig glanced uneasily about him, but then, without taking his leave he turned and walked away.

Scotia watched him go. In her father's court, a man would have been killed on the spot for such insolence. But that was not her way and, besides, she did not want to turn Gregorian's funeral into a battlefield. This was to be a testing time for her, there was no escaping that.

*****

"The girl escaped the Parzule?"

The voice was quiet but it had a cold power that could turn a mountain to dust.

Ardbeg remained on her knees, her eyes staring intently at the black marble floor in front of her.

"We made her lose the brooch, and even now a Wraith is being summoned. The forces around the confluence make influence difficult, but it will not be long. Besides, the other gods have already forsaken her."

Anput, sitting on her high throne before Ardbeg, considered this for a moment. She sat tall, three hundred feet tall if dimensions meant anything in this place. They did not.

Anput was glorious and terrifying. Classically depicted, she often wore a dog's head, like her husband. Now, she appeared simply as a beautiful woman in a black silk robe with deep silver-black skin. Her eyes were deep pits that a mortal would drown in had they the misfortune to behold them, and her long black hair was tied up and exquisitely pinned.

"Are you sure?"

Ardbeg did not need to look at her. The old god's presence was so strong that she felt every detail of her appearance burned in her mind's eye. Not for the first time, Ardbeg found herself wondering if the deal she had made was really going to pay off. Such thoughts were quickly banished though, for she knew her mind was not private in this place.

"They are fickle. They look to influence another."

"Indeed? Well, this could well turn to our advantage. Keep them busy and their attention elsewhere."

"Yes, my mistress."

"Now, be gone before they notice you are missing."

"Yes, mistress."

Without looking up, Ardbeg turned and walked out of the throne room. Quietly she calmed her fears.

She had had enough of the lowly existence of a minor goddess, gently fading into eternal slumber. When the new order was established and Anput was returned to power on earth by the rising of the Leviathan, she would be glorious and majestic at her right hand. The thought of such power was truly intoxicating. She just had to stay in favour. The prospect of failing did not bear thinking about.

Besides it would be over soon. The girl would be under their control within hours, that old fool folk-singer could not protect her for long.

*****

Dougie awoke to the sound of a car going past. It was light, the sun shone through the windscreen and he could hear the sound of crows squabbling in a nearby copse. His clothes were damp from the morning dew or rain that had splashed through the open driver's side window. Crap! He had fallen asleep waiting for the Stone to be collected. He was cold and hungry and he needed a pee, desperately.

He checked his watch: six fifty-four. He had been asleep for four hours in the driver's seat. His face was sore where it had been resting against the sill. *Why was he doing this?* He found himself asking again.

He had to get back home, have a proper kip, rest up for tonight, the big one. Clearly, he had missed the pick-up. It was time to stop playing detective and get to bed.

He was so busy berating himself that he almost failed to notice the Range Rover turning down the narrow track where he had stashed the stone the night before. Immediately, his perspective shifted. Once again he felt the compulsion to learn more about what was behind all this. After all, he told himself, he had waited out here all night already. It only made sense now to see where they were going with that thing and what they wanted with it.

He had to wait another twenty minutes or so until the maroon Range Rover re-emerged. There was one driver and one passenger. It turned away from where he was watching and headed back up the lane. He waited until it was just out of sight and then started his engine and set off after it, his tires swishing as they rolled over the rain slicked tarmac.

Dougie had to stay fairly close. With all the turns on the narrow road, it was very difficult to make sure he didn't miss a junction. There was little chance that they hadn't noticed him, he just hoped that they were not expecting to be followed.

They passed through a couple of small towns but stayed mostly to the back-roads. Eventually, after several miles, he saw them turn into a large driveway with a sign by the gate that read "Perthshire Grange."

Dougie drove past the entrance and turned at the next corner ahead. He pulled off the road, brought the car to a halt on a grass verge and took the key out of the ignition. What now?

He rubbed his eyes and looked blearily at the steering wheel in front of him. Once again he thought of the importance of heading home and getting ready for tonight's mission but he had come this far and he needed to at least find out who these people were. He took a deep breath and opened the car door.

He started to work his way back toward the gate, on the one hand trying to look like he was just out for an early morning stroll, on the other hand trying to keep beneath the level of the hedge so that he could not be seen from the house. He succeeded at neither.

Fortunately, no one seemed to notice as he opened the rusty iron gate with a loud screech and made his way up the tree-lined drive.

He could hear birds twittering in the trees but everything else was quiet. The Range Rover was parked outside the front of the house. Next to it was a white BMW.

Dougie could see the Stone in the back of the Range Rover, covered with a blanket. He tried to focus. He was looking for information, names of people – even some idea what they were up to. Maybe there would be some documents in the vehicle. Then again, it could be alarmed. A safer option caught his eye.

Around the side of the garage, pretty much out of sight of the house, he saw of a large steel dustbin. It took a little grubbing around amid potato peelings and old spaghetti but eventually he found just what he was looking for... a letter. It was an invitation to contribute to a retirement plan — a dull professional form letter, but it was fully addressed to "Assistant Chief Constable Mark Struthers, Perthshire Grange."

Very interesting. Dougie had been fairly surprised at how ineffective the police had been against the SSA, the only reported arrests were foot soldiers. None of the organisers had been caught. A few, well-placed contacts in the police force to "lose" the right pieces of evidence and throw the investigation off the scent would really help. All power to you, Mark Struthers, he thought.

His reflections were disturbed by the sound of voices coming from the direction of the house.

"...aye, well, we'll see I don't think it'll be as scary as all that." said one voice.

Dougie shrank silently back into the shadows by the side of the garage.

"I'll let you take that up with her," came the reply.

"So, I'll see you this afternoon, Mark."

"Three-thirty sharp, mind. Don't forget, we are bringing

the centrepiece. She'll want it carried up and put in place before they can start."

"I hope there'll be someone there to help. We'll not get that thing far on our own."

"Don't worry, we'll all be there – who would miss it."

"Alright then, till three-thirty."

There were the sounds of a car door slamming, and engine starting up and finally a car pulling away. Dougie heard the front door closing. He waited a little while until he was sure all was quiet and then, as smoothly as he could, he headed back down the long drive to the gate and turned up the road towards his car.

Pausing to relieve himself against a tree, he considered what he had learned. There was definitely a mystery here. They needed the Stone for something, a "centrepiece," but what? And could this woman they referred to be his superior?

He was supposed to do the final job tonight but somehow he knew that this was more important. He had to find out what this was all about. He decided he would take it easy today. He would head back to the town and buy himself the greasiest breakfast he could find. Then maybe a couple of pints and some lunch and before he knew it, it would be time to come back to follow the stone to its final destination.

Inside Perthshire Grange, Mark Struthers watched the less-than-discrete, SSA operative zip up his flies and return to his car. He frankly could see no possible value in letting the boy follow them, but his instructions had, as always, been very explicit.

*****

"You see," remarked Ardbeg, "so much easier than steering that wretched girl."

"Indeed," replied MacAllan. "Almost too easy, don't you think?"

"Come now, let's not look our gift horses in their mouths. All we need is someone to disrupt the ceremony and the confluence will pass."

"Confluences ain't like that Ardbeg," exclaimed Dufftown, from the back. "Ya can't tell with confluences. That's the whole point."

The rain had stopped, but the dark clouds still hung heavily over the loch outside; its clear waters looking drab as they reflected the ominous sky.

Oban and Talisker stood, once again on the far bank, leaving only part of themselves in the council chamber with the arguing gods.

"I fear we are being led astray here, Talisker," Oban began. "This new direction of Ardbeg's, to use the boy, is too easy."

"You may be right, though I thought it could help."

"Perhaps but it feels wrong to me."

"Then why not just tell the others to drop it. There might be some disagreement, but they would follow your decision, my Lord."

"Indeed, they would," replied Oban, casting his gaze back toward the distant council chamber, "but I wonder if we might have more success if our enemy continued to believe that we were following this alternate course. Our influence over the events around the Heart has been very weak and we are limited to subtle adjustments at best. If you were to just quietly keep an eye on her and nudge things in the right direction from time to time, perhaps we could still affect the outcome. I think she could use a little of your particular brand of luck."

"Very well, my lord, I will do so."

"And, Talisker."

"Yes, Father?"

"Don't get too flamboyant."

*****

The MacDonalds did not show for the council, nor the Mac-Greggors. In all, eight out of the twenty-three major clans did not appear. It was a foreshadowing of grim times ahead.

The council itself went well. There was some debate but the outcome was seen in advance by the wise and few ultimately opposed it. The decision was clear and, for such things, quickly reached. Scotia was to take over as High Thane in Gregorian's place.

Scotia was crowned in a grand ceremony. At its height, she seated herself upon her new throne, which had been built to accommodate the Stone at its base. The same priest who had married her set a simple crown upon her head and the assembled Thanes swore allegiance to her rule.

She moved quickly even as the council was still assembled and began preparation for war.

The war came, but it did not seem to pack much of a punch. All of Scotia's enemies seemed to be overcome by extraordinarily bad luck. A crazed dog bit the Thane of the MacGreggors, the wound seemed unable to heal and quickly became infected. He grew ill and eventually died. The whole MacDonald army, the day before battle, all drank and bathed in a brook that, it turned out, was poisoned, polluted by the rotting corpse of a dead cow further upstream. The whole army faced their opponents with green faces. There was no fight left in them and they quickly fled.

So it went. Everyone who stood against Scotia was undermined by ill fate or betrayal. There were whisperings of witchcraft but only from the foolish. And all this with very little loss of life. Many were expecting a bloody war that would split the country but it never came. Very soon all the other clans came to pledge their allegiance until it was only the MacDonalds who had not.

*****

Mari woke up very late the next morning. The sun was well up and bathing the small room in a bright, warm light. The bed beside her was empty. Katie was up already. There was the sound of light chatter coming from the direction of the kitchen, wafting in amid the mouth-watering aroma of frying bacon and almost-burning toast.

Mari had never been one for cooked breakfasts, but there was something about the homely atmosphere, the late start and her weariness from the previous day that made her demolish a respectable plate of bacon, eggs, mushroom, sausage and fried haggis.

It was past ten o'clock by the time everyone had had a third round of toast and their fourth cup of coffee.

"Alright, ladies and gentlemen, it is time we were getting out of here. It's a fair old way to Loch Ness and we have to be there around sun-down. That old tractor of yours, Dee, is not exactly the speediest way to travel, so we'd best get going. Do you think we'll all fit in the trailer?" asked Connor.

"What do you mean?" replied Dee, with a strange look on her face.

"Old Bessie or Daphne..." said Connor, waiving his hand vaguely.

"You mean old Mollie...?"

"That's it, Mollie. You can take us on Mollie... right? Hitch up the hay trailer to the back."

"Mollie's up there in the top field, threw a piston rod last summer, hasn't moved since. I'm afraid you'll not be travelling on Mollie."

"Don't you have another tractor, or a car?"

"No. Never really needed a car, and I'm getting too old to farm the fields."

Connor looked blank for a moment.

"So how are we going to get to the Loch?" he asked, finally.

"You'll have to go into the village and hitch a lift."

"What? We don't have time for..."

"Don't worry, something will turn up. I'm sure of it."

It took a long time for them to say their goodbyes. Dee walked around them all and insisted on giving each one of them a hug and a kiss, even William. Mari got hugged three times before she eventually made it out of the cottage door.

Armed with little parcels of food and a clutch of old umbrellas, which they promised to return, they set out along the road towards the village.

Mari, who was back in the white Faerie Flag dress, zipped her black leather biker jacket up tight as they began to trudge up the road. The early morning sun had been lost behind some gray clouds and a brisk northerly wind picked up. It was going to rain.

It fell softly at first, as if unsure that it really meant to, but it was not long before it settled into a thick West Coast downpour. It was rain of a fine, mist-like quality that seemed to hang in the air rather than actually fall in the way rain should. Despite the old umbrellas, they were drenched long before they reached the village.

"Jolly decent of Dee to loan us these brollies," said William, breaking the sombre silence as they trudged down the road.

"What planet are you from, William? Who says things like 'Jolly decent', honestly?" exclaimed Mari, suddenly, and then wished she hadn't.

William looked embarrassed and said nothing.

"Look, the village is just round this corner," said Connor. "Keep your eyes open and watch out for anyone who could give us a lift to the main road."

*****

Gendrig MacDonald kept a careful watch on the approach from the mainland these days. He had finally developed a level of respect for Scotia, but it was the sort of respect that one had for a deadly snake. To his frustration all the other clans seemed too frightened, or too stupid to see this witch-queen for what she was. Even the MacGreggors had given her their allegiance.

He knew that Scotia was behind the apparently accidental death of his father and the poisoning of his army. He also knew that he dare not stand directly against her, for, even in spite of her unearthly assistance, she had the support of the rest of Alba. He also knew that he could not remain undecided for long. In time, she would come after him.

So, he entertained her ambassadors, he traded with her people and he made show that he was coming around to join with his kinsmen, but all the while, he plotted.

He searched first for a mage that might stand against her but he found none who would rise to the task.

Then he hit on an idea: Everyone knew that she had come here from some distant land, but no one knew why. Why had she left? Why had she never gone back? Was she really, as some had said, a princess?

Whatever it was, she had kept it a secret and that suggested that there was something there that he could use.

He called on his cousin, Carther, and sent him forth in a chartered ship in the guise of a merchant.

It was to cost him heavily in gold, but Gendrig was sure it would be worth it. He was confident that once he found out who she was and where she had come from, there would be a weakness he could exploit. Everyone had a weakness.

*****

"We've been walking for half an hour and no one has passed us yet," said Mari, stating what they were all thinking.

"Don't worry," replied Connor, "if Dee says we will get a lift, then we will get a lift."

"But...what if we don't make it?"

"Mari, you have to learn to trust."

The 'village' seemed rather grandly named. There was a post office, which was closed, a church, three or four houses and a stone bus shelter.

They stood in silence in the shelter, holding their tattered, dripping umbrellas. Waiting.

Eventually, a brown Volvo swept past its windscreen wipers flat out. Connor stuck his thumb out but the driver didn't even slow down. A large woman in the passenger seat turned to peer at them intently as it pulled away.

"Well, so much fe' local charity..." his grumble was interrupted by the sound of another approaching vehicle.

This time Connor was clearly taking no chances. He stood out in the middle of the narrow road and waved both arms in the air.

With a loud squealing of brake discs, the vehicle pulled to a halt. It was perhaps the strangest sight that you could expect to see in the Scottish highlands. A double-decker bus, painted purple, with yellow highlighting and a proud skull and cross bones across the front.

Mari watched from the bus shelter as the doors opened with a characteristic pneumatic hiss. A sign over the bus door read: 'Purple Pirates Tour Company, Welcome aboard mi hearties'.

Connor mounted the steps and talked to the driver for a few minutes before returning to the others.

"So, the good news is he's going to Loch Ness, but the bad news is we have to buy tickets."

"How much?" asked Mari.

"Twenty quid each."

"Twenty?"

"He says it's a three day pass – cheapest they have."

"OK"

"So, um, does anyone have any money?" Connor looked hopefully at William who shook his head.

"I was just out for a walk – I left my wallet in the cottage."

"Mari?"

"I have a tenner."

"Let's see." Connor dug hopefully in his pockets, but then stared forlornly at the result in his hands. "Seven pounds thirty one. Hmm…"

"Just a second," said Katie suddenly brightening, "I know him!" She pushed past Connor and started towards the bus.

"Graham? Is that you?" She waived to the bus driver. "We're in a bit o' bother" she explained as she mounted the steps. "D'ya think you could help us out?"

Katie re-emerged from the bus after a couple of minute's hasty negotiation and beckoned the other three on board.

"Ya see, Graham is my best-friend Sally's big-brother," she explained. "He's been a purple pirate all summer, till term starts up again."

"Shiver mi' timbers," exclaimed Graham, with limited enthusiasm as the four mounted the bus. "I've not seen ya an' a don't know anythin' about ya," he said, deliberately keeping his eyes on the road.

The doors hissed closed and the bus lurched forward down the windy road. The new passengers found seats as fast as they could.

There were only three other passengers. A Scandinavian-looking couple in bright yellow matching anoraks sitting at the front with a pair of backpacks that looked about as big as they did and a long haired man in his mid-twenties in a dark-green jacket sitting about half way back. He was fast asleep with his head resting impossibly against the window.

There was a loud but low quality music system on the purple pirate bus that seemed to play a continuous mix of rock sea shanties and eighties pop.

Mari wedged herself hard against the seat in front and stared at the raindrops as they wound their way across the bus window. As the bus lurched around another corner she found herself wondering if that big breakfast had really been a good idea after all.

*****

Carther MacGreggor left his home and sailed south. He had travelled more than most in his clan but this was to be a much bigger voyage than any he had known. It was his considered opinion that the trip was ill conceived. How likely was it that he could find anyone that remembered a pair of travellers from so many years ago?

Still, he was careful to keep this opinion to himself. He had no objection to seeing more of the world. His cabin was grand and what's more he had spending money to keep him in wine for a good few months. All he had to do was sail around for a while; enjoy the trip at his cousin's considerable expense and return with some tale or other of runaway lovers. There would be plenty of time between ports to dream up the details.

He took a deep breath of the fresh sea air as his island home disappeared out of sight in the distance. This was going to be a grand few months he told himself with a grin.

*****

The 'Purple Pirates Tour Company' is a backpacker's cheapest way to visit Scotland's highlands and islands (well, some of them). They started with two second-hand buses, bought when Glasgow city council privatized the bus service. From there they have grown from strength to strength. They are cheap, clean and cheerful and visit all kinds of out-of-the way places you'd need a car to get to otherwise. Don't rely on their schedules though. Their antiquated fleet is always breaking down. On occasion they have been known to be more than a day late in arriving.

— The Backpackers Pocket
Guide to the British Isles

*****

To Mari's immense relief, the fourth rendition of "What shall we do with the drunken sailor" arranged for rock guitar and bagpipes, was cut mercifully short as the bus gave one last irritated snort and Graham turned off the ignition.

It had been making a loud clanking noise for the last mile and, as William had pointed out, the fumes coming out of the back looked blacker than they probably should.

"We'll stop here for a break. Everyone meet back at the bus in an hour," announced Graham. He thought for a moment, then added, "Better make that an hour and a half."

They had collected a surprising number of passengers on the long bumpy ride, all of which shuffled out with very little comment or complaint. It seemed that the regulars were used to this.

When Connor reached the front of the bus, Graham was fussing with some small tattered bits of folded paper and a very old looking mobile phone that bore the lettering in permanent black marker pen "For emergency use only!"

"Do you know how long it's going to be?" asked Connor. "We really need to get to Loch Ness, *today*."

"Who knows," said Graham, with resignation. "Might be out 'a here in a couple o' hours, then again... you might have to wait for the next bus."

"And when's that?"

He looked at his watch.

"Tuesday," he said, with a grin.

"This is really important!" exclaimed Mari, in frustration.

"Aye, I'm sure it is," he replied, as he dialled a number from the paper, "but if ya had a ticket, ya'd be able ta read the back of it where it says — in bold letters - 'schedules cannot be guaranteed.' But since you don't, I'm not sure why I'm even havin' this conversation. Nice outfit, by the way. Where did you... oh, excuse me. Hello is that, Iain? It's Graham here..."

Despondent, they left the bus and walked slowly through the drizzle to the low building in the distance. From here they could just make out the green and blue neon sign that read "Barry Ramsbottom's – the Biggest Fish and Chip Shop in the World."

*****

Barry Ramsbottom's is a remarkable testimony to the American cultural adage that "bigger is always better." The humble fish and chip shop has been the cornerstone of British fast food since long before the discovery of the plastic burger and fries that is now so prevalent.

Imagine a small cafe with imitation-wood tables and wipe-clean plastic-covered chairs. Everything on the menu is deep-fried and most of it is battered and the only condiments available are salt, malt vinegar and ketchup.

Now take that cafe, drop it into a roadside location in the middle of nowhere and add seating for another 200 or so and you would have a Barry Ramsbottom's.

It has to be said that, despite the feeling that you are eating in a warehouse, we found the food to be actually very good and this is really at the heart of the success of these unexpected restaurants. They are located so as to provide tourists, particularly coach parties, with a convenient place to stop for a meal. Their menu is pleasantly familiar to the locals and represents an opportunity for the visitors to try Britain's most infamous gastronomic delight.

— *Food for Thought,*
The gourmet's guide to the U.K.,
J. D. Platter

*****

Dougie was hungry again. He ordered another plate of chips and carefully checked his watch. It would be time soon. He thought about getting another dram but decided against it. He'd probably had too many already.

He'd spent the day pretty much in the local pub reading the paper, drinking whisky and ordering bar food. This would be his third plate of chips and he was no longer sure how many drinks he had had. The papers were full of his exploits from the previous two nights. He had read four from cover to cover, relishing every speculation about the origin and high professionalism of the perpetrators. It gave him a warm feeling inside, or maybe that was the whisky.

Several times during the day, he had stopped to wonder exactly what he was doing here. He should be getting ready for the big raid, the final attack. Instead he was snooping on his own team. He had got up to leave, to drive home at least four times and each time something had distracted him, a fresh pack of cigarettes, or another paper with a big set of photos of Edinburgh Castle walls bleeding and somehow he would find himself back in his seat with a fresh glass in front of him and, well, you couldn't leave with a full dram.

He was feeling anxious. He knew that he was disobeying his orders and betraying his people by staying here. However, he found the whisky helped to calm him and it was always very easy to have another. In fact, he decided, maybe he would have one last shot for the road.

*****

"You don't think that we might be overdoing it?" asked Jura. "The boy will collapse."

"He'll be fine," said Ardbeg sternly, "this is no time for half measures. He is our last hope."

"But what use is he going to be if he's so drunk he cannae even walk?" asked Laphroaig, despairingly.

"The drink makes him malleable," said Ardbeg.

"It'll make him fall over!"

"Look, he doesn't have to dance a jig out there, just run out and steal the sceptre, that's enough."

"If he can run..."

"Trust me, Laphroaig, he can play his part."

*****

At three o'clock, feeling now *very* calm and full of chips, Dougie got in his car and started back to the distinguished residence of Assistant Chief Constable Mark Struthers.

Somewhere in the back of his mind, it struck him that he was driving to the house of one of the most senior police officers in the country significantly over the blood-alcohol limit, but somehow the thought didn't trouble him. He knew that what he was doing was *very important*, he could feel it deep inside him, he just wasn't entirely sure why.

*****

Carther smiled gently to himself as he walked away from the Tavern. His belly was full of wine and roasted goat. It was a warm night and there was the pleasant scent of lavender in the air.

He simply could not believe his good fortune. At only the third or fourth port they had visited, he had, almost accidentally, come across an old tale of some Egyptians that were travelling in search of their princess. The runaway Pharaoh's daughter had almost become a myth and the closer he got to Egypt, the more widespread the rumours.

At first, he could see no connection between this phantom princess and his cousin's nemesis but he recognized immediately a good story when he heard one. This was exactly the sort of thing that Gendrig would just lap up.

As time went on, however, he began to see more connections between the story and the Alban Queen. The timing of the story seemed to coincide pretty well with Scotia's arrival. The descriptions of the Egyptian princess, of her husband and of the ship they sailed, all matched. Very few claimed to have seen the princess and many were emphatic that she had never existed but everywhere he went, Carther found stories of Egyptian soldiers who had come in search of their Pharaoh's daughter.

The aspect of the rumours that he found most intriguing – the part that kept him heading for Egypt rather than returning to give his cousin the news – was the gold. It was said that the Pharaoh, who was the richest man in the world, would pay dearly for the information that would lead to the capture of his runaway daughter. Estimates of exactly how much he would pay varied from the informant's own weight in rubies, to a pile of gold that would reach to the sky.

As he strolled back to his boat, Carther found himself gently dreaming, once again, about how he would spend his vast, new-found wealth. He was so lost in his plans that he never even saw the three, darkly clad men step out of the shadows and barely felt the blow to the back of his head before he lost consciousness.

*****

Dougie's head nodded and he blinked himself back awake. He sat watching the gate of Perthshire Grange. At three twenty-one, he saw a car entering – the same white BMW he had seen leaving that morning. At exactly three-thirty, the Range Rover emerged.

He started his engine, pulled off the muddy grass verge and followed it up the quiet lane. They drove back through the village and joined the A9 heading north.

*****

Mari's tea was as cold and gloomy and grey as the evening outside.

They sat against the wall in the empty multi-acre café. Connor spread a map on the table and squinted at it as if by staring he could somehow reduce the remaining distance that they had to cover to get to Loch Ness.

Mari watched anxiously through the window as Graham's mechanic showed up and spent a long time examining the bus. Eventually, he came back to Graham, and had a long conversation over a cigarette that involved a lot of shrugs and head shaking and sharp intakes of breath. Then he left in his truck.

Graham started working his way around the Purple Pirates passengers a table at a time.

"He says it's too bad to drive any further and he doesn't have the parts to fix it," he explained, when he reached Mari's group. "I've a list of guest houses, hostels and camp sites in this area, if you're interested. They're going to try to send a bus out for us tomorrow. Of course, you folks will probably have to buy tickets if you want to get on that one..."

Katie and William went around the other restaurant customers looking for a lift but they came back after twenty minutes with no success. The only party they found who admitted they were heading for Loch Ness was a family with three kids and they had no room for hitchhikers. Most of the other Purple Pirate passengers had left to sort out their accommodation.

Mari glanced again at the darkening sky outside. They did not have much time but maybe that was a good thing. Maybe if she wasn't there she wouldn't need to find out whether the prophecy was true. Maybe the world would save itself – even Dee could tell what the outcome was going to be.

Something felt wrong. Mari couldn't tell what it was at first, just a sense that something was out of place.

"Where's William?" she asked.

Katie was playing with the saltcellar. "He went to the toilet."

No, it wasn't William. It wasn't even their travel problems. There was something else. Then she started to feel it, like a cold chill running down her spine. It was coming from something out there in the empty café.

Mari started to feel very strange. The world around her was fading in and out of her perception. She stood up, barely aware of her chair falling backwards to the floor with a clatter.

In front of her, she could see a shape starting to rise out of the floor, first a head, then a body as the figure of a man floated through the tiles. She couldn't see any face beneath the dark hood of its tattered robes but she felt its stare on her. She could feel the bitter cold the emanated from it.

It seemed to pass through the floor and the surrounding furniture as if they were no more substantial than air. Its form was translucent and through the dark folds of its cloak she could still see oblivious diners tucking into their fish suppers. Once clear of the floor though, it started to become more opaque and substantial.

Mari's spoke low and fast. "Connor! What is it? What do I do?"

Conner's eyes were searching the room, but he looked right through the apparition in front of her.

"Mari, I can't see it – tell me what's there."

Mari felt the cold becoming more intense as the figure approached. It reeked of death and the tattered rags and cloth that were draped over it seemed to move, to writhe of its own accord. The movements, she saw, were from tiny maggots that seemed to pass in and out of the robes and wrappings eating at the flesh beneath them.

"It's a hooded figure. Its clothes are tattered and maggot-ridden and it smells of vomit."

"Crap," said Connor.

"What?"

"It's a Wraith. Quickly, Mari, grab hold of my staff, you, too, Katie."

Connor planted the wooden staff firmly on the floor and held it upright between Katie and Mari. They both took hold.

"Now, listen, carefully. The Wraith is going to try to take you, Mari, by sucking you onto the ethereal plane. If it can get you there, it can take you anywhere – literally. So, you need to focus your attention on being here."

She could feel the smooth wood under her grasp. She had hold with both hands and felt its warmth. A soft tingling ran up her arms.

Connor leaned closer. "You need to be totally present, Mari. Don't think. If your mind wanders, you'll give it a crack it can use to start prying you away. Focus, Mari. Feel the staff under your fingers, feel the strength of the mighty oak that it came from, feel how solid and rooted it is. Hold on to that. Feel that rootedness inside you. Katie, you can help Mari – do the same."

The power of the staff kept the Wraith back. It seemed to be glowering but, beneath the hood, Mari saw nothing. She found herself starting to imagine the horrors that the darkness might be hiding, the decomposing face staring out from empty eye sockets writhing with maggots. The image burned in her mind's eye, feeding her fear. She felt colder and colder as panic rose within her. Why couldn't she concentrate?

"Mari!" Connor yelled. He was standing right beside her but he sounded distant, as if at the end of a tunnel.

"Mari, you must focus – we're losing you. Remember the staff."

Mari tightened her grip and brought her attention back to the warmth from the staff. She felt the energy grounding her against the pull of the Wraith.

She calmed her breathing and brought her attention back to the staff; the ghastly visage started to fade back to darkness. It became smaller and less substantial and eventually was gone. Then the darkness cleared and she saw in front of her a beautiful image of a tree, a glorious old oak with majestic, sweeping branches. It sat alone in a meadow of soft waving grass and the sun glinted through its rich green leaves as Mari looked up at it.

She realized then that the Wraith had gone. She opened her eyes to meet the concerned looks of Connor and Katie.

"It's gone," she said, confidently.

Conner's look of concern deepened. "That was too easy. There's something else going on."

"What?"

"I don't know. That's what bothers me." Connors eyes were scanning the restaurant. Mari's gaze followed his, searching for a sign of the Wraith or what might follow it. Several of the other diners were looking their way with anxious curiosity.

Then, out of the corner of her eye Mari caught sight of it. She could only see it in her peripheral vision, but there it was the creature passing across the restaurant, moving relentlessly toward... William.

"William!"

She yelled across the vast room, drawing the attention of everyone, but it was too late. The Wraith was already upon him.

Mari saw the look of surprise and horror on William's face as he left the ground. Then, both he and his captor became translucent. His arms reached out for her, his mouth formed a silent scream as the creature propelled him straight through the wall of the cafe and out into the night.

*****

Wraith – A creature of the undead that dwells primarily in the Ethereal plane. Formerly a living person, a Wraith is created by a powerful curse that turns their life force in on itself.

They are usually perceived as ragged, hooded figures, often suffering missing limbs or covered in maggots. Their horrific appearance is a material representation of the torment of their continued existence.

They are masters of the Ethereal Plane and can shift back and forth with the material world at will, taking people and objects with them that they can then rapidly transport through the Ether. They move slowly in the material plane and are only usually visible to their victims.

They are relatively easy to conjure but notoriously difficult to control. Their ultimate loyalty lies only to the gods of the dead because it is they alone who can lift the curse that binds them.

Gimwald's Cyclopedic
Daemons and Demi-gods
of the Ancients

*****

Thutmose II looked down with merciless disdain at the prisoner before him.

Cather MacDonald sagged between the two burly guards who were holding him up. His fancy merchant's clothes were in tatters. The ripped cloth, exposing a mass of festering cuts and sores. He was barely able to focus on the floor in front of him. One eye was so swollen shut. The other was little better. After weeks in the stuffy confines of a boat, they reached Memphis. His questioners had been relentless. They had beaten and tortured him for days.

"We have checked his story, my Lord," said the inquisitor. "He clearly speaks of your daughter. She is now queen of a distant land. Her husband is dead but she has a child."

"You know where this place is?" asked the Pharaoh quietly, not taking his eyes off the prisoner.

"Most definitely, my Lord. It is too far to send an army, but an assassin..."

The sentence was left hanging.

"Ahmos," said the Pharaoh to one of the men by his side, "I want you to handle this personally. Go there and kill them. Kill them all — the mother, the child and the people of this land. You will return with Neferubity's head and news of the destruction of her new dominion. Go now."

Without a word Ahmos left.

Cather, his eyes still averted, said a silent prayer to his gods. Surely, he was of no more use to them now – they could let him go. He'd find a way back home, eventually.

The Pharaoh took one last look at the pitiful figure of the prisoner, as blood dripped from the poor man's mouth onto the throne room floor.

"Kill him," he said, quietly.

*****

"Where is he?" demanded Gail for the fourth time.

"Look, I – don't – know," replied Brian.

They were sitting in Gail's car on a side street in the outskirts of Edinburgh. The darkening sky was heavy with rain clouds and the air thick with a gentle but consistent curtain of drizzle.

The car was parked beside a children's play-park that was deserted except for a pair of lonely kids trussed up in hooded raincoats pushing each other on the swings. Their mothers sat off to one side on a park bench, smoking cigarettes and gossiping.

Their breath was fogging up the windscreen as they waited. Dougie was more than half an hour late and they were getting nervous. Dougie had never been late before.

"They must've got him," she declared, biting manically at a fingernail. "He told them. They'll be waitin' fer us. Ta catch us, red handed, like."

"Nah."

"What?"

"Nah – no way!"

"How do ye know?"

"Look, if they knew what we were plannin', we'd be in prison by now."

"Aye, well, maybe."

"C'mon Gail, let's just pick up the stuff and get there. You know the deal: if he doesn't show, we continue without him."

"Do ya think he might 'a bottled like?"

"Dougie, scared? – nah, why would he?"

"Well, this is the big one."

"So?"

"Brian, don't ya see. Tonight people are gona' die, and it'll be our fault."

*****

Mari stood for several seconds looking dumbly at the wall that William had just been carried through – literally though the brickwork.

The other customers had not seemed to notice William's disappearance but everyone was looking over at Mari and her companions, though they were careful not to make eye contact.

"We have to go after him," said Mari with quiet determination.

"No, Mari," said Katie, "it's too dangerous. I don't want ta loose ya, again."

Mari looked at Katie. There were tears in her eyes.

"Katie, he saved ma life. He's part of our team. We've got to help him."

"C'mon, Mari, he's only English!"

Mari looked at her in disbelief. How could her little cousin say such a thing? And yet she might have felt that way herself only a few days ago.

Suddenly it all started to make sense. She knew that Connor was right, she could feel the hatred in the country, like a worm eating its way to the core of an apple and she could feel the horror of the future that approached. It was time to act. Now.

"Don't you see Katie, that's what this is all about? Our hatred of the English is what is fuelling this whole thing. We *have* to go after him. It's important."

"We will go after him," said Connor. "We know where he is; we just have to work out a way to get there. We still have time. Sit down. We'll get another cup of tea and then we'll decide what to do."

"No," declared Mari, "we have to go, now."

She picked up her jacket from the back of the fallen chair and started toward the exit.

Grabbing up their things, the other two followed her a few paces behind.

"Hold on, Mari," called Connor, "let's think this through."

They caught up with her by the door.

"We're going out to the road," explained Mari, "and we're going to flag down every car that comes past until we find one that will take us to the Loch."

Outside the cafe it was already dark. On the far side of the car park they could see the lights of the cars passing on the main road. As Mari spoke, the single headlight of a motorcycle approached and pulled up right in front of the cafe doors. The driver jumped off and rushed into the cafe heading for the toilets. In his haste, Mari noticed, he had left the keys in the ignition.

It was a gift. That bike had been left there for her. She knew it and she knew what she had to do.

Before the other two had realised what was going on, she was sitting on the bike and had the engine rumbling.

"Look after Katie," she called to Connor as she slipped the clutch and sped across the car park.

"Mari, wait!" Connor called after her but she didn't even slow down. With barely a glance at the oncoming traffic she leaned the bike over sharply and accelerated out of the car park and up the main road, her hair flying in the wind and white skirts flapping crazily about her.

*****

The wind roared past his ears as Oban sped across the glen, his dark hair flowing behind him, his feet racing across the soft turf. He grinned. He was starting to gain on the stag.

It was a powerful, majestic beast but he had been chasing it now for several hours and it was growing tired.

The stag came to a halt on the edge of a tree line. Oban closed the distance a little and then stopped himself. The wind had changed and the animal could no longer sense him, but still he did not want to get too close. He pulled the bow from his back, strung it and selected an arrow from the quiver. He kept his gaze steady though he was careful not to look directly at it, for animals can sense if they are being watched.

Calming his breathing, he notched the arrow on the string and drew it back. He took his time. It was a long shot, almost half a mile. He took careful aim, feeling the path the arrow would take, allowing for the gentle breeze.

"My liege," said a youthful voice behind him.

The bowstring slipped from his fingers, loosing the shaft. It flew impossibly fast across the valley, missing the stag by a few feet, burying itself deep into a nearby tree.

The stag froze for a second and then Oban watched with frustration as it took off, reaching the cover of the trees in a single bound.

"Talisker," rumbled Oban as he turned around.

"My Lord, this is important," insisted Talisker, nonplussed at the wrath of his father. He was dressed in a deep purple robe that was thrown over one shoulder and tied around his waist.

"It had better be," replied Oban. "What in the world is that thing you are wearing?"

"I believe it is called a 'Toga' my liege."

"Well it looks ridiculous. Now, what is the reason for this rude interruption?"

"There are some strange events afoot in the world of the mortals," said Talisker.

"The mortals? What is it now, another war between the squabbling clans? Why do you trouble me so with these trifles!"

"More grave than that my liege. You know of the foreign queen?"

"The witch? Yes." replied Oban with disinterest.

"The people like her, she is popular."

"What of it?"

"Well, her father has finally found her and wants to exact his revenge."

"Again, Talisker, I say what of it? These affairs need not concern us."

"Well, father I believe that they may. There is high magic being brought to bear and other gods are...."

"Talisker? What's happening?" interrupted Oban, in alarm.

"There's something drawing our essence..."

"I feel it, something is... pulling us..."

"We are being summoned, father."

"Summoned?" cried Oban. "But I am a god! This is *not* dignified..."

Suddenly the glen was empty.

*****

Ahmos pondered the task before him. The Pharaoh had given him a direct command and he knew it was to be obeyed without question, but the destruction of a whole nation? Still, how grand it would be to accomplish it, if anything would earn him a throne in the after-life surely it was this.

He was powerful, an unrivalled mage and a ruthless statesman. He knew it was going to take everything he had to complete his mission. He was going to need help, but he knew where to go and he was prepared to pay. He smiled at his own cruel boldness. If he succeeded there would be none who would dare stand in his way.

*****

Mari's feelings soared as she sped down the road. All the fear and worry left her. She was finally doing something. It almost didn't matter what.

The bike was an 850cc hybrid, smooth and tight on the road but with the high suspension and tires to eat up a dirt track. It had so much more power than her little bike – and she *loved* it.

She leaned hard into a turn and then pulled out into a long straight that ran past a loch. The bike roared as she opened up the throttle to make the most of the open road, watching the speedometer inch past ninety-five.

She'd had to sit on her dress to stop it from flying up but the cool Scottish air chilled her bones.

She dropped down to seventy-five for the next bend. She had no helmet, but she was trying not to think about it. Suddenly, she caught sight of a blue flashing light behind her, lighting up the road in front. She glanced back in the mirror – a police car.

She'd made her choice at the cafe. Now she was going to have to live with it. She twisted the grip and opened up the throttle. The bike leapt forward. "Live fast, die young," she muttered to herself as she accelerated smoothly past one hundred. This was going to be interesting... if she lived through it.

*****

Oban and Talisker found themselves in a rough stone hall, a meeting place of some sort. Chairs and tables had been hastily pushed aside to make way for the trappings of a ritual. They had appeared in the centre of a circle scratched in the dirt floor. In front of them was a low altar with various pieces of arcane paraphernalia. On one side of the room, a young goat was tied to the leg of one of the larger tables.

Behind a makeshift altar knelt a woman with dark hair and dark eyes, clothed in a simple pale-blue dress. She looked up at them.

"What is this?" asked Oban, irritably. "I'm not used to being treated like this." He walked forward, but as he approached the edge of the circle, he sensed, at once, that he could not leave it.

"Forgive me," said the woman. "I apologise for bringing you here in this way."

"Who are you?"

"I am Scotia, queen of this country of Alba, your dominion."

"The witch."

"If you like."

"So, what are we doing here?"

"Time is short and I need your help."

"I can't say I'm feeling very helpful right now," exclaimed Oban, gruffly.

"My Lord, Oban, I beg you hear me out. You know that your form and your power comes from the people of this land."

"Aye?"

"Well, they are in grave danger, all of them, and with them, so are you."

"What do you mean?" Oban glanced at Talisker, he was liking this less and less. "Talisker, what do you know of this."

"My liege, I know that she speaks the truth. I came to tell you of this. I suggest that we listen to her story."

"Very well, lady, proceed."

"Lord Oban, the High Priest-Assassin Ahmos has been commanded by my father to destroy this land. To do so he called on Anput, the goddess of death and made, with her, a pact." Scotia stood up. "The pact he has made is a terrible bargain. Anput has given him the means to destroy this land and all the people in it. And in return he will arrange that the souls of those who die go, not to their natural resting place, but instead to feed Anput."

"Can he do that?"

"I believe he can, although he fails to recognize the powerful consequences that would arise for so flouting the natural order. Lord Oban, these are my people, as they are yours and I am sworn to stop him."

"We can do that, by thunder. We will tear his puny body apart."

"Powerful though you are, my Lord, I suspect that we may need help."

"Help? Dealing with a single mortal?" exclaimed Oban.

"My Lord, I mean no offence, but he comes from a different land, a different people. Consider how easily I summoned you and I tell you he is far more powerful than I and he has the protection of Anput."

Oban considered this grimly for a moment. The idea of a mortal with greater power than his own was new and uncomfortable. However, he was wise enough to see the danger.

"I believe she speaks truthfully father," whispered Talisker in a low voice.

"Then what can we do?" asked Oban, eventually out loud.

"We call upon one more powerful still." She gestured to a second circle. "We must call upon Anput's consort, Anubis, Lord of the Dead."

"And what do you need us for?"

"I have not the power to do this alone. I need you to lend your will to my spell. I believe I can carry out the summoning with your help."

Oban turned back to Talisker. "What do you think?" he asked.

"My liege, she speaks truly. This is a grave challenge. I believe our very existence is at stake."

"Very well, we will help you," he announced.

"Then, ready yourself and lend the force of your will to my

rite."

Scotia began work on the elaborate ritual. Each act was smooth and precise. Her hands and body flowed in a rhythm as she consecrated each device upon the altar, burned incense to the gods and scattered herbs and flowers. Precision and attention to detail were essential in this complex and dangerous rite. After over an hour of preparation, she finally crossed the room and led the goat to the altar. Taking the animal by its small horns she raised a long curved knife. It bleated forlornly.

"Lord Anubis, god of the dead, guardian of souls, here my request. I beg you to accept this life. Come forth that we may speak with you."

The knife came down and with one swift blow she separated the head from the body. Blood sprayed from the open neck, spattering Scotia's face and clothing. The carcase fell to the floor, where it twitched and continued to bleed profusely.

Scotia paid the blood no heed. Her attention was focused entirely on the second circle before her. There was a swirling of smoke and haze as a shape began to take form. Gradually at first and then very rapidly the swirling patterns began to form into the tall dog-headed humanoid form of Anubis.

"Neferubity," he said, slowly in an impossibly deep voice. "You are bold, like your mother."

Although he addressed her, his gaze was fixed on a point far in the distance as if she were simply too insignificant for him to look at.

"O Great Anubis, Master of the Ultimate Truth, I beg your forgiveness for disturbing you."

"Who are your helpers? You appear to have some pet gods?"

"Great Anubis, allow me to introduce Lord Talisker and Lord Oban, who have graciously agreed to help me in this act. They are gods of this fair land in which I have been living."

Anubis did not look down.

"Your father has been seeking you."

"He has, my lord, and recently he discovered my whereabouts."

"I see. And why do you disturb me? Can it be that you seek

my help in evading your father?"

"Great Anubis, I have determined that the High Priest Ahmos has made a pact with Anput to destroy this land and all who live in it."

"That is between Anput and Ahmos."

"Great Anubis, they have agreed that Anput will be given the souls of those who die."

At these words, the great canine head turned for the first time to look directly at Scotia. She averted her eyes immediately but nevertheless felt the overwhelming power of that gaze, like a physical blow that nearly drove her to the floor. For many long moments that gaze bore into her soul until, at last, Anubis looked up and spoke again.

"I see you speak truly. But this cannot be, that would defy the Truce of the Nine Bows. The heavens would be ripped apart by the conflict that would ensue. It cannot be allowed to happen"

"I was hoping, my lord, that you might intercede."

The dark canine face stared intently into the distance, its black featureless eyes seeing everything, yet looking at nothing. Eventually, the corners of its mouth turned up in what Scotia hoped was the dog-equivalent of a smile.

"Indeed you are bold, Neferubity," he said, at last his voice so low it was barely more than a rumble. "Very well, I will intercede. This pact cannot be fulfilled. However, I suspect that you ask for more. You want me to spare the lives of your people?"

"My Lord, I do."

"I can do this, too, but there will be a price to pay."

"What price my Lord?"

"What would you be prepared to offer?"

Directly in front of Scotia, a globe of light formed, bigger than a man's head. Inside the globe could be seen an image. It was an image of a sleeping child – Scotia's daughter.

Scotia's calm broke. Her hand covered her mouth in horror.

"No!" she said, quickly.

"Well, daughter of the Pharaoh, what is your price?"

"Great Anubis, you may take my life in payment, but I beg

you, guarantee me the safety of these people against the wrath of Anput."

The dark god appeared to consider this for a moment.

"Very well," he said finally, "your people will be saved and I will stay the hand of Anput so long as your daughter's bloodline walks the land."

"Thank you, Great Lord." She touched her fingers to her forehead, in respect, and bowed deeply. Then she turned towards the Scottish gods. "And thank you Lord Oban and Lord Talisker for your assistance."

Oban nodded to her stiffly. He was very uncomfortable in the presence of the great Egyptian god and very ready for this whole experience to be over.

Scotia made a pass in the air with her hand and muttered a few words. Suddenly, she was alone in the dark hall. Stunned and exhausted she stared unseeing at the empty room. Then like a wave rolling inexorably up the shore she felt emotions building inside her, fear and relief, anger and loneliness and for a moment, she gave in to them.

Her soft sobbing was the only sound that broke the silence of the night as she fell to her knees in the goat blood.

*****

Dougie worked hard to stay awake at the wheel. He felt very sleepy after all that whisky and wished he had grabbed a coffee on his way out of town. The rush of cold air through his broken window certainly helped, but despite that he felt his head nod forward more than once.

Following the Range Rover had been easier than he had expected. He lost it at one point on a roundabout but he managed to find it again. In fact, it was almost as if they had slowed down and waited for him. In any case they didn't seem to notice that they were being followed. When he started out, he'd been concerned that the broken window would make the car appear conspicuous but he was clearly much better at this than he had thought.

They had led him all the way up the A9, almost as far as Inverness. Then they turned south onto a smaller road that took them through a series of little towns Tombreck, Farr House, Bailebeag. The old stone-built town-houses and the modern pebble-dashed shoe-boxes blurred past in a comfortable whisky-soaked haze. The fields and hills swept past almost unnoticed as Dougie tried to focus on the maroon Range Rover ahead.

Eventually, they turned off the main-road and started down a narrow single-track lane that wound its way down through the rich countryside.

As he rounded a bend, Dougie saw the Range Rover pull up at a gate leading into a fallow field to the left of the road. He drove past, glancing casually over his shoulder to see what they were up to.

One of the passengers had opened the gate and the vehicle was halfway down a rough track, which led up the side of the field.

Dougie kept going down the road until he was sure that he was out of sight from the gate and then pulled over to the side.

The car came to a halt and Dougie turned off the engine. It had been a long and noisy drive. He closed his eyes for a moment and his head spun. The quiet stillness sucked him in. He had to wait a few minutes before he could follow after the Range Rover. It would be okay, he told himself, to take a quick snooze. Within moments, he was asleep.

*****

Scotia's mind wandered again as she tried to bring her attention back to the matters of state before her, some minor land dispute between two of the smaller clans.

Ahmos was near now, she could feel it and he was brewing something; it could not be long in coming. It was in the air, the anticipation, the dread. Then there were the dreams, such dreams as she had never had before; dreams of chasing and being chased; dreams of death. He was coming for her. She knew that. Tonight was the night of the dark moon, when the forces of destruction were at their most powerful. If Ahmos were going to try something, it would be tonight.

The Stone had been strangely quiet lately. It usually spoke frequently, but she had heard nothing from it for a week now. Ahmos knew that she had it; perhaps he had a way to disrupt her connection with it.

She had taken to holding court in the open outside the great hall. Proud though her people were of the hall, she found it gloomy and smelly and would only retreat there when forced to by the elements. The afternoon was drawing on and the crisp chill of the approaching winter could be felt in the breeze. It would not be long before the rain and biting winds would drive them back into that smoky den. Scotia breathed deeply, relishing the sharp clear air and brought her attention, once more, back to the matter at hand.

"...so, my Lady, we hold that, by dint of these various ancestral petitions, the land to the east of the Taye tributary clearly belongs to the McCreed clan."

There was a pause. Scotia felt all eyes turn on her expectantly. They were waiting for a decision. She floundered for a moment trying to recall whatever she could about the dispute. There was something about a marriage and the wife had died, or maybe it had been the husband, or both of them? The land had been part of the dowry, or was it an inheritance? It was no good. She had not been listening.

"Thank you, fellow clansmen, for your disposition. I will consider the matter overnight and give you my decision on the morrow."

She knew that this was a poor response but no one seemed to care. They accepted her word these days. Too bad she would not be around to help them for much longer. She had left instructions with the council of Thanes over her successor, naming Alanth of the clan MacCleland to take over as head of the council. No one had objected but she doubted, in truth, if Alanth really had what it took to hold the council together. It was frustrating, but there it was. There was little more that she could do.

She had also made provision for Scandia. The twelve-year old girl would be in danger, once Scotia could no longer protect her. She and her offspring might one day be royal pretenders, but also her bloodline was tied now to the safety of Alba. To destroy the country, as Ahmos meant to do, he would have to kill Scandia. The only safe course was to hide her. Scotia's maid had agreed to take the girl in and raise her as one of her own extensive family. She should be safe, or at least as safe as any of them.

"My Lady, a matter for your urgent attention."

The voice snapped her back to the present. Before her was Crenald, her Captain of the guard. Her heart leaped into her throat. This was it.

"Court is adjourned," announced Scotia. "Crenald, in my chambers."

She climbed quickly from her throne, ignoring the clansmen who were trying to catch her eye as she withdrew. There was always something that someone wanted to bring to her attention. She marched rapidly to the door, leaving a wake of disappointed statesmen. Crenald had to trot behind her to keep up.

They entered the low portal that led to her private audience chamber. It was dark inside, lit only by the glowing embers of a fire in the corner and a small oil lamp.

Scotia turned quickly to her trusted Captain. "What is it, Crenald?"

"My Lady," he began, unable to look her in the eye. "I do not know how it happened. It is devilry of the deepest kind. There were guards posted all around the building, as we agreed. I spoke to them myself, and they saw nothing, and yet, she is gone."

"Gone? Who?" asked Scotia, feeling dread rise within her.

"Your daughter, my Lady."

*****

Dougie awoke with a start. Blearily he looked around at the grey fabric interior of his car. He glanced at the dashboard clock. It was late. He had probably been asleep for less than an hour but the light was fading, and it would be dark soon. He was already too late to make the rendezvous with Brian and Gail, but if he set off now and floored it all the way back to Edinburgh he could probably make it before the mission was over.

Somehow he couldn't bring himself to do it. There was something about following the Stone, about being here that was more important. He sighed, wishing his head were a bit clearer so he could think this through properly.

The gate opened onto a rough track, which led to the far side of the field where there were several cars neatly parked, including the Range Rover. Beyond the cars was a narrow footpath that led down to a small brook and then up the rocky slope on the far side.

At the top of the rise, the trees gave way to a grassy clearing. From here, a tufted grass slope tumbled gently down towards the Loch in a broad tract that was bounded on either side by copses of old, weathered trees. The grass ended at a shallow beach of coarse grey shale, and beyond that, the dark waters of the loch.

The sun dipped low towards the horizon. The wizened trees cast long grotesque shadows across the grass. The air was still, as if the earth itself held its breath in anticipation of some great event.

On the grass just before the beach, a circle of torches had been planted on posts in the ground and at its centre of which was a table, covered in a black cloth. Around the table stood several figures dressed in, what looked like, Halloween costumes: long dark robes with deep pointed hoods that hid their faces. He could hear a chanting coming from them, a low monotonous dirge. It was a grim, foreboding sound.

This whole thing was getting weirder by the minute. He had not known what to expect when he had followed a senior police officer across Scotland with the Stone of Scone in the boot of his car, but it had not been this. In any case, the people under those hoods must be the leaders of the SSA. He had to find out more about who they were and what they were up to.

He slipped quietly into the trees and made his way through the undergrowth towards the circle. The ominous chaning became louder and clearer as he approached. Finally, he reached the edge of the trees close to the circle and was able to look out from behind a tall patch of bracken.

The altar was a little over waist high and covered in black cloth. Set into it he could make out the pale yellow of the Stone of Scone, which protruded slightly from the top of the black-cloth surface. On top of the altar lay a tall man in a long woollen coat. At first Dougie thought he was dead, his limbs looked stiff and rigid and his face was very pale and drawn. However, his eyes were wide and fixed on the figure who stood over him. As Dougie crouched low to the ground, he could see the look in those eyes and it sent a shiver down his spine. It was a look of abject terror.

*****

Scotia clung tightly to the back of the great horse as it galloped over the dark ground.

She had never liked riding much. However, she was sparing neither herself nor the horse, for everything she loved and cared for depended on her haste this night.

As she rode her mind relived again and again the last few hours. How could she have been so blind? Upon hearing that her daughter was missing, she had gone at once to consult with the Stone, but the oak chest, in her private chamber lay empty. The Stone too had been taken. She felt the fear and anger rise within her again just as it had done when faced with that empty chest two hours earlier. She had become lazy, relying on the Stone to warn her.

The horse continued to plunge through the darkness. At times she followed roads, at other times, game trails. For a while she splashed wildly down a small waterway. Much of the time she galloped across open country.

The ritual would take place upon the rise of the dark moon. That had given her five or six hours from when she heard the news. It had not taken her long to work out where it would be.

True, she no longer had the Stone, but Ahmos had taken her daughter, to whom she was eternally tied. There was nowhere that he could take her on this earth that Scotia could not find her. It had taken all her skill and training to calm her fears, but once at peace she could feel Scandia, and knew at once where she was. It was a place of dark magic on the banks of a loch, a big loch on the mainland. Even now she could feel it. The energy of the ritual was already collecting there. Whatever Ahmos was planning, it was to be big.

On she rode. The cold wind gnawed at her and her fingers went numb in spite of her thick cloak and the heat from the great horse. Branches whipped at her face in the dark and thorns tore at her legs but she clung tightly to her swift and sure-footed steed, who found his way in the starlight.

And so she galloped on, with speed born of desperation, always drawn to the gathering of the dark power ahead of her.

*****

Mari gripped the handlebars tightly as the motorcycle plummeted through the dark night. The howling siren of the pursuing police car spurred her on.

Another corner appeared and she leaned the bike hard over. The wet road was so close; she could have reached out her fingers and touched it. Miraculously, the tires held their grip and the corner swept smoothly past at amazing speed. Then, for an instant, her concentration wavered and she pulled out of the turn a fraction late and found herself on the wrong side of the road hurtling into the oncoming traffic. The car horn ahead of her blared out as she swerved wildly to avoid it.

Mari caught her breath as she brought the powerful machine back under control. She was taking the corners too fast, and she knew it. She could not keep this up for long. At some point, her luck would run out.

She twisted open the throttle again, accelerating hard down the next straight. The bike responded instantly, consuming the dark road ahead.

She went tearing through the next small town at over seventy, ignoring the thirty-mile-an-hour speed limit, ruthlessly overtaking the slower moving town traffic.

The police car was falling behind. She had a lead of several seconds now but she needed to find a way to lose it for good.

Then, a little way beyond the town, the beam of her headlight picked out exactly what she was looking for, a farm house by the side of the road with a garage and several small outbuildings.

She pulled hard on the brakes bringing the bike to a bone jarring halt and then turned quickly in to the open driveway. She drew the bike deep into the shadow of the buildings and switched off the engine and lights.

Ducking down against the smooth cold metal of the petrol tank, she held her breath and waited.

The wail of the pursuing police car was rapidly approaching. Then the headlights lit up the driveway in front of her and, for a moment ,as it passed, Mari and the bike were bathed in blue light, but then it was gone.

She breathed again.

She was shaking. Her hands were actually shaking when she lifted them from the handlebars. A surge of relief, mixed with fear and anxiety started to bubble up inside her and threatened to erupt in tears. "Come on, Mari" she said to herself, silently. "You've no time for any of that nonsense."

Instead, she turned her attention to her next move. She clearly couldn't follow the police car; eventually he was going to work it out and double back. The driveway she was on turned into a farm track that led across a nearby field. It headed toward the Loch, as far as she could tell. Of course, it might not go very far, but, if nothing else, it was a night for taking risks and somehow this felt right.

She powered up the bike and started down the bumpy farm track as fast as she dared in the gloom of the wet night.

*****

Oban nodded. "The girl is doing well. Providing that motorcycle was a nice touch, and very subtly done. I didn't feel your influence at all."

Talisker shook his head, "that wasn't me, father. It was very fortunate, though, do you think she has help from someone else?"

Oban scratched is beard. "As we get closer to the confluence, we will see more strange turns of fortune. The Universe itself needs this to happen a particular way. Mari will be there."

*****

Mari was lost. The rough dirt farm track had led her across country for several miles and had emerged on to a small road. She could see the road disappearing into the distance in either direction. The question now, was left or right?

She killed the noisy engine and looked up and down the road looking for anything that might help her. She was really starting to regret riding off the way she had done. What use was she going to be to William if she spent the whole night riding round muddy fields in the dark?

It was cold now. The darkness had brought with it a damp chill which the faerie flag dress failed to keep out even with the heavy biker's jacket over it.

She looked up and down the road. There was nothing, no lights, no signs of life, just the dark shapes of twisted trees.

"Come on Mari," she said to herself. "Left or right?"

She sat for a moment paralyzed with indecision, feeling the cold, feeling the quiet. Suddenly she realised that maybe she didn't actually want to get it right. Choosing the right direction could mean her death. Then again, choosing the wrong direction could mean everyone's death – including William. She calmed her breathing and dug deep, letting thoughts and fears fall aside. She held that place of no thought and started up the bike.

She pulled forward slowly, wavering for a second and then watched as she turned down the road to the left.

*****

Connor waved his arms wildly at the rapidly approaching headlights. It had been over an hour since Mari had taken off and in that time he had been desperately trying to find a way to follow her. He had lost count of the number of vehicles he had waved at now. Most of them didn't stop but the half dozen who had pulled over had been either full or heading in the wrong direction.

He turned back to Katie, who was sitting on a bench by the side of the road, looking cold.

"Don't worry," he said, "we'll get a lift. You'll see."

Katie looked at him; she had not been listening.

"Do you think she'll be alright?" she asked. "Mari, I mean. Do you think I'll see her again?"

"Och, aye, if she doesn't kill herself on that infernal motorcycle, that is." He said with a wink. "She'll be fine, you'll see. Our Mari's made of tough stuff, tougher than she knows."

He sat down next to her on the wooden bench as they waited for the next car. Katie was obviously thinking about something and he, too, had plenty to occupy him.

"Connor, can I ask you a question?" she asked, finally.

"Aye," he replied, confidently.

"Do you hate the English?"

"Well, suppose so. In a way," he answered, noncommittally.

"I do," she went on. "I'm a *true*Scott and I *hate*the English. I have always hated the English. There was riots and bombs going off since I was wee. Everyone I know hates the English. It's part of being Scottish. It like *defines*being Scottish. But if what you said last night is true, then it was all a trick, a sham, a pack o' lies and... well, if that's true, then who am I?"

She fell silent, leaving the question hanging.

"You're right Katie," Connor replied, slowly. "All of us are gonna have to rethink a few things if we get through this. But the answer to your question is that you are the same person you were before, you've just come to understand something about who you are not. We are not defined by hatred or flags, where we were born or how we talk, the size of our wallet or the colour of our skin. What defines us is deep inside. It is our connection to the world but it's easy to lose sight of that, for all of us."

Katie said nothing as she thought about this. Another pair of headlights appeared down the road.

"Here we go again," he declared, jumping forward to the very edge of the road. He started waving his arms like a windmill.

The headlights started slowing and came to a stop with a hiss of pneumatic brakes. In the dark, it was difficult to tell what the vehicles were until they got close. This one, it turned out was a large, articulated truck. The markings on the side showed a cartoon of a smiling pig with a napkin around its neck, holding a knife and fork; underneath it read "Scottish bacon — a crackling good breakfast."

He went around to the driver's side and watched as the window wound down. A woman looked out at him, at least he thought it was a woman. She had a round saggy face and looked more than a little over weight. There was a cigarette hanging from her mouth and an earring in her eyebrow.

"What's up?" she asked, without taking the cigarette out.

"Err, the wee lass and I are having a bit of a bad night," began Connor. "See, our car's broken down and we really *have* to get to our camp site. My other daughter is gonna be there all on her own and d'ya know, I don't even know if she could put up the tent herself."

She considered this for a moment.

"Where's it at?"

"We're camping on a little beach on the shore of the Loch before Foyers."

"Alright," she said, "I'm heading that way. You'd better get in."

*****

Mari sped down the small winding road, forcing herself to take it slowly. If she put this bike into a ditch now there'd be no help for William. It was couldn't be far.

Just then, she caught sight of a cluster of cars parked on the far side of a field, off the road. There was something going on here, maybe it was the something that she was looking for. She rode the bike up the dirt track to the cars and pulled up on the far side next to a white Mercedes.

Beyond the cars was a trail leading up the hill. With only the dim light of the stars to guide her she, splashed through the brook and ran up the wooded slope on the far bank.

As soon as she crested the hill she could see the circle of torches by the loch shore below her and hear the menacing chant of the ritual. She could see the altar. There was a figure on it. William? Her heart leapt. Was he still alive? Was there still time to save him?

Mari could just make out the dark shapes of a line of trees to one side of where the torches were set. She crept quietly down the slope, staying close to the treeline and its covering shadows. Once she was about as close as she could get, she ducked behind a patch of bracken and peered out from between the leaves.

It was definitely William lying on the altar. There seemed to be nothing binding him and yet clearly he could not move. His eyes were staring wildly at the figure in front of him with a look of terror. The figure was dressed, like the others, in long, dark, hooded robes. Unlike the others, it was brandishing a short, black rod.

Cynthia Farrow and her nasty toy. What had Connor called it? The Sceptre of Something-Or-Other? She was obviously using the Sceptre to hold William – no wonder he had a look of fear in his eyes.

The chanting was low, long, rhythmic and monotonous, if there were words they were none that Mari recognized. Nevertheless, the chanting was somehow demoralising as if it were sucking at her motivation or her power to act.

Ms. Farrow would occasionally utter something and the others would answer back. One of the figures held a gong that seemed to be struck periodically; another had a vial of some sort and was sprinkling it occasionally around the circle.

As she watched, a plan started to form in Mari's mind. The key, it seemed, was the Sceptre. If she could move fast enough to take Ms. Farrow by surprise, maybe she could grab the Sceptre and release William from the spell. She felt pretty sure she could out run Ms. Farrow and without the Sceptre they wouldn't be able to complete the ritual. It wasn't much of a plan, but it could work as long as she could take them by surprise.

Suddenly, she heard a noise coming from the undergrowth beside her. She looked around and saw a man crouched in the trees a few feet away. He was looking straight at her.

*****

The tension in the council chamber was palpable and the gods continued to watch the events unfold on the tabletop before them. The moment of reckoning was rapidly approaching; they could all feel it. Like a climber seeking finger-tip holds on a sheer rock face, they continued to seek purchase that would allow them to influence the outcome.

"So, I'll tell ya what we do," roared Laphroaig. "We've two of our own on the ground now. We get one of them to create a distraction while the other one runs in an' grabs the sceptre. We pitch the sceptre into the loch and it's all over."

"Risky," replied Oban. "The boy is too confused, and too drunk, to do anything very coherent without us taking direct control and that would just give Anput more rope. He could certainly create a distraction but that means Mari would have to go in. If she were caught, things would be much worse than they are now."

"She can do it," insisted Laphroaig. "That girls got real grit!"

"We must not underestimate that Farrow woman, though," replied MacAllan, "and remember, Talisker has intervened directly a couple of times now. Anput has not. She still has some powerful cards to play."

"In any case, there's no stoppin' the ritual directly," asserted Dufftown, wheezily. "This moment has been prophesied for centuries. Now that we are here, there's just too much momentum behind it for it to be turned aside. We have to be more subtle."

"All we need," agreed Talisker, "is to tip the scales. Everything is being thrown up in the air. The smallest tweak at the right moment could completely turn the outcome."

"We'd better make sure we tweak things the right way then, eh?" remarked Ardbeg, dryly.

*****

"Come on ya lazy get." Gail hollered, as she climbed to the discrete marker at the top of the grassy slope.

"Aye, all right, I'm coming'," he hissed back. "Next time, you can carry the bloody launch tubes up the hill."

They stood at the top of The Crags, in Holyrood Park, a cliff face that represented the little brother of the small mountainous hill in Edinburgh city known as Arthur's Seat. The nighttime cityscape of Edinburgh twinkled before them. Thousands of little windows shone with light. Behind each window was a person or a family. People all over the city were eating their evening meals, putting their children to bed, watching TV, doing ordinary things. None of them knew what they would wake up to in the morning.

Brian dumped his pack heavily on the ground next to Gail and began unloading and assembling the mortars. They were tubes with legs that clipped into place and allowed them to be adjusted to the right angle.

Gail set down her pack of shells and helped Brian with the job of aiming and calibrating the weapons. Getting the angle correct was probably the most critical part, but they had calculated the details well in advance. All they needed to do now was allow for the light easterly wind.

Below them was their target, the new Scottish Parliament building. The lights there blazed, too. It was late on a Sunday night but the government body was in an emergency session discussing a motion to grant new powers to the police to help stem the rising tide of terrorist activities. It was something of a controversial bill given the strong public sentiment in favour of the terrorist point of view and the feeling that the Scottish police were really just pawns of the English government.

"It doesn't bother you, then?" asked Gail, suddenly, looking down on the gleaming new building they were about to destroy.

"What?"

"Killin' all those people, it doesn't bother you?"

"Well? They're English, who cares, like?" he shrugged, non-committally. He had not really given it much thought.

"Brian, ya plonker, they're *Scottish* Members of Parliament, they are ne English."

"Aye, but, ya know, they're part of the establishment, like. It's like they're workin' fer the English against us."

"Och, well, that's okay, then!"

"Look, this is a war, people die, okay?"

"But what did they do?"

"What are you sayin'? You want to call it off? Now?"

"No, I'm just saying, like."

Brian made the last adjustments to the equipment. Gail stuffed her hands in her pockets and stared down at the city, lost in thought.

*****

Scotia rounded the crest of the rise. Her horse was thick with foamy sweat and shaking. Before her, she could just make out the black outline of the great Loch, stretching off to the horizon. Below her, between two thickets of trees, she could see a circle of torches. That was it. She urged the tired horse down the slope.

As she slowly drew nearer, she could see Ahmos alone in the circle. He stood with the Stone at his feet and pointed a dark sceptre toward the sky. The ritual must be almost complete. Scotia could feel the intense power in the air. At least Ahmos had not noticed her; he was fully bent toward his intent. He let out a loud cry, voicing the true name of the horror he was summoning, calling it forth. His words echoed out over the Loch.

Scotia stopped the horse as close as she dared and dropped to the ground, cursing silently as her aching legs almost buckled beneath her.

Ahmos was still now, staring out at the Loch as if looking for something. Then she saw something else at his feet. It was Scandia. She had been hidden in the deep grass. She could sense something else. It was a soft, gentle sound, the Stone seemed to be humming gently. Then she understood, it was singing to Scandia, a soft calming lullaby.

Scotia, still unnoticed, dropped to one knee and pulled the bow off her back. She took an arrow from her quiver and then very carefully opened a vial she had in her belt. She dipped the arrow tip into its sticky black contents and notched the it, taking great care with its poisoned tip. Drawing back the bowstring, she looked down the length of its shaft at the assassin in the circle.

Kneeling down, Ahmos lifted the girl onto the Stone so that her upper back rested across it. With one hand he took a handful of her hair and roughly pulled her head back to hold her in position. With the other he raised the Sceptre over her heart and made ready to strike.

At that moment, the horse let out a loud whinny. Ahmos spun around, leaping to his feet. In the darkness he could only see the horse.

"You are too late, Neferubity," he called out to the land around. "The beast has been summoned. You cannot stop it. It will destroy your people and it will destroy you. There is nothing..."

He fell silent as his body dropped to the ground. The poisoned arrow lodged deep in his chest. He died instantly.

In moments Scotia was by her daughter's side. She cut the ropes that bound her hands and held her daughter tight in her arms, as a few silent tears ran down her cheeks.

Scandia sobbed as she clung desperately to her mother.

"It's alright, now," Scotia soothed as best she could.

"It's not that, Mama," said the girl, between sobs. "I don't want you to go away. I don't want to lose you!"

Scotia blinked back the tears that stung her eyes. She had thought to keep her fate from her daughter, but the child had the sight. She already knew what was about to happen and she knew it could not be prevented. What a burden for a child to have to bear.

For a few moments longer, the two held each other for what would be the last time.

"Now, my child, you must go," Scotia said, softly. "Take my horse. He is tired, but he can lead you home."

Scandia did not protest.

"I love you, Mama," she said, bravely, blinking fiercely at the tears that continued to roll down her face.

"I love you, too, my dear, so much," replied Scotia. "Now go and do not look back. Do not look back."

Slowly, the child picked up the horse's reigns and led the tired animal up the path, over the rise and out of sight.

Scotia watched them go and then painfully turned her attention back to the Loch. She could feel the beast out there, feel it starting to rise. It would not be long now.

It began as a gentle disturbance on the surface of the Loch, as if a squall was whipping at the water. There was stirring in the air, a rustle of wind high in the trees on either side. Then, came the bubbles, one or two at first, then more and larger, until it looked as if the Loch were boiling. The wind began to grow in strength until the rustling became a howl, flattening the long grass and bending the mighty branches of those great trees almost to the ground. The waves that a moment ago had been little more than ripples began to roll in from the loch like ocean breakers in a storm, crashing against the shale.

Finally, amid this tumult, the creature started to show. At first Scotia could see just the crest of its back as it rose above the water line. Then it started to emerge, like a nest of giant vipers. The tentacles came first, slimy grey feelers, writhing in the air, exploring the sensations, the smells, the tastes the feel of this material dimension. Then, came the head like an island appearing in the water. Huge black eyes, ancient and evil, stared out of either side. It grew impossibly out of the dark waters until it towered over the land.

It opened its mouth at the centre of a wreath of smaller snake-like tentacles, displaying line upon line of pointed teeth the size of swords and screeched, a deafening sound that filled the air with the terror of many ages past. It was the lustful call of a hunter that would finally gorge on its prey. The air became filled with the putrid stench of rotten flesh.

Undaunted by the chaos around her, Scotia knelt in the centre of the circle. She could feel the Stone. It was not talking to her so much as crooning, soothing her, much as it had done for Scandia. It knew what was about to happen. The wind whipped at her hair and cloak.

The sight, sounds and smells of the monster beat on her senses, evoking deep animal fears and yet she had found a place deeper inside, a place of stillness that even this spectacle could not disturb.

She had made her choice. She knew what she had to do and she was no longer afraid.

"Anubis, God of the dead, Guardian of souls, here my call." She spoke the words quietly, without force or emotion but despite the noises of wind and water and the cries of the beast, the words seemed to carry and echo in the hills around. "Anubis, banish this creature to whence it came, and place your blessing and protection on this land and its people. I give you, in payment, this life."

The creature continued to advance relentlessly toward Scotia, its massive body still submerged in the water. It reached out is writhing limbs toward her. She was the wielder of the Sceptre and must be the first to die.

Scotia could feel the anger and hatred that emanated from it. The smell of death that surrounded it was now almost overpowering.

She stood up and held the sharp point of her dark sceptre to the centre of her chest. Then with simple grace, she let herself fall forward so that the sharp black jet pierced her body, cutting through bone and flesh. She felt intense pain for a brief moment and then death overcame her.

The monster let out one more deafening screech of defiance, but then reluctantly started to retreat back into the foaming waters. In moments, it had disappeared from sight. The wind died down and the waters stilled.

Aside from the dead bodies on the shore, there was no sign of the powers that had been unleashed and subdued that night. The only one left to tell the tale was a lonely young girl leading a horse through the open country, with tears streaming silently down her face.

*****

Dougie continued to watch the weird rite play out in the torch-lit circle before him. He felt strangely transfixed by the semi-hypnotic chanting and the repetitive cycle of actions. The principle figure in the centre would point or sign with a black rod and pronounce some foul guttural utterance. The others would respond in chant. Sometimes, one of them would sprinkle the contents of a vial, flicking it around the circle or across the prostrate body of the man on the altar. At one point, a silver chalice was taken around the circle and each of the participants sipped of its contents. Incense, strange smelling powders and herbs burned, and all the while the low, rhythmic chanting continued.

Dougie could feel the power of the rite. It was both captivating and repulsive. He felt a dreadful fascination building and, with it, a lust for blood, a desire to inflict pain and suffering. He knew that the man on the altar was going to be hurt, maybe even killed. The prospect was delicious.

Then a movement caught his eyes. He could see a person approaching in the shadows just outside the light of the torches – a girl dressed in a long white dress and a black leather biker's jacket. She looked a little like she had walked off the set of a fifties teen musical. This whole thing was getting surreal. Her eyes were fixed on the ritual; she hadn't seen him.

He started to retreat but a noise caught her attention and she turned to look straight at him. For a moment they eyed each other warily.

"Who are you?" he whispered.

"My name's Mari," she replied quietly, afraid they might be discovered.

"What are you doin' here?"

"I'm trying to stop that," she nodded to the ritual.

"Wha' is it?" asked Dougie.

Mari gritted her teeth.

"Look, I don't have time to explain, but the simple part is that they are going to kill that man."

"What? Like a human sacrifice?" Dougie asked, almost in awe.

"Yes."

"What fer?"

"Does it matter? They're bloody loonies, alright! The important thing is that they have to be stopped."

"But..." started Dougie. His mind was full of questions vying for attention. He was feeling the effects of the ritual and the craving for blood was with him. Should he help her? Should he try to stop her? What would happen if they were discovered?

Then, like the lifting of a curtain, all Dougie's questions and doubts were brushed away. He suddenly knew why he was here, and what it was he had to do. It was clear as day. He almost laughed at himself for not understanding it earlier.

He stood up and walked calmly forward into the torch light.

Mari watched with growing trepidation. What was he going to do?

"She's here," called out Dougie, in a loud clear voice, "in the trees."

The chanting stopped at once and all the cowl-draped figures turned to look in the direction Dougie was pointing – directly at Mari.

*****

"What the hell happened there?" yelled Laphroaig, unable to believe what he was seeing. "That was an intervention. Some god did that."

"Yes," said MacAllan. "I felt it. But who did it?"

Pandemonium broke out among the gods. They had all felt it. It was not the gentle, subtle influencing of a person that they usually indulged in, but a direct modification of their perspective. It had been so blatant.

"Silence," called Oban, striking his staff loudly against the floor. He spoke softly but forcefully and the bickering and accusations quickly died away. "At last, we see Anput playing her hand," he said, sadly.

"What d'ya mean?" asked Laphroaig.

"You know we have been building up a debt. Talisker's interventions have been fairly direct."

"Not like that!"

"I suspect that you will find that this last act balances exactly our actions earlier. What do you think, Dufftown?"

"I think yer right there," responded the old god. "She's a canny one and no mistake. As near as I can guess it they balance exactly."

"It's not the sort of trick I would expect from an ancient, though," remarked Lagavulin, pausing her knitting for a moment. "It doesn't feel like her style."

"She had someone else doing her dirty work for her," declared Talisker, with unusual venom.

"Wha?" yelled Laphroaig, rising to his feet. "What d'ya mean? What is he talkin' about?"

"We have suspected for a time that there has been a traitor in our midst."

"And ya did nothin?" cried Laphroaig, in disbelief.

Oban sighed.

"My son, I judged it best to play along until we knew more. I thought there might be an advantage in keeping our suspicions quiet and I did not know, without doubt, who it was. But now, alas, perhaps too late, she has revealed herself."

"Who?"

"Look around – she is no longer here."

"Ardbeg!" said Jura, suddenly.

"Why that sour old bitch!" cried Laphroaig. "I'll teach her a lesson or two with the sharp edge of my axe." He started to swing the mighty weapon about his head in fury.

"Laphroaig! Everyone! There is no time," said Oban, urgently. "We must all try to focus and see if there is anything left that we can do while the game still plays."

*****

Mari stared out of the bushes for a moment, blinking like a rabbit in headlights. The boy's actions had been completely unexpected and for a moment sheer panic set in. She closed her eyes and breathed and then took the only course of action left. She charged headlong out of the bushes towards Cynthia Farrow. Her only thought was to get her hands on that sceptre.

Ms. Farrow watched the girl approach from beneath her hooded robe with gentle amusement. She was so hopelessly earnest, just like her mother. She waited until the girl was inside the circle of torches, almost within reach of her goal and then turned the full power of the sceptre on her.

The fear gripped Mari instantly. Her legs went limp and she crumpled to the ground like a marionette whose strings were cut. Rough hands hauled William from the altar. He caught sight of Mari on the ground as he was dragged away and his eyes went even wider, but he was still unable to move.

The same hands grabbed Mari and set her in William's place upon the stone altar. Things were really not going the way she had hoped. She stared defiantly at Cynthia Farrow. She felt the Stone of Scone beneath her and the fear seemed to bleed from her at the touch of that hard surface. She regained enough control over her body that she could talk.

"Let him go," she said, bravely. "He has nothing to do with this."

Cynthia Farrow regarded Mari strangely from under her cowl. This close to the sceptre, she should be completely incapacitated.

"You are growing strong, my little Mari," she remarked, softly. "Too little, too late, though."

She gestured to Dougie.

"Take the Englishman and tie him up."

"No!" cried Mari.

"Hush, my dear, you have much more important things to worry about."

"You can't win," cried Mari. "Scotland will never fall for your hate campaign."

"Ah, but, my dear, Mari," replied Ms. Farrow with a smile that was lost in her hood. "They already have and now that I have you, there is nothing – truly nothing – that can stop me."

She turned away.

"It is almost time," she announced to the group.

At once, the chanting began again, this time more feverish, more urgent.

Mari could feel the build up of fear and hatred that were part of the spell. Its dark energy made her skin crawl and the hairs on her arms stand on end. She struggled to move but the power of the sceptre held her fast.

The chanting built to a crescendo and Cynthia Farrow let out a cry in a long, loud voice that echoed across the glen. Suddenly, there was silence as everyone waited, watching the Loch.

Mari continued to search for an escape. Something was going to happen. Something had to happen. It couldn't end like this.

"Goodbye, my dear," smiled Cynthia Farrow as she lifted the Sceptre into the air. She uttered a short verse in the same alien language and then brought the point of the stone sceptre down with all her might.

Mari watched, in disbelief, as the sceptre descended towards her chest. Time seemed to slow. She could see every detail of the intricate engravings cut into the black stone. She saw the manicured nails and the veins on the back of the hand that clutched it. She watched the graceful arc it traced through the air towards her prone body.

Some saviour she was. She had failed both herself and her people and all to try and save William. This couldn't be happening. She felt as well as heard the sickening crack as the sharp dagger-like stone pierced her sternum and then buried itself in the tough meat of her heart. The world became pain. For a brief moment, every sense, every nerve screamed at her in agony.

Then all was black…and there was nothing.

*****

Mari found herself walking down a tree-lined lane. Autumn was about her. Dry leaves covered the trees and seemed to fall all around like golden confetti. Everywhere there were the gentle colours of red and yellow and auburn.

She had this strange sense that she had something important to do, but could not remember what it was.

Ahead of her, in the centre of the lane, she could see someone; someone waiting for her. She continued to walk toward the figure. At first she felt a vague sense of familiarity, then a clear feeling of recognition and finally she knew the person to be her mother.

Mari ran forward and fell into the waiting arms.

"Oh mum, mummy," she said weeping, "I missed you so much."

"I missed you, too, Mari. I have been waiting for you for a long time."

"What happened, Ma? What happened to you?"

"It's a long story."

"But why did you leave us, me and Dad?" Mari's looked into her mother's face, her eyes suddenly full of pain. They held the accusing look of an abandoned child.

"Oh, Mari, you know I would have done anything…"

"But why, Ma? What happened?"

"We were betrayed by one of our coven, a witch by the name of Cynthia Farrow."

"Who?"

Even as she said it Mari started to feel memories tugging at her awareness – she knew that name.

"She used to be one of my oldest friends but as time went on she became seduced by power. She found a prophesy, that speaks of 'the coming of a darkness ruled by a dark queen in the land of the Picts,' and of course she cast herself in the lead role. She found allies in the gods and, since I represented the biggest threat to her scheme, her first act was to bring about my death. I trusted her. I had no idea that she would be that ruthless."

Mari's mind reeled. The mention of the Dunvegan estate manager suddenly brought back the last two days; her escape from the hellhounds, her ill-fated rescue of Katie and her foolish flight to save William.

"Mother, I have failed. I failed them all. Cynthia Farrow has won."

Her mother smiled.

"Nonsense, my dear," she replied, lightly.

"Mum, it's true! I am dead. That's why I am standing here talking to you." said Mari, starting to feel angry.

"Death is not always the end."

"What do you mean?"

"Your task is not yet over."

Then, Mari began to feel something else, a tugging, a pulling at her centre.

"What's happening to me? Are you here to save me, Ma?"

"No, my dear, Mari, you have already done that for yourself."

"What do you mean?"

"The Flag, you are still wearing the Faery Flag. You went up against Cynthia Farrow, and most importantly, not for yourself, but for another. A McLeod that goes into battle, true of heart, baring the Flag cannot be defeated."

Mari found herself leaving the ground. She was being swept up into the air. She looked down through the falling golden leaves at her smiling mother as she was drawn past the naked branches. She felt as if all the pieces in the complex puzzle of her life had just fallen into place. There was still something she had to do and she was returning to do it.

"Will I see you again?" she called out. "I don't want to lose you!"

"Mari, you will never lose me. I am with you always."

"I love you, mummy."

"I love you, too, Mari." replied her mother. "Now go, go back and finish what you started."

The words echoed in her mind as she lost sight of the trees and everything around her went white.

*****

Cynthia Farrow grinned in triumph as she stood over the lifeless body. Warm blood spattered across her face and covered her hands. It still gushed from the fatal wound in Mari's chest, soaking the snow-white dress and running in sticky trails down the sides of the altar.

With a sickening sucking sound, Ms. Farrow pulled the bloody sceptre from the wound and absently wiped it on the hem of the dress. Her attention was fixed on the Loch. It would not be long now. Everything was going so beautifully to plan. In moments, she gloated, she would be the most powerful person on earth. With the Leviathan now undeniably subdued and under her control there was nothing that could stop her. The final culmination of her plan was approaching its ultimate and inevitable fruition, when she would become the Dark Queen.

The chanting had stopped and all eyes were now fixed on the Loch. For a long time, nothing moved. It was more than still, as if time had frozen in the glen. Then the wind started. It grew with unnatural speed from a whisper to a roar, as the wind grew, so did the waves on the loch. Its glassy black surface became first rutted and then torn apart as white-capped waves raced over its length.

William was tied to a tree. His eyes were not looking out at the loch but were fixed on the horrific sight on the altar. He was in shock, unable to rip his eyes away from the grotesque sight of Mari's broken body as it lay there in the blood soaked dress.

Tears began to form in his eyes, blurring his vision. He blinked them back, wanting to hold on to that last image of the girl he loved. It was then that he saw something that all the others had missed. It seemed as if there was less blood on the dress than a few moment before. At first he thought it was just his blurry vision playing tricks, but as he watched, it became clearer. The blood seemed to have reversed its course. The red stains were growing smaller. It was almost as if the blood were returning to the wound. Dumbfounded, William continued to look on as the dress returned to its original pure white colour and the rent in its front repaired itself. Then, to his astonishment, Mari's eyes opened and with a heaving gasp, she began to breathe again.

Cynthia Farrow gazed out at the loch, searching for the first signs of the evil she had summoned.

The wind was reaching a frenzy now, tearing madly at everything in sight. Only the rocks of the hill itself were unmoved by its rage. The torches in the circle were guttering wildly and several had been blown out. The waters of the loch mirrored the anger in the air. It foamed with white rage as great waves, like walls of heavy black water crashed up on the shale beach, throwing stones and spray in all directions.

Then she saw it. The grey green rubbery-looking skin of some appendage surfaced. Then another, and another as the water became alive with the seething tentacles of the emerging monster.

Her grin broadened as the power of the rite mixed with the elation of certain success. She raised the sceptre and made ready to channel the terrifying power of pure hatred that emanated from the beast. It was truly the beginning of the end. Millions were going to die at her hand – she felt drunk at the prospect.

Then she noticed the movement out of the corner of her eye: Mari's first breath. She looked down in disbelief. The wound and the blood were gone. The sacrificial victim, whose death was critical to controlling the dragon-daemon she had just summoned, *was breathing*. Her dream of victory came crashing down about her.

With speed borne of fear and desperation, she raised the sceptre in order to plunge it once again into Mari's heart but this time Mari was too quick for her. She swung a punch, connecting solidly with the underside of the estate manager's delicate chin.

Ms. Farrow staggered back in shock and pain.

The loch boiled as a dark head emerged at the centre of the serpent-like tentacles. Blindly the limbs tasted the energies in the air around them searching for food. The beast could sense the anger and hatred in the land around it and it rejoiced at the prospect of feeding again after so long a sleep. It could feel the place of the ritual and the power of the sceptre and it realised with an ancient delight that, for the first time in millennia, the ritual sacrifice had failed.

It started for the shore.

Mari smiled grimly and swung down from the altar. She ignored the approaching monstrosity, the gale-force wind and the aching pain in her hand. The sceptre was the key, she told herself. Grab the sceptre!

The estate manager had been taken by surprise, but she had not been beaten. She looked at Mari, her face set in grim determination, and held out the black scepter.

The wall of fear hit Mari like a bus. It was stronger this time, and not just fear, but hatred and anger too. She could feel the power of the Leviathan being channelled through the sceptre, a power that could destroy whole civilizations.She staggered and tried to catch herself on the edge of the altar, but it was too much and she slid miserably to the floor. The fear overwhelmed her, the paralysis draining the strength from her limbs. She could not fight that. She was beaten.

Then from deep inside, she heard a voice, her own voice. It was calling out to her, "Ya what? You just died ya daft bitch! What's left to be afraid of, eh? Now, get up! Get up!"

It wasn't that she no longer felt the fear, it was still there, but she became aware of herself beyond the fear. It was just an emotion, a reaction of her body. She was more than that. It could not control her. She stood up.

She could see Cynthia Farrow's knuckles going white, as she gripped the sceptre manically. With wide eyes, she advanced on the girl holding the sceptre out. Fear poured from the black rod, a palpable emotional pain that bombarded Mari like a physical blow. She felt the terrifying energy, the strength of the attack was many times what had overcome her before, and yet she could now contain it, hold it, like an electric ball of barbed wire, feel its power but remain untouched.

Mari swayed toward the altar, pretending to be driven back. Ms. Farrow continued to advance on her like a spider stalking a trapped insect. Mari waited until she was within arm's length and then swiftly turned and grabbed the front of the older woman's robes. She pulled down and swung her forehead up, smashing into Ms. Farrow's face with every ounce of force she could muster. The 'Glasgow kiss' struck home with satisfying crunch of bone and cartilage.

Cynthia Farrow fell backward with a shriek. Her left hand covered her mouth and nose as blood flowed freely down her face behind it. Seizing the moment, Mari wrenched the sceptre from the estate manager and made ready to run.

"Get her!" shrieked Ms. Farrow at the startled watchers. "We need the sceptre."

Mari suddenly realised she was surrounded. The robed figures on all sides started to move in. She knew she could not let them have the sceptre. So, she did the only thing she could think of. She drew back her arm and hurled it, as hard as she could, out into the foaming waters. The jet-black rod was hard to see against the dark sky. It soared through the air in a graceful arc, flipping lazily end over end, until it passed out of the range of the torchlight and was lost from sight in the darkness of the loch.

As it fell, a scream arose from Ms. Farrow, a hoarse animal wail that rose above the howl of the storm.

"No!" she cried. "You stupid, ignorant bitch. May all the gods in hell curse you for that. You have killed us all. That sceptre was the *only* way to control the beast. It will devour everything now, everything and everyone!"

The advance of the robed figures faltered at the sound of these words. A couple of them turned to glance out at the loch. Beneath the dark hoods, Mari saw looks of terror. Then, as if they had made the decision with one mind, Ms. Farrow's followers broke out of the circle and began running madly away from the loch, up the slope and back toward their cars. The boy she saw in the woods was with them, running as if his life depended on it.

"Come back, you fools" shrieked Ms. Farrow at their backs. "There is no escape."

But the cry simply fuelled their fear, hastening their flight.

She turned back instead to Mari. Her hand was still clasped across her broken face, but there was a fierce fire in her eyes.

"We are both dead now, Miss McLeod, but at least I can have the satisfaction of being the one to kill you." She drew the hand across her face ineffectively trying to wipe away the blood. Then she pulled a long ceremonial dagger from inside her robes and pounced on Mari.

The speed and ferocity of the attack took Mari by surprise and she ducked backwards only just in time as the dagger swept through the air within inches of her face.

"Its too late." Mari said, playing for time, as she tried to put the altar between them. "You're beaten Farrow. I'm wearing the Faery Flag, there's nothin' you can do."

"That old rag won't save you. I'll tear it from your back." She attacked again slicing at Mari.

Again Mari dodged, but she caught the corner of the altar and the knife sliced into her forearm. Her armed burned like fire as blood welled and started gushing from the cut. With the pain came anger. An intense anger at this woman who had killed her mother, who was trying to kill her, and who was about to destroy her country.

In fury, Mari grabbed a handful of the sandy soil at her feet and flung it at Ms. Farrow's face. The older woman shrieked and Mari made a grab for the blade.

Ms. Farrow clung to the weapon with a talon-like grip but Mari smashed the bony hand against the altar and with a gasp of pain the knife fell free. Grabbing the knife, Mari threw herself at her opponent with the full force of her anger. Ms. Farrow, still blinded by the sand was taken by surprise. They both fell to the floor with Mari on top of the struggling estate manager.

She pressed the knifepoint hard against her adversary's throat. The struggles stopped.

"Go on then, kill me!" Ms. Farrow spat, her eyes filled with defiance. "It makes no difference now."

Mari could feel venomous rancour pumping through her veins. She *hated* this woman. She could think of nothing else but to destroy her.

"Don't you worry, I'm gonna kill you," Mari replied, her eyes wide, "an' I'm gonna enjoy it."

To emphasise the point she twisted the knifepoint until a trickle of blood emerged.

Mari was ready to force the blade through her neck and watch as her life-blood spill in the dirt. She was going to kill her and it would be glorious, but something held her back. A bubble of awareness rose slowly in her mind and popped gently. The anger wasn't coming from her. It came from the creature in the water; *and she was feeding it.*

She felt the anger insider her and just as she had done with the fear, she found she could step out of it. With a deep breath, she pulled the knife back and stood up. "You're not worth it." She muttered.

Ms. Farrow stared at her in disbelief and then she saw something behind Mari and her eyes grew wider. Mari turned to see the grey tentacles of the monster starting to extend up the beach towards them, searching and tasting as they went.

Ms. Farrow started to run, staggering across the sand. Sensing the movement the tentacles shifted to follow her. One of the tips found her foot and fastened around her ankle. She fell hard and started to get dragged towards the water.

It was too much for Mari to watch, she couldn't let anyone fall to that creature, not even her enemy. Without a thought for her own safety, she rushed to Ms. Farrow's side and in moments, she was stabbing brutally at the tentacle that was pulling at her leg. But even as it released her, three more took its place; then others followed, grabbing at the estate manager's wrists and body. Mari slashed desperately at the thick rubbery limbs but there was little that she could do.

Ms. Farrow grabbed at Mari, as she was lifted from the beach but her hands were ripped away. As she disappeared, Mari could just make out her final words. "Its no use, Mari." She spat. "You have *lost*. You *can't* fight it."

Mari could feel the black emanation of dark emotion that spilled from the beast. She moved away as tentacles continued to search the waters edge. They were getting closer. It had tasted its first meat in a thousand years and it would soon be back for more.

"No, Mari," she said quietly to herself, "You can't fight it. It's fuelled by hatred, conflict, resistance. Fighting it would make it stronger. You have to take away its fuel."

As she spoke, she realised that the words were not coming just from her. At that moment she felt her mother and her grandmother and her great grandmother all the way back to Scotia who had stood in this same place over three thousand years ago and faced the same terror and died to overcome it.

"You can't run, and you can't fight, so what's left? Surrender and death?"

But Mari was not going to die, not again.

A deep calmness came over her, she felt alive in a way that she had not done before. The world was vibrant, she could feel the life all around her. Above it all, she felt the dark bitter hatred of the creature emerging from the loch. There was one other thing, too, a low soothing song. It spoke to her in feelings. It was coming from the Stone.

Mari walked over to the altar and climbed on top of it and stood with her feet on the sandstone block. She looked out at the monstrous horror that was emerging from the water and, facing out to the Loch, she began to sing.

The song came unbidden to her lips. It was a song she had known all her life. Her mother had taught it to her and her mother to her and now she understood what it meant:

Hush now, hear the silence.
Let it wash your fears aside.
Hush now, feel the stillness,
The gentle strength inside.

Keep the darkness from the threshold,
Fill your heart with light.
Love will triumph over darkness,
Softness over might.

The song arose from deep within her, from the Stone and from her ancestors. All around her the rocks, the trees, the fish, the birds, all lent their power and vitality to her spell.

Hush now, feel the calmness.
Still the winter's rage.
Hush now, sense the turning,
Of another page.

Gentle touch like falling leaves,
Like petals from a flower,
Soft and tough like moon-bleached silk,
Find your hidden power.

The sound of Mari's voice rose effortlessly above the din of the waves. It filled the ears and minds and hearts of all those that heard it. It echoed through the Great Glen and then like a distant bell or the roll of far off thunder, it swept across the country.

Hush now, sense the dawning,
Of a bright new day.
Hush now, calm the anger,
Turn the hate away.

Night is darkest 'afor the dawn,
When fears and shadows reign.
Lift the fears and light the shadows,
Rejoin with truth again.

For a timeless instant the souls of all Scots were brought together in a still, absolute, peace. For that one instant, they forgot all worries and cares. There were no troubles or problems, no fear or hatred, no English and Scottish. For one instant, they were truly free.

It only lasted for a moment but that moment was enough. Like puncturing a giant water balloon, the putrid sludge of human malevolence that was bottled up in the collective psyche of the nation sagged and deflated. The beast shrieked in frustration as it felt the power drain away, for there was nothing it could do. The hate that gave it form and substance on this plane fell away like dead leaves from a winter tree. It thrashed and roared one last time and then, defeated, its massive bulk sank backward into the dark waters of the loch.

When the song came to an end, the wind had died and the waves subsided and the loch was back to its dark, silvery calm and the glen was still. Exhausted, but strangely happy, Mari climbed down lightly from the altar.

She heard distant shouts from up the hill. She turned to see two familiar figures running towards her. It was Connor and Katie.

Katie came running up to Mari and caught her in a wild hug that almost knocked her over.

"Oh, Mari, thank god you're OK," she sobbed.

"And you," replied Mari, holding her tight.

Connor followed some way behind, wheezing terribly from the exertion. He was looking at her very strangely.

"Wha'?" she asked, a bit perturbed.

He smiled. "You did good lassie, you did good."

She smiled back.

They heard a muffled cry over by the trees. It was William. Mari ran over and untied the gangly Englishman.

"That was amazing," said William, gesturing at the altar. There was awe evident in his tone.

"Thank you," said Mari smiling, and unexpectedly finding herself looking into his eyes.

"You saved my life," he said.

"Well, that makes us even," she shrugged, but still did not look away.

"It was beautiful," he said. "You are beautiful."

How could she possibly look beautiful – what with crawling through the mud and dying and all. Then she noticed that she was still holding his gaze and a more urgent thought came to her.

"William," she said, in a warning tone, "whatever you do, don't you even think about kis...."

Her words were lost as his lips found hers. To her own surprise, she did not pull away.

*****

"It's time," said Brian, looking at his watch. "Let's get them ready."

Reluctantly, Gail opened the pack of mortars and handed half to Brian. A soft, but chill, breeze blew over the dark cliff top, rustling the grass.

"You really sure that you want to go through with this?" she asked. "It just doesn't seem right."

"Och, now don't start that again," groaned Brian. "We have a job to do. Get the first shell ready."

"Okay, but..."

"Alright, we fire together on ma mark, three, two..." Brian stopped. He felt something, something inside. It was as if all his life he had been alone, separate, and suddenly, just for a moment, he felt connected, connected to everything, the grass, the hill, the city, the world. He felt whole and complete, at peace. The feeling only lasted for a moment or two and then it was gone, but something changed for him.

"...well?" asked Gail, after a long pause.

"Did you feel that?"

"What?"

"Somethin', somethin' happened."

Brian suddenly looked at the shell in his hand, and at the launch tube. Then he looked out at the brand new parliament building and finally he looked back at Gail.

"Why are we doin' this again?" he asked.

"Because we hate the English..."

"Well, yeah, I mean we do hate the English, *obviously*. I've always hated the English. Ma dad hates the English. Ma mates hate the English. Even ma wee sister hates the English. But, ya know, I don't *feel* it all of a sudden."

"Feel what?"

"The hate," he replied.

"Aye, it's gone."

He set the shell down on the ground and sat next to Gail. Together they looked across the city. At the far end of the royal mile, beyond the spires of St Giles Cathedral, Edinburgh castle rose up out of the sea of rooftops, its stark battlements floodlit against the night sky.

"You know," said Brian, softly, "I never really noticed before but it's really beautiful up here."

"Aye it is."

*****

It was a grand funeral, more grand even than that of her husband. The whole country seemed to turn out to mark the passing of Scotia. There were rumours of traitors and foreign spies. Many dark stories hung around the body of the man they found with her who died with her arrow in his chest. But even though no one really understood how she had come to die, every one knew, somehow, that she had died for them.

Alanth of the clan MacCleland took his place as king of the land. He was crowned, just as Scotia had been, seated on a throne containing the Stone that had been retrieved with Scotia's body. Its place in the history and mythology of the country was secured.

Alanth's first act was to mark the passing of his predecessor. To ensure that she would be always remembered in the hearts and minds of the people, he issued a royal proclamation. Henceforth, the land of Alba would take the name of its late queen, Scotia, it would be called Scotland and its people would be known as the Scots.

*****

"Did you find her?" asked Oban, trying to size up the distance to the green from the sandtrap.

"I did not," replied Talisker "She could be anywhere, a blade of grass, a piece of shale, a mouse."

"Perhaps she will show herself, in time." Oban scooped the wedge skilfully into the soft sand.

The ball chipped into the air and sailed in a graceful arc towards the green. It landed short and started to roll slowly back down the slope. Picking up speed, it bounded over tufts of grass and fell back into the bunker, finally coming to rest a few inches further from the hole than where it started. Oban frowned.

"What will you do if she does?" asked Talisker.

"Well," he replied, "it is difficult. She is a part of Scotland just as much as you and I. If we are to heal, we must welcome her back, despite what Laphroaig may think. We will do so cautiously, though, for sure."

Talisker was on the fairway less than a dozen yards from the green. He looked at the bag of clubs and, after a moment's thought, selected a driver.

"You're not supposed to use that one from here!" declared Oban, emphatically. "It's a chip shot. You need to use one of those metal ones."

"Does it matter?" asked Talisker, with an innocent smile. Then holding the club in one hand, he swung it nonchalantly at the golf ball at his feet. The ball lofted beautifully into the air, shooting over the green and gaining altitude as it went. It looked as if it would land halfway down the next fairway. Then, suddenly, it hit a tree trunk on the far side of the green; it ricocheted up into the branches and rattled back and forth for a moment; finally, it dropped to the ground in the centre of the green, bounced twice and then fell neatly into the hole with a gentle "plunk."

"Do you know, Talisker," said Oban, with exasperation, "I don't believe you are taking this game very seriously."

*****

Connor sat back in the worn but exceptionally comfortable armchair by the fire, cradling his generously poured tumbler of whisky. It was one of Dee's very best and it was not a night for half measures. He just dropped by to warm his "innards and outards," as he put it, before retrieving his boat.

Outside, the sun set into the sea and the sky warmed to a remarkable pinky-orange, which just happened to match the enormous flowers on the pattern of Dee's dress.

"I think she did pretty well, don't you?" remarked Connor, for what must have been the ninth or tenth time.

"So, she did," answered Dee, patiently, taking a sip from her own glass, "and you didn't do too badly yourself."

"Why thank ya, kindly, Ms. McDee," he replied with a smile, raising his glass.

"Will ya be sailing back to Skye?" she asked.

"Aye, eventually. I might just take a short trip first, though."

"Oh?"

"I was thinking of wandering south a-ways, just for a few weeks."

"Down ta England?" pressed Dee.

"Nah, probably just as far as, maybe, Jedburgh," admitted Connor, eventually.

"Oh really! Visitin' Nancy Braidburn eh?" said Dee, triumphantly.

"Well, I might just drop in..." began Connor, defensively.

"Now, far be it from me to try and predict the future," said Dee, "but I'm wondering if Nancy might not pin you down one of these days.

*****

It was a remarkable bunch of flowers. The biggest, grandest, most purple, thistles Mari had ever seen. Rich, dark, green leaves, with prickers that would pierce leather and fat swelling buds the size of golf balls bursting into rich feathery plumes. There was a note attached. It read: *To Mari McLeod, The Flower of Scotland, No other has deserved the title more. Your father will be better soon. Love, Dee."*

The front room of the cottage was almost back to normal. William had helped her board up the broken window and they had swept up all the glass and debris. They'd moved a bed in there for her father to make it easier for Mari to take care of him. He'd need to be in bed for another week, at least. Mari set the flowers down in the jug on the mantle.

"It was nice of you to come," Mari told William, who was standing by the window, "and thanks for getting Katie to the train."

"Of course," he replied, looking at her in his puppy-dog way that she was very concerned she was starting to like.

"I'll stay with him for a while, in case he wakes up."

"Okay," he replied. "I'll see you tonight then?"

"Yes, seven o'clock."

He stood for a moment, just looking at her. "Bye," he said, eventually.

"Bye", she said, with a grin.

William blushed, and strode purposefully to the door. In spite of himself, though, he glanced back over his shoulder as he closed it. She did like him, but had the feeling that this behaviour was going to drive her crazy.

She sat down by the bed and took her father's hand. The doctor had said that he should make a full recovery but he had lost a great deal of blood and was still weak. He had a fractured skull and his head was wrapped in a pale brown crepe bandage. They said he would need to sleep a lot but he should feel much better in a few days. He looked so peaceful lying there.

Over in the corner of the room, the TV news was coming to an end. She picked up the remote and turned the sound up.

"...once again the main headlines of the day: In a surprise move the Scottish Separatist Army has called a ceasefire and announced that it plans to hand over its remaining weapons.

"Police are searching for a missing woman named as Cynthia Farrow, estate manager for Dunvegan Castle on Skye.

"And finally in other news, experts are reviewing a video posted on the Internet a few days ago, by tourists, who claim that it provides the final proof of the existence of the Loch Ness

Monster."

Mari smiled to herself as she turned off the TV and sat back down to watch her sleeping father.

Suddenly she heard a knock at the door.

"Er, excuse me, Miss McLeod? I hope I'm not intruding," muttered an old man as he bustled in through the door. It was Ally, the game-keeper from Dunvegan, unmistakable beneath his bushy brows.

"Ally?" she asked, "what are you doing here?"

"Och, Miss McLeod, I'm so glad you're alright, and that lovely cousin o' yours."

"How do you know about that?"

"Listen," he went on, ignoring her question, "I found this. I thought it must be yours, 'coz it has your name on it, and sure enough here you are." With a huge smile he handed her an object.

It was a small key attached to an ornate silver key fob. It bore the symbol of a thistle, and underneath the inscription. "Mari McLeod, The Flower Of Scotland".

"Wha' is this Ally?"

"Come and see lassie" he replied, still smiling. "I've some friends out here who'd love to meet ya."

Mari left her father and followed Ally outside. There, in front of the cottage, waiting for her was the strangest group of people she had ever met. They were talking among themselves as she approach but when she stopped in front of them, they all turned to smile.

"Mari, I'd like ya to me ma' family, and friends," announced Ally.

There were a couple of older men in kilts. Next to them were two ladies, the first with light brown hair and hazel eyes. The second was younger and incredibly beautiful. Next to her was a very broad man with long hair and a shaggy beard who looked like he would have the strength of a horse. Finally, at the end, sitting on a bench, was an elderly couple, a woman working intently on her knitting and a very old man puffing gently on a small clay pipe.

As she looked down the line, from one to another, they all smiled and nodded to her as if they had met her before and she somehow felt as if she were among old friends.

"Well done, Mari McLeod," said the man with the cane. "Well done."

He stepped forward and shook her hand, and then all of a sudden she was being kissed and hugged from all sides. She was passed down the line like a sack of potatoes but found herself laughing and hugging back as tight as she could.

"Alright, you lot," announced Ally. "Give her some air. It's my turn."

The others stood back. Ally, she noticed seemed to have changed a little, his nose was no longer as bulbous and his eyebrows were much less bushy than they had been.

"Well, what do you think?" he asked, pointing.

Mari turned, there, leaning on a kickstand, just where her old Yamaha used to be parked was the most beautiful sight Mari had ever seen. Gleaming in the setting sun was a sleek, sports motorcycle that looked almost capable of flying. It was painted in purple and lavender with white and silver detailing, including an ornate thistle on the petrol tank. Sitting on the seat was a matching helmet.

"Triumph Daytona, 955i", said Ally. "It's a special edition that never went into production. Only ten of these babies were ever made, and o' course, it's a custom paint job."

Mari ran to him and gave him a huge hug.

"You'd better give it a try," he said, with a grin. "See how she handles."

She started toward the bike.

"Och, Mari, I almost forgot," he said, pulling an envelope out of his pocket and handing it to her, still grinning. "License and insurance, just in case you get pulled over."

She sat on the bike and pulled on the helmet. It fit perfectly, of course. She turned back to wave, but Ally and his friends were gone.

She looked at her watch. Still at least two hours before she was to meet William. Her father was asleep and surely wouldn't miss her.

The sky glowed an impressive orange with wispy salmon-pink clouds that criss-crossed it like the wild brush strokes of a mad painter. She turned the key, started the engine and set off down the road, wondering gently to herself just how fast the bike would go.